Ours are the Streets

Sunjeev Sahota is the author of *Ours are the Streets* and the highly acclaimed The Year *of the* Runaways. He is a Granta Best Young British Novelist 2013, and lives in Yorkshire with his wife and two children.

Praise for **Ours are the Streets**

'The great strength of Sunjeev Sahota's debut novel is that, while it lays bare Imtiaz's emotional and moral confusion, it also presents his experiences of community in his father's home village and, most especially, his religious conversion as genuine . . . this makes for uncomfortable reading. Expecting to see in Imtiaz the model of an angry young terrorist, we instead discover a boy who feels more keenly than others the real injustices done to his community – and to the common good. That this community is something that he virtually invents, to fill the vacuum that he has grown up in, makes his dilemma more poignant – and it is this invention that marks *Ours are the Streets* not just as a topical novel about "home-grown terrorism" but as a moral work of real intelligence and power' – **John Burnside**, *The Times*

Sunjeev Sahota

OURS ARE THE STREETS

PICADOR

First published 2011 in paperback by Picador

This edition published 2011 by Picador
an imprint of Pan Macmillan
20 New Wharf Road, London N1 9RR
Associated companies throughout the world
www.panmacmillan.com

ISBN 978-0-330-51581-8

9 8 7 6

A CIP catalogue record for this book is available from
the British Library.

Printed and bound by CPI Group (UK) Ltd, Croydon, CR0 4YY

Visit www.picador.com to re[...]
and to buy them. You will als[...]
news of any author events, ar[...]
so that you're always first to [...]

Ours are the Streets

At last the page is stained. Feels like a relief, truth be told. Sitting here hovering over the paper with my pen and waiting for the perfect words weren't getting me nowhere fast. And already the light's coming. A dark blue morning mist spreading thick across the window. The time's sempt to have flown by and I've spent so much of it worrying about how to kick this thing off that I'm not going to have chance to say all the things I wanted to in this my first entry. Inshallah, it'll get easier from now on. It wants to. I want to leave something behind for you all – Becka, Noor, Ammi, Qasoomah, Tauji. Abba, too. I guess knowing you're going to die makes you want to talk. But right now I can hear the voices of angels in my ears and they're calling me to prayer. Ameen.

————

Another night. A better night. It's only just touching ten and I'm already managing to get a few good words down. Alhamdulillah! Not sure what good these words are going to be to you, mind. Now that I've left you. I know that it'll be hard for you all to get your heads round the fact that only a few months before you read this I were here at the window-desk in Ammi and Abba's old room and making the final preparations. That's what I think this is probably all about. Crossing the i's, dotting the t's. The last few steps before the ground falls away. I know you'll be upset when I'm gone, and – I can't lie – that brings a sense of relief to my bones. I don't want to leave this world without having staked my claim on someone. But remember that you mustn't go overboard. You know how Allah (swt) doesn't approve of making a spectacle of your grief. Think of it like this – if you do start crying a great river of tears, how will I ever make it across? I'll be stranded, won't I?

Just remember that it's into His arms I'm heading. Me, Aaqil, Faisal, Charag. We're all with Him now. We're all of us unafraid. Remember that, B. We're an unafraid and fighting people. We are better than they can ever hope to be. So stand tall and fight it out and let your faith be your shield. Protect your brothers and sisters by singing louder than their guns. I'm speaking especially to you, Noor. I don't know how many years will have passed by the time you're old enough to read this but I want you to grow up and be a fighter like your abba. You understand? This is going to be a long and hard fight and we'll need you. You won't find it easy, I know, but don't listen to what the newspapers and TV will have said about me. None of it is true. They don't know me. They don't know that when it's just me on my own in this room, the loneliness takes hold of my gut. I look out the window and all I can see are row after row of semi-detached houses, Toyotas parked out front, and I don't understand how these people can invest so much hope in those things.

I'm ashamed to say your abba weren't always a strong believer, Noor. I used to hang out with my mates and wear their clothes and be part of their drift towards nothing. The only good thing that came out of all that was that I met your ammi. She didn't always used to believe either, you know. Oh, yes, it's all coming out now! We were both very different back then, weren't we, B? When we met at university we were both of us very different. Do you remember?

It were a student night so it must've been a Thursday and a bunch of us from the course had gone to the Leadmill here in Sheff and I were there without beard or kufi and naked as the girls who were there to tempt me. They laughed and danced on the fuzzed-up flashing squares. I felt my chest expand. Away from home even if only for the night and all this creamy pleasure on show just for me.

There were a tap on my shoulder. It were my Rebekah.

In those days she didn't care so much for modesty. She let her dark red hair hang short and loose, skimming her jaw. Her slim shoulders were bare and packed tight with freckles. She had a short white dress on, I remember, with big green lotus flowers printed down the front of it. It pushed her small breasts up for all the men to gawp at. She had her arms folded, as if she were waiting for an explanation. I think I beamed I were that happy. Happy and nervous, the way you get when someone so far out of your league approaches.

'Evening,' I said.

'I'm disappointed,' she sighed.

'Yeah, I know. Me too.'

'I expected better if I'm honest.'

I nodded. 'Totally. Personally, I blame Ronald.'

She made a face. 'Who's Ronald?'

'No idea. What are we talking about?'

'You know exactly what we're talking about.' She coughed then, and creased up her brow in what were meant to be an impression of me. 'Oh no, Rebekah. I'm not, like, going out tonight. I'm, like, way too busy and want to, you know, like, finish that assignment.'

She pressed a finger into my chest, and I wished to God she'd just move in and let me ride my hands up behind her. 'Imtiaz Raina, I'm accusing you of lying to me.'

'Firstly, the impression? Like a mirror. Twicely, I don't tell lies. Only fibs.'

'Hmm,' she said. 'We'll see.'

In the silence that followed, she were the first to look away. When she looked back she sempt to want to say something to me, but then she just shook her head and said she'd better get back to the others. But it were the way you pulled back your shoulders, B, and put a bit of pace into your step that gave you away, like you were telling yourself to get a grip. I knew there'd always been an attraction between us, ever since that time you came and sat next to me in the library and asked to borrow my notes. ('Hi, I'm Rebekah,' you said, and I remember being floored by the fact you felt the need to introduce yourself.) But it weren't until that night at the Leadmill that I figured out how much you were into me. I played on that, I know. No point hiding anything now. Time to open myself out, wound on wound.

I left for the toilets, just to psych myself up a bit, and sat on the bog in one of the cubicles I popped a pill. I didn't do that often, but it always did the trick. It made everything better. It were like it dulled all the rats inside my head, even if for only a little while.

When I walked back out into the union, the music sounded sharper, the jokes came quicker, and talking to girls felt like the easiest thing in the world. Across the floor, I spotted this one girl who were on the same course as me and Becka. Blonde, top-heavy, orange-baked. You know the sort. I went over. We got chatting. She probably told me something about her life. I were too busy making sure to stand where I could see Rebekah. I wanted to know how messed up she'd get by me talking to this girl. And it worked. Rebekah were looking across, which just egged me on more, and the more I could make this blonde girl – Donna? Debbie? – laugh, and the more I leaned in and held her shoulder, the harder I could see it were for Rebekah to concentrate on her own conversation. The more sips she took of her drink. The more effort she had to put in to stay cheerful in front of her friends. Cheap thrills on my part. I recognise that now. Then too, if I'm honest. But I know I loved being aware of your eyes on me, B. Made my whole body fill meatily out, like I were the king around here.

Towards the end of the night, I dropped the blonde and made my way back across the dance floor. I caught Rebekah looking at me. What? I mouthed, hitching up my shoulders. She just shook her head, all sad. With hand on heart, I gave a little bow. And just like that she forgave everything. She did a curtsy. I tapped my wrist – it's getting late. She mimed sleep. I waved her over. She dropped her friends and came at once.

'Do you wanna dance?' she asked, beaming.

'I don't do dance.'

'Oh, come on. Sure you do.' She reached for my hand, but I snatched it back.

'Seriously. I never dance.' Just the thought of making a twat of myself in front of all the girls caused me pain. Becka looked annoyed, like she thought she'd just made a fool out of herself by coming over. I grabbed her hand. 'Come on. Let's get out of here.'

We walked out of the club and all the time as we walked side by side there were this horrible tension in the air, like a tingling up and down my arm. My stomach felt raw. I'd never had that feeling before. I thought there were something wrong with me. It weren't normal nerves, because I'd been with a few girls by then. I used to keep on imagining them in the corner of the common room afterwards, laughing because I'd not measured up. But it felt different now with Becka, and it were only later that I worked out that those warm tight sticky pangs in my stomach as I walked beside her were simply because I wanted to impress her. Which just meant that I wanted her to like me.

We ended up behind the big green recycling bins at the back of the Novotel hotel. I'd been telling myself all the way up to be confident, in control. Be firm but make her laugh as well.

'It's only my dingle. Don't know what you're so scared of.'

She laughed at my saying dingle, like I'd hoped she would. 'Who's scared? I just don't want to, that's all.' She moved to kiss me again. 'Where were we?'

I turned away from the kiss and started jiggling my jeans

back up. 'Up to you.' I made my voice all annoyed. 'We might as well head back, then.'

She sighed. 'Well, if you're gunna be such a kid about it.'

I felt a bit panicky, as if she'd taken the upper hand. 'You don't have to.' She crouched down on her heels and stretched my briefs out over my cock. 'But, you know, if you insist . . .' She raised her eyebrows at me, warning me not to push my luck.

I remember they were my best jeans so I kept hold of them around my thighs because I didn't want them to get mucky, and with my other hand I tidied her hair back off her face and held it there. I liked watching her stroking me off, and then my cock disappearing inch by inch into her mouth, and I loved the feel of my weight cushioned inside her like that.

Just when my balls were starting to clutch, she stopped and stepped away.

'What the fuck? What's the matter?'

She shook her head. 'You can finish yourself off.'

'Oh, brilliant.'

I came up the wall, the hem of my T-shirt gripped under my chin. Somehow, that weren't how I'd planned on the evening ending.

'Thanks for that,' I said. 'Remind me to leave you half-cocked next time an' all.'

'Come again?'

I gave her a look. 'That's not even close to being funny.'

But you'd started giggling, and that set me off too. And we stayed there looking at each other, laughing, like we couldn't really believe we'd done this behind the back of the Novotel, as if we were a couple of stupid schoolkids again. We carried on laughing until we heard footsteps on gravel and then I took your hand and we hurried round the corner.

It were a long walk back to your bus stop. You were hugging yourself warm, I remember, nodding in thought like you were working up to say something. I stayed silent. I didn't want to risk spoiling things. It might be easy to say this looking back now, but when I laid in bed afterwards, smiling my face off, it honestly did feel like a real turning point in my life.

Eventually, you said, 'You doing anything tomorrow night?'

''S Friday. I'll be at the mosque.'

'Really? Didn't know you were that into it.'

My guard went up. 'Why? That a problem?'

I saw her smiling to herself. 'Nope. Not at all. In fact, some of my best friends are Muslims.'

I loved that you could make me laugh. 'Yeah, yeah, okay. Sorry.' We carried on walking. ''S just sometimes I get "the Friday feeling", you know?' I made air-quotes.

'Guilt, probably. Wash off the sins of the week.'

'Summat like that. Maybe.'

Up ahead, shadowed in orange under the dark glare of a lamppost, two giants were talking on the iron bench at the bus stop. But as we got closer I saw that it were only that the two blokes were perched up on the back-rest with their feet on the seat. They were smoking. Their chunky uniforms had large loose gold buttons. They were speaking some tongue-filled language. Porters from the hotel, probably. I put my arm around your shoulder and pulled you to me. We moved inside the bus shelter, away from the two blokes. The bus didn't look like coming any time soon.

I knew the answer, but anyway I asked, 'Do you like me?'

You looked surprised, amused even. 'What are we? Twelve?' Then: 'Why? Do you like me?'

I made sure to get your eye. 'Yeah. I do like you. As it happens.'

It did the trick. You pressed your face into the side of my neck, sucking it, and lifted your arms around my head. Behind you, the porters ground out their cigarettes and nudged one another. And then I remember steering one hand around you, and around your waist, and thinking that it sempt made to fit my hand.

———

I used to always wait with you at the bus stop, and I never minded, B, not once. But sometimes the bus took ages to arrive and we could do nothing but sit shivering on the bench, sharing chips from a paper cone.

'You know, I'll have a car soon enough,' I said. 'It won't always be like this.'

'Like what? Chip?'

It must've been Christmas Eve because I remember the church music starting up behind us and then the doors opening and all these old people came shuffling past. Coats buttoned up to their chins, white hair blazing against the tall black sky. The frost crackled under their feet. They smiled at us and I knew exactly what they were thinking. What's she doing with him? Freezing to death at a bus stop in this weather. What kind of a boyfriend is he? And I remember thinking that of course they were right. What were I thinking! It's obvious she were too good for me. And, like I know I always do, I kept on building it up and building it up inside my head, going over and over our conversations, picking them apart and looking at them from every angle. I shook my head violently.

'What's got into you?' you asked.

'Cold, that's all. 'Nother chip?'

You tipped the cone upside-down. 'All gone.'

'Fatty.'

'Oi!'

I balled up the chip-paper and lobbed it towards the bin. It bounced around the rim, then dropped in. I were stupidly glad. 'See that? Did you see that?'

'Well done,' you said, all droll.

'It's all in the wrist action, you know.' I demonstrated. 'You see, the crucial thing is the flexibility in the wrist' – I pointed to my wrist – 'or the pivot, as we call it.'

'The pivot. Right.'

'Right. And the angle of release, which, of course, depends on how far the basket – or receptacle—'

'Not bin?'

'No. Not bin. Please. I'm explaining here.'

'Sorry. Carry on.'

'It's like I said. It's the wrist action, which is all about the pivot-angle ratio.'

'The pivot-angle ratio. Right. And you learnt this . . . where exactly?'

'Oh, well, of course to some of us it comes naturally. It's' – I reached for the word – 'it's intuitive.'

'Intuitive,' you said, impressed. 'Well, I always did say you have a pretty intuitive wrist action.'

I loved it when you were cheeky like that. I leaned in and

said, 'Still not as intuitive as yours, though,' and then we kissed for the longest time, interrupted only by the sound of the stupid bus grinding up the road.

Thinking about it, I might be getting things mixed up a bit. I must be thinking about the bus stop on the other side of the duck park because that's where the church is, isn't it? There's no church by the Novotel, I don't think. But I've got the basics right, haven't I? I mean, that's how it were, weren't it, B? Oh, I know I've probably got little bits wrong and I know you're all probably at some point going to say that you didn't say that or that never happened or how that bit's the wrong way round, but this is how I remember things. This is how it feels to me.

—

Sounds like your chacha's just got in from work, Noor. Can hear him rustling about downstairs. More than likely you won't remember him. He's a soldier like your abba. We're going into battle together. You'll probably only know us from photos and old videos. The 'cousin bombers' they'll label us. I wonder what you'll make of me! Hope you'll agree that your abba were a pretty dashing fellow (as they say back home). Ask your ammi. When we first started going out she were always touching me, the way girls do, wedging her arm in mine, or slipping her hand into my back pocket. She said I had the nicest eyes. Apparently they make up for my nose. Which

you've inherited! Your chacha's making a lot of noise downstairs.

—

Not long to go before dawn and then maybe I can get some
sleep. He were in the kitchen, were Charag, gathering up the
tins rolling across the lino. It makes me so angry to see him in
that stupid yellow pizza uniform with that shameful hat that
looks like a boat got turned over on his head. Serving drunks
who only give him grief. I keep on telling him to quit. What's
the point any more? But he says we should keep on acting
normal, so people don't suss. But I think there's something
else too, something he's not telling me. I think he just wants
to keep on sending money back home for as long as he
can. He'll want to make sure his abba has enough to cover
Qasoomah's wedding.

'Sorry, bhaiji,' he said, pushing the tins back up onto the
worktop. 'The bag was splitting.'

'Take that stupid topi off at least. You're not a servant
here.' I shut the door to. 'I phoned Aaqil today.' I waited, but
Charag didn't say nothing. 'Aren't you even going to ask how
they're doing?'

He apologised. 'How are they?'

'Don't you miss it all?'Again, he said nothing.'Because I do.
Loads. I wish I were still there. Do you remember when—?'

'What did Aaqil say?'

'Nothing much. I just wanted to talk to him. He'll be going through with it soon, Inshallah. Another month. Two, tops.'

'Right. That is good,' Charag said quietly, and started putting the food in the fridge.

'They've paid one of the guards. He said it should be easy from now on in. Just driving up to Islamabad. They've already found out which days the embassy's busiest.' Charag twisted round, smiled, nodded, then ducked back down. 'He asked how far we were from being ready.'

He closed the fridge, keeping hold of the handle. 'What did you say?'

'I said we're always ready. What else were I going to say?' I took out a piece of paper torn from a notepad. 'He gave me the number of a brother in Bradford who says he can make the vests. Do you want to come with me?'

He looked at the number and shook his head like a frightened child. He's so nervous about it all. So am I, if I'm honest, but one of us has to stay strong.

'Okay. Don't worry. I'll go alone.' I smiled at him. 'But you'll have to come for the fitting, acha? Try on your new clothes.' He said he would. 'And then we need to start sussing out where, okay?' I turned the paper over. 'I've made a list. You know, the kind of things we need to think about.'

'A list?'

The door opened behind me then, and Rebekah stood there in her grubby long-sleeved top and quick-wrap black headscarf. Me and Charag stared, wondering how much she might've heard. 'Sorry,' she said. 'I heard crashing.'

'This clumsy fool,' I said. 'What were you shopping for, anyway?'

'Just some things bhabhiji was asking me to get.'

I looked to Rebekah. 'I was joking,' she said. 'You didn't have to.'

He shrugged and went to lift the next bag. His skinny arms jerked down with the weight of it.

'For Godssake, just leave it. I'll put them away in the morning.'

You know, B, you can be really ungrateful sometimes. 'He were trying to do you a favour. You don't have to snap his head off.'

'Please, it is fine,' he said.

She turned to go, then stopped at the doorway. 'Are you coming?'

'Soon. I'll be there soon. I just don't want to miss fajr. And I'll only wake the baby if I come in now.'

'I doubt it. That walk tired her out.' That were me, Noor. I took you to the masjid so you could meet some of your uncles. 'What are you doing holed up in that room at night anyway?'

Writing this, B, writing this for all of you. 'Nothing. Just du'a. Don't want to miss the dawn call. You can join me if you want.'

'Maybe.'

I never meant to lie to everyone. But now you know what I were doing all along and you'll understand why I couldn't tell you. I do want to. I want to say let's just be as good as we can together in these my final months with you and the baby. Let's not argue like we have been doing. But I weren't totally lying. Because all this is just a form of du'a, isn't it? That's what these pages are all about. A form of prayer. Wanting to be found out, which is only another way of wanting to be known. Sometimes, when I'm out the house, I wish that you'll be in here going through this desk and finding these words.

The night's beginning to lift and I need to bathe before dawn. After that I'll come and join you, Rebekah, and slide quietly in beside Noor, just like you asked. Because you're not going to come and join me, are you? Like you said you might. I guess you must've had a change of heart. Ameen.

———

We must've been going out for a good six months or so when Becka said she wanted me to meet her mam. We were at the back of some business studies lecture, trying to follow what the hell the Sri Lankan dude at the projector were going on about.

'What do you mean she wants to meet me? Why would she want to meet me?'

'You are sleeping with her daughter . . . What did he just say? Who's Captain Blonde?'

'Capital bond. Bond. She knows you and me . . . ?'

'She knows I'm not a nun, if that's what you mean. Look, there's nothing to worry about. It's normal.'

That were exactly it, though. The normal thing would've been to take you to meet my ammi and abba as well. But I couldn't do that. I couldn't do the normal thing for you. I think you mistook the look on my face for nerves or something.

'For once in your life don't think too much about it. She's going to love you.'

The lecturer banged the table, about to tell us off, but then the bell went and his words got trampled under all the feet making for the exit.

—

Becka held my hand as we walked up the path. There were small neat flowers all round the postage-stamp front garden.

We went in by the back door and into the kitchen. Theresa were checking on something in the oven.

'Hey, Mam,' Becka said, as her bag slipped down her arm and onto the floor. I stood by the door, a bit nervous.

'Hello. Hello, Imtiaz. Tea'll be best part of half an hour yet so why don't you two go into the front room and watch some TV.'

I followed Becka, sticking to her side.

'And Becka,' said Theresa, still poking about in the oven, 'take your bag with you, please.'

I sat in the corner of the settee, hardly speaking. I think 'Countdown' were on.

'You alright?' Becka asked.

'Yeah, course. I'm cool.'

Theresa brought in a drink of orange for us both, and that were the first chance I had to get a proper look at her. She were pretty old-school. Long skirts and blouses with ruffled necks. Nice-hearted, though. She went back into the kitchen. I heard the back door go again, and then a man's voice.

'Who's that?' I whispered.

'Gerald,' Becka said, all surly. 'Mam's latest heartbreak.'

I heard Theresa telling him to keep his hands to himself and go get changed – they had a guest.

'Becka and Imtiaz, can you plate up, please?' Theresa shouted.

The settee moaned loudly as we got up. 'I bet there's a new one coming next week,' Becka whispered into my ear, and then back in the kitchen Theresa said, 'Sorry about the settee, love. I've got a new one being delivered next week.'

I put the knives and forks out and then just hung around by the table not really sure what to do with myself. Becka did the dishing out.

'Sit yourself down anywhere, Imtiaz, love, except there due to that being Gerald's place, or there as Becka likes to sit there, but she might give it up, just for you.'

'Since when has Gerald had "a place"?' Becka said.

'Don't start, Rebekah.'

Gerald came down, rubbing his hands. 'Ah, smells good.' He sat opposite me. 'Nice to meet you, Imziat.'

I shook his big clean hand. 'And you . . . sir.' I'd been wondering what to call him and that just slipped out. I could see Becka biting her lip from laughing and Gerald looking a bit surprised. Everyone were now sat down and Theresa said to start eating before it went cold.

'Well, Imziat, I hope your intentions for Rebekah are honourable?'

'Excu—?'

'Oh, Gerald, stop it,' said Theresa. 'Can't you see the poor boy's having kittens enough as it is. Ignore him, Imtiaz. He's only trying to be funny.'

'And failing,' muttered Becka.

'Tell me,' Theresa said hastily, 'Becka says you live near the Common?'

'Just at the bottom end, by the old folks' home.'

'Oh, I know it well. We had to put Becka's Nan in there for a few years. She died not long ago.'

I stopped eating my lamb and tried to look sad for a few seconds.

'Is the food not okay?' Theresa asked.

'Yeah, thanks. It's great,' and I tucked back in.

'I did ask Becka if there was anything you didn't like. If you had any, you know, special dietary requirements, but she said you eat anything. Apart from pork, obviously.'

'Pretty much,' I managed, still chewing.

'You'll fit right in, then.'

Gerald spoke. 'So you got any plans for yourself after university, Imziat lad?'

'Lots, yeah. But I want to see what graduate schemes are around first. See what turns up, like.'

Gerald nodded. 'P'raps you'll lend some sense into this one. She wants to stay on. As if she's not put her mother in enough debt already.'

'And what's it got to do with you, anyway?' Becka said.

'Eh up,' Gerald said, laughing. 'She's a firecracker, this one, Imziat.'

Becka opened her mouth, but Theresa spoke first. 'More peas?'

'What kind of jobs are you looking at?' Gerald went on. 'I'm in the car trade myself.'

'Do you have to interview him?' Becka said. 'And it's Im-ti-az. Try saying it?'

'I really don't mind,' I said.

'I'm not interviewing him. I'm interested. He seems like a nice—'

'He seems like a very nice—'

'I'm just talking to the lad—'

'Hassling, more—'

'How're the vegetables, love, not too—?'

'No, really, they're fin—'

'Imziat, am I hassling—?'

'Why did you even invite—?'

'No, not hassling, def—'

'See?'

'I've got ice-cream for afters if that's—?'

'Well, he would say that cos—'

'Strawberry or—'

They carried on like this for all of the meal. Talking over each other. I just kept on staring from one to the other not sure who to answer. And then I just sat back and ate my food, smiling to myself. This is funny, I remember thinking. Them chatting and arguing like that. It felt really nice to be around.

After ice-cream Theresa told Becka to give me a tour of the house.

'Should take about ten seconds,' Becka said.

I followed her up the stairs.

She pointed out all the rooms from standing in one spot on the landing at the top of the stairs. She started with the bathroom straight ahead and just went round to her left. 'That's the bathroom. It's pink. That's Mam's room. That's pink too. And that,' she pointed behind her and to the right, 'is my room. It's not pink.'

'Let's have a look in there, then.'

When we got back downstairs I thanked Theresa for the meal. She were washing and Gerald were drying.

'You're very welcome, Imtiaz,' she said. 'I hope we'll be seeing much more of you in the future.'

'If you can handle a night out with us, come down to the Butcher's Arms on any Friday. We're always in there,' said Gerald.

'I wouldn't say always,' Theresa came in quickly. 'Wouldn't want you to think we're a bunch of old soaks.'

And then Becka opened the back door for me. She kissed me on the lips. I checked but no one sempt to bat an eyelid that she'd done that.

After that first time I were always getting invited back to Becka's. She only came to mine once before she met Ammi and Abba. It were a Sunday and everyone else had gone to some wedding and I'd sneaked Becka round to the house. She didn't force me or nothing but I just wanted her to see our place. I didn't want her to think I were ashamed or anything. But the plastic wrapping all over the settee were a bit embarrassing now I come to think of it. And on the remote control. But Becka said it made perfect sense to keep things new as long as you could. She really slays me with some of the things she comes out with sometimes. She spent ages looking at the photographs in the wall cabinet.

'That's you?' she said. It was the one of me with my railtrack braces on.

'Yeah, yeah. Move on.'

She picked up the one of all of us. Abba, Ammi and me. The one we went to that studio to take, Ammi, with you and Abba sat on chairs and me stood behind you.

'You look like your dad, don't you?' She put the photo next to my face. 'Same nose. And mouth, big and sulky.'

'Whatever.'

'He's handsome, though, your dad. Still got all his hair.'

'He's alright.'

'Your mum's got gorgeous eyes.'

'That's lucky. Seeing as that's the only bit of her you can see.'

I showed her round upstairs. We took our shoes off before going into Ammi's prayer room, and I explained what we did and a few things about what all the different prayers mean. She listened like she were really interested, like at that moment I were the only boy in the universe. Which just kinda made me feel really good and sad at the same time. And then we went into my bedroom. We didn't shag, Ammi, so don't go having a migraine. We just sat on my bed and messed a bit and I played 'Wonderwall' on my guitar because it's the only one I know how to play. She went through my CDs and laughed at some of them. Then she found some papers by the TV.

'What are these?'

I looked up. 'Oh, nothing. Ammi were making me clean my cupboards out. They're from way back.'

'They're stories, aren't they?'

'Just crap from when I were bored.'

She came and sat next to me. 'What they about?'

'They're about shit.'

'This one's called The Burning House.'

'Don't remember it.'

She looked at me. 'I didn't know you were into writing.'

Me neither, B. But thinking about it, I really did enjoy English and Art and stuff like that. And wondered about growing up and writing plays or something, like the ones Miss Shepherd took us to see in our GCSE year. Knew it'd never happen, like. For all the usual boring brown reasons. But I'm loving writing this. It's really helping. It's like normally I'm walking round and I'm just confused about how I'm feeling or what I'm thinking. But when I'm writing it's like I'm rummaging about inside myself, and I can just keep on rummaging until I find something that's not far off what it really is I want to say. Ameen.

———

The days are passing over me. Don't think that I'm writing every night. Sometimes I just like to sit here at Abba's desk and look out the window to the flashing red light of that TV mast. It must be miles and miles away but I love that light. Like it's speaking only to me, calling out for me. It's grown up with me, that light. Even as a kid I used to stay up on weekends to watch it flashing red, convinced it were a secret code meant only for me. I'd sit at the window with pen and paper trying to work it out, but then Abba'd come in from a night's taxiing and shoo me back to my room.

'But I've nearly worked it out.'

'You are a very clever boy. But go on now, time for your bed.'

He'd try to pick me up by the waist, but I'd resist, my little hands holding onto the windowsill with its peeling white paint. Abba'd prise my fingers off and send me on my way. 'You never let me stay up with you on Saturdays,' I'd grumble, mooching across the rough corded carpet. I'd hear Ammi giggle, then, as she stood in front of the mirror and slowly unwound her scarf from around her face. But Abba'd cough like I'd embarrassed him, and he'd follow me to the door and slide in the bolt after me.

No matter how far I stretched out the window, I couldn't ever see the red light from my bedroom – one time I thought

I could, but it turned out to be a motorbike. So instead I'd just climb down and grope about under my bed for the books Ammi had brought back with her from Pakistan one time. I loved reading those stories. Of Ala-ud-din and his cave of treasures. Of Babur the Tiger, squat and fat and plodding slowly into battle on his poor donkey. The paper were made of soft brownish tissue, I remember, and I had to be careful not to rip it when turning the page. A faded yellow label stuck to the front of each book said 'Product of Sunderdas College, Lahore City, India'. They must've been from before Partition. I'd sit there for ages, cross-legged on the floor with my back against the bed. I can remember how the Ala-ud-din one ended with a list on the inside back cover of his top nine 'most especial achievements', and how happy it always made me to read that number one were 'repairing forts'. I thought of Ala-ud-din the night in Kashmir when I were repairing forts too. And it felt good to remember him, to know that we were all connected.

Maybe you like to sit here at this window and watch the red light too, Noor, thinking how someone out there needs your help. I can lose hours doing that, falling into thoughts of rescue missions and eternal gratitude. So even if I don't write for a few days, don't think I'm not here. I'm always sat here with these pages held down with Abba's old cigar case, waiting it out for the dawn call.

It's amazing how quiet this city can get. Sometimes I can hear drunks making their way back from town. Sometimes a Paki bombs down the road in his souped-up wheels. But usually, like now, the city goes quiet and it all looks and feels as ghostly as an abandoned fairground. I can see across the whole city from here. It's like it's built on these huge great grey waves. Off to the right up ahead there's the floodlights poking up from Bramall Lane. On the other side, I can see Meadowhall with its shiny dome wrapped in some sort of dim halo. And between them the vertical red sign of the Leadmills buzzing in its half-arsed neon way. The bored and dirty river's way off west. So quiet the city is. Everyone sleeping contentedly. So indifferent to the crimes of their land.

Noor, my little soldier, I learnt when I went away that any land that attacks your homeland or your Muslim brothers and sisters has to face the consequences of its decisions. Always remember that and carry it with you. Don't be scared. These people think that what happens to our people in Palestine and Kashmir and Iraq and Afghanistan is just what happens to people whose lives are meant to be lived in a different way to theirs. That's how they think.

I'm not sure if you'll still be living in this city, mind. Or even in this house. They might move you, and then you won't remember that you ever lived here with your abba. I've lived here all my life, in this house. It's not much, an old-style terrace, but your baba were very proud that he'd paid the mortgage off and owned it fully. He cared about material things like that. About how he compared to others. I hope Allah (swt) has been merciful to him. I hope that I, his son, can wash his sins and earn him entry to jannah. But I know it's not up to me.

—

The last time I remember being happy – properly happy, wind-in-my-hair happy – were when we went away for Becka's twenty-first. She'd been dropping hints for ages that she were expecting something special.

'Paris, Rome, Milan. I'm not fussy.' We were queuing up at the main uni canteen. 'It'd be good to get away for a bit. Do —'

'Something nice,' I finished for her. She were always wanting to do 'something nice'. 'Don't worry. I've got it all in hand.'

'You have?' She sounded doubtful.

'Of course. It's not every day one turns twenty-one, you know.'

'Oh, is it not? Well, I do hope you have something good prepared. Do we have reservations?'

'Absolutely. In a very exclusive establishment.'

'A good table, I trust?'

'With the most perfect view, of course.'

'Marvellous!'

I took her camping. One of Abba's taxi friends were in Pakistan and I'd managed to wangle his motor for the weekend. We found a great little spot in the Peaks. It were green and empty and just us for miles. I pushed my sleeves up to my elbows and set about pitching the tent up. I wouldn't let her help – I wanted to do it myself – so she just waited a way away, shivering as the hem of her yellow anorak whipped about her knees.

'I don't believe you. Camping? Fucking camping?'

'What?' I said, scuttling round to hammer the next peg in. 'It's what you wanted. Just me and you.'

'Let's not forget Daisy,' she said, all sarcastic, and the cow in the next field groaned, as if it knew.

It were dark by the time the tent were ready for us both. We left the flap unzipped to let in some moonlight, and Becka brought in the hamper from the car.

Afterwards, we got into our sleeping bag and undressed. We started messing, and she reached down and began tugging me to life. It were then that I saw in my mind's eye the pack of condoms tucked inside one of my textbooks. And the textbook still on the shelf. In my bedroom. At home.

'Fuck,' I said. I got dressed and drove down to a pub we'd passed on the way up, but I couldn't see a condom machine in the toilets, and I didn't want to ask if they knew where I could find one. I even stopped at a small countryfied petrol station, but they didn't have any either. Plenty of organic gerbil feed – 'cos who doesn't need that? – but no fucking condoms. Becka were lying on her side when I got back, reading a magazine with the light from her mobile.

'No luck,' I said, undressing again, getting in beside her. 'You'll just have to keep your grubby paws off me for once.'

'I'm only human,' she said.

We picked up where we left off. Tongues, teeth. Your legs scratching hard against mine. You sempt desperate, and that were hot, letting me handle you a bit roughly. I think being alone in the outdoors made us lose our heads a bit, B, because it were almost like we were fighting. Squirming and pulling at each other. I remember the sleeping bag kept getting in the way, and us laughing and kicking it off until it were just the two of us naked in the tent, my hand on your warm pouchy stomach. Or at least I thought we were laughing, but when I looked your eyes were wet. I pulled back. You said it were nothing, just that you'd never felt about someone the way you felt about me. That pretty much slayed me. I sat up, on my

knees, and without really thinking said, 'Let's get married.'
You laughed. 'What? I'm being for real.'

'Sorry. It's just hard to take seriously when . . .'

You gestured, and I looked down to where my erection
were pointing straight at you. I moved on top, lengthening out
along your hot body. I love the feeling of my chest rubbing
coarsely against you. I moved your knees apart.

'Imz,' you said, all caution.

'It'll be right. I'll be in and out. Promise.'

You shrieked with laughter, but then snapped your hand
over your mouth, as if there were someone around who
might've heard.

—

It were about nearly two months after that, Noor, when
your mum told me she were pregnant with you. It were the
summer holidays after our exams and we were just sitting on
the swings in the park. Becka were quiet for ages, but then she
said, 'I still haven't come on.'

I didn't say anything. She looked at me.

'I said, I—'

'I know. I heard. But you said before you're sometimes not
regular.'

'But I've never been this late.'

I remember rocking a bit on the swing, my trainers scraping the ground. 'Do you think you should get it checked out?'

'I took a test this morning.'

I looked hard at the floor and then I heard you sigh, B, and begin to cry and that told me everything.

She said she were going to tell her mam that night. I said I'd go with her if she wanted, but were relieved when she said she'd handle it better on her own. 'And your mum and dad?' she said. 'Or are you just going to keep this a secret as well?'

'Don't.'

'Why? Why the hell shouldn't I?'

'I know what they'll say. They'll say you'll have to revert.' I looked across, but still she didn't say anything. 'B? How would you feel about that?'

She stood up, wiped her wet face. 'One thing at a time, yeah?'

Later that evening, I heard Abba coming through the front door and putting his keys on the phone-table on his way to the kitchen. I went down and sat opposite him at the table. Ammi were plating up his dinner.

'Are you hungry?' she asked. I said I wasn't. 'Are you sure? You've not eaten a thing all evening.'

'Why?' Abba asked.

'Don't feel like it.'

Ammi put the back of her hand to my forehead. 'You've got a temperature.'

'Have I hell. I'm just not hungry.'

'The surgery is open tomorrow,' Abba said. 'I'll take you down.'

I sighed, dragged my hands down my face. 'Imtiaz?' Ammi said. 'What is the matter?'

'Ammi, can you sit down as well, please?'

I told them that there were this girl called Rebekah who I'd met at uni, and how she'd been on the same course as me, and that she lived Meersbrook way and how we'd been going out for a couple of years now.

Ammi interrupted. 'Is she pregnant?'

I nodded, looked up. Tears under Ammi's eyes, smudging her kohl. I could tell by the way her niqab were fluttering in and out of her mouth that she were breathing hard. Abba reached over and patted her wrist.

'Abba?' I said.

'Abba what?' he replied, calmly. 'What use asking us now? Now you have already done everything?'

'She says she'll revert,' I said, and that sempt to turn things a bit.

'That is something,' Abba said.

'I think it's quite a lot, actually.' I felt my position strengthen. 'It's not every girl that'd agree to that, you know.'

'It is not every girl that is being pregnant before marriage,' Ammi said, and then, in a quieter voice, 'Only certain types of girls are doing that.'

'Don't,' I said. 'Don't ever call her that.'

I left before we got into a fight, and then halfway down the hill I rang Becka to tell her what had happened. She weren't picking up, so I decided to just go round instead. I were still pumped up from the way I'd handled my parents.

Becka were at the kitchen table when I walked in through the back door.

'Hey,' she said and reached for my hand. I sat down in the chair next to her. No one said a word for the longest time.

'You staying for dinner, Imtiaz?' Theresa asked, not looking back from where she were washing dishes at the sink. She were scrubbing so hard the plates squeaked.

'No. No thanks.'

'Right. You'll be running off instead, will you?'

'Mam,' said Becka, warning.

'Well, I feel I've got a right to know. Is he going to be sticking around or am I supporting the bairn?'

'I'll support my kid well enough on my own if I have to,' Becka said.

'You're not going to be on your own,' I said quietly.

'What, then?' Theresa said. 'You've got a job lined up, have you? You're a kid yourself, for Chrissake. Both of you.'

'I can go out taxiing with my dad.'

'Imz can do what he wants,' Becka said. 'If he wants to stay, he can. If he wants to leave, he can. It's up to him. I'll survive.'

'It's not as easy as that, young lady.'

'I'm not saying it's easy, I'm saying I can make it work.'

Theresa banged her hands in the sink water. 'I've been a good mother.' She were sobbing. 'I thought I'd brought you up well.'

'You have, Mam. But these things happen. And we just have to get through them as best we can.'

Theresa looked to the ceiling, shaking her head, even smiling in a sad way.

'I won't hurt her,' I said.

'I'm sorry, Imtiaz, but I don't see how you can make such a claim.'

'Because I'm in love with your daughter, Theresa.'

With that simple honest sentence, the whole evening sempt to shiver and change. Theresa peeled off her rubber gloves and placed them next to the sink. She had a few things to do upstairs.

We waited to hear the bedroom door click shut. 'And I thought my folks took it badly.'

Becka fell back against the chair. 'You're still alive. Can't have been that bad.'

'Yeah,' I said, very slowly. 'I did kind of . . . I might have given them the wrong impression.'

'What impression?'

I scratched my head. 'They might be thinking that you're happy to revert.'

'Imz!'

'It means so much to them, B.'

'But what about me? What about what I want?'

'It's a way for us to be together. That's what we both want, isn't it?'

She groaned in frustration. 'You'll just have to go back and give them the right impression. Tonight.'

'Look. Let's not be hasty, yeah? Come talk to the imam. Swear down, you'll be surprised.' And, B, you said you would. Ameen.

———

In case you don't remember your first home, Noor, I'll describe it for you. This used to be your baba and bibi's room.

The ceiling's white and high, from Victorian times, with a big round plaster flower pattern in the centre. The yellow wallpaper's going soft and bubbly in parts. Damp. That time of year. There's a clean white bed with not a crease on it, like it's never been used, and apart from the almari with its long grubby mirror there's not much else. The window's cut into squares. Your baba always wanted to get the place double-glazed, but it just never sempt to happen. When the wind picks up, the corners of my pages flicker and the few wire coat hangers in the almari rattle against each other. Your bibi took all her clothes with her to Pakistan after your baba died. I keep on meaning to call her. But I know she'll guess something's up and say she'll cut short her visit. I don't want that. I want to walk out of this house without having to say goodbye to you, Ammi. That would be too hard. It would only remind me that I were leaving you alone here, in this country where people point and look at you. Just for covering yourself like our beloved Prophet (sAas) asked. If I had to look you in the eyes before I left, it would only remind me what I've always known about you and Abba. That I've always been an undeserving vessel for your affection. And then I'd start hating you for making me feel like that.

It's like that time when I finally brought Rebekah home to meet you. When I tried to get you to take the plastic wrapping off the settee.

39

'But it's embarrassing,' I said.

Ammi slapped my backside with a rolled-up wet towel. 'Do not touch it!'

'That hurt!'

'I said, leave it. It is keeping it clean for guests.'

I didn't have time to argue – the doorbell went.

'Arré, look how fast he runs!' I heard Abba laugh.

I slowed down into the hallway. Rebekah were blurred by the thick mottled glass. I opened the door. I don't know what she thought she'd come as. Long purple skirt. High-neck black blouse with big floppy cuffs. Every inch of her from the chin down were covered up.

'What?' Rebekah said, looking down at herself. 'You said dress modestly.'

'I best switch the heating off.'

'Well, I didn't know. I've never met your parents before.'

'That your mam's brooch?'

'Right!' She thrust the flowers at me. 'I'm going back to get changed.'

I grabbed her hand and pulled her inside. 'Don't talk shit. You look fine.'

In the hall, she hitched up her skirt and slid out of her shoes, leaving them outside the lounge. I loved that you did that without me having to ask you to.

'What you smiling about?'

I shook my head. 'Ready?'

I could hear Ammi and Abba arguing in whispers from behind the door, but as I showed Becka in Ammi's fingers leapt away from Abba's tie. Abba were beaming, hands behind his back. And the way Ammi's cheeks plumped up around her eyes told me that she were smiling hard under her niqab too. Ammi came forward, arms held out, and there were a bit of a kerfuffle while flowers were handed over and hugs given. I said that we'd better get to the restaurant or they might give our reservation to someone else.

I'd booked a table at the Lal Gulaab, just off West Street. It's easily the best restaurant in town with its purple wallpaper and gold stencil tigers. All the tables were round and covered in thick white tablecloths with a brass vase in the middle, a yellow rose drooping over the lip. The place were packed. Ammi and Abba looked nervous as we waited to be seated. I don't think they'd ever been to a restaurant before. The waiter arrived, as thin as the stubby yellow pencil angled behind his ear. His name badge said Rakesh. He mumbled a bored welcome.

'We've got a table booked,' I said. 'It's under my name.'

He looked to me, waiting for me to carry on, but when I didn't his gaze turned upwards, like he were asking Lord

Rama how he'd washed up in this cheap dhaba in this cold-as-kulfi city waiting on idiots like these. The guy were a regular riot. Eventually we got to our table. The seats were covered in furry velvet.

'This is nice, huh? Ain't this nice?'

'It's lovely, beita,' Ammi said. 'Very good choice.'

We opened our large plastic-crinkled menus and I made a point of studying mine closely, as if I were making a really important decision. But Abba and Ammi just kept on glancing at each another. The menu were all in English. I'd not thought it through, and now you looked embarrassed and it were my fault and I didn't know what to do. I just sat there with this prickly heat climbing all up my neck. My fingers gripped the menu harder. I didn't hate that you hadn't learnt to read English properly in all the years you've been here. I hated that I knew you weren't saying anything because Rebekah were there. I hated that you felt you were embarrassing me. Rebekah shut her menu.

'Well, I think I'll go for the lamb tikka, Mr and Mrs Raina.' She nodded a lot, like she were trying to convince them. 'It's really nice. I recommend it.'

Abba shut his menu, relieved. 'In that case, I shall have that as well.'

'Me too,' Ammi said.

'We can't all have the same,' I said. 'We'll look like right chumps. I'll have the' – I looked down the list – 'the prawn curry.'

Ammi shook her head. 'Always having to be different.'

Rebekah reached over and laid a hand on Ammi's forearm. 'Tell me about it.'

And I thought that were really nice, B. They way you touched my ammi's arm like that. And I know you'd probably noticed how they were struggling with their menus and that's why you came in like you did. It's what I love most about you, if I'm honest. It's a kind of intelligence you have. Not grades and exam passes and stuff, but some other higher kind of intelligence that I don't know how to put into words.

The waiter came with our food, throwing it on the table like it were offending him. We started eating. Abba started with the questions.

'So, Rebekah! What now after university? Did you pass?'

'I got my certificate through the post the other week.' She put a hand on her chest, as if presenting herself. 'Mr Raina, you are looking at the holder of an Advanced Diploma in Business Administration. With distinction.'

Abba looked to me. 'Diploma?'

'A degree for dummies, kind of.' Which got me a thwack on the shoulder.

'He says!'

'Do not worry, Rebekah,' Ammi said. 'These days his head is getting very big. What is he doing that is so good? All day now sitting about whatnot.' She turned back to Becka. 'But now he will be getting a job. You will be too busy looking after my grandchild.'

Becka looked to me. I looked to my food. 'Well,' she said, 'I do hope to do some work after the baby's born.'

Ammi retreated back into her seat. 'That is your choice.'

'As long as you'd be able to look after the baby, of course. I don't think I could do it without you.'

Ammi nodded graciously, always happy to be flattered.

It were then that those slappers came in, drunk. Skirts so tight their splotchy stomachs mushroomed over. They were laughing and swaying and swearing at each other and the whole restaurant sempt to straighten its back as the waiter herded them to a table. Thank fuck they weren't next to us, I thought. I could feel you were nervous, though, Abba and Ammi. The way you went quiet over your food. Like you were trying to make yourselves as small and invisible as possible. And when I said I were going to the toilet, Ammi looked frightened and asked me not to go, as if any movement away from the table were asking for trouble. Like this were our little corner and we should just stick to it.

'I won't be a sec.'

'Do you need some money?' Ammi asked, reaching for her purse.

On my way back, I saw that the women were on a hen night, and that the podgy one with frizzy blonde hair piled up like a frothy pineapple had a 'just married' sign hanging across her back.

'Wouldn't want to be the one marrying that,' I said, re-taking my seat.

'Shh!' Ammi said. 'We are not making trouble.'

'No one's making trouble,' I said.

Abba patted his napkin neatly around his mouth. He cleared his throat. 'These people are exactly what is wrong with this country.' He spoke loudly, as if to show that he didn't care who heard him, but not loud enough that his voice might carry. 'I am seeing it every night, Rebekah. I tell you, people were never being rude when I was first coming to this country. They had some respect,' he added, angling his head to the side.

'Arré, Baba, please,' Ammi said. 'They will hear you.' She sounded full of nerves.

'I am not afraid,' Abba said, turning his volume right down. 'Maybe if there were more brave enough to speak out like me we would not be having our children driving planes into buildings.'

There were a yelp then, and the whole restaurant turned round to see the drunk bride tipping back in her chair, falling to the ground and taking the tablecloth and all the plates smashing with her. The waiter came running over, shouting, 'What's this! What's this!' But the bride's friends rolled her back up onto her feet, and put a few notes in the waiter's top pocket. They got moved to the table next to us and while the waiter got them seated he looked across to Abba as if to say he were sorry for having to do this.

They got louder, drunker. Ammi, I could see the sweat across your eyebrows, like you were waiting for them to pick on you. And Abba, the way you just kept on looking down at your food. You looked scared.

I stabbed my fork through a prawn. 'How's the food, huh? Why's no one talking?'

'It's great!' Rebekah said. 'Mrs Raina, how's yours? It looks delicious!'

'It's fine, beiti. Very nice. I am just not a big eater, you see.'

'Oh, I'm the same. I go through phases. What about you, Mr Raina? Is your lamb cooked well?' You were trying hard, B. I took a breath.

'Why don't you at least ask her to call you by your first names?'

Abba looked to me, confused.

'She's been calling you Mr and Mrs all night, and you haven't even said she can call you Rizwan and Nausheen instead. That's what normal people do.'

'It's not an issue,' Rebekah said. 'Really, it's not. Don't make something out of nothing, Imz.'

'We didn't know,' Ammi said quickly.

That was just it, though. You just didn't know.

Abba pushed his plate aside. 'We were not aware we were so embarrassing for you.'

The table went quiet, until finally Ammi said, 'Rebekah, Imtiaz is telling us you are happy to revert.'

Rebekah swallowed, nodded. 'We've spoken about it. And Imz has explained how important it is to him. So, yes! We've got a meeting with the imam next week.'

'And your mother? She is happy with your decision?'

Rebekah made a so-so face. 'She's coming round. She thinks the world of Imz, so I'm sure she'll be fine in the end. It'll just take some getting used to, won't it?'

'You don't have to,' I said. 'You don't have to revert if you don't want to.'

Becka pulled back, getting a proper look at me. 'You've changed your tune!'

I shrugged. 'It don't bother me. You can stay as you are, far as I'm concerned.'

Abba's eyes went wide. 'This is nonsense. You are knowing how important it is.'

'You don't have to do anything. We don't even have to live here. In this town. We can just move somewhere and be alone. Away from everything.'

'What is this?' Ammi said, sounding worried. 'Moving where? Away from your family? Say something, ji, what is he saying?'

'We can go somewhere where no one can find us. Leave everyone here behind.'

'Stop it!' Abba said. 'Look how upset your ammi is getting.'

'Oh, we'll visit you,' I said, all casual. 'Every now and then. If we've got time, that is. Won't we, B?'

It were one of those times when I felt as if there were something that didn't quite fit about my mind, as if it had been put together in the dark. I'd've carried on and all, twisting and twisting it in, if the drunk bride hadn't turned up at our table, swaying beside Abba.

''Scuse me, love. But you wouldn't be a star and take a photo of us all for me, would you?' She held out a cheap camera.

'Here, I'll take it,' Rebekah said.

'No, no,' Abba said, as if to prove a point. 'I can take it.'

The woman went back to her table, sitting on someone's knee. Abba held the camera to his eye and clicked once.

'Ta, love,' she said, and took the camera back. 'Here, how about me and you have one taken, too?'

Abba looked pained. 'No, no. Thank you, but I am sorry.'

'Aw, don't be all shy. It's me wedding tomorrow. I'm getting married!'

'My congratulations,' Abba said.

'Here, Wendy! Take a photo of me with this here mister. It'll be a nice touch for the album.'

A beanpole of a woman with a helmet of black hair and a tattoo of a sun on her shoulder came and took the camera. The bride crouched down and threw her arm around Abba's shoulder. The stench of beer and smoke came off her in fat waves.

'Give him a kiss!' Wendy said.

The bride puckered up.

'Please,' Abba said, 'you are shaming me. I am sorry.' There were bright sweat on his forehead.

'Just a teeny-weeny kiss.'

'I am sorry.'

He kept on saying that like it were the only three words he knew. The whole restaurant were watching. She didn't care.

'Come on. Cop a feel of them if it makes you feel any better.' She jiggled her tits in his face.

'Please. I am sorry.'

'Don't be sorry, love. We're all same underneath, ain't we?'

'Not a tit man, is he?' Wendy diagnosed. 'Some blokes aren't, are they?'

'That true, love?' I looked up. She were talking to Ammi. 'Woman to woman. Your fella here not a tit man.'

My fist came down on the table. The cutlery jumped. 'Get the fuck lost.'

She looked at me, blinking as if to get my face into focus. She were all perplexed. 'What's up with you? I'm just talking to this here lovely man.'

An older woman came and took the bride by the elbow. 'Come on. Leave these folk alone.'

'But I didn't mean owt by it, Mam. I weren't being funny or anything. You know I weren't, don't you, love?'

Abba gave a shaky smile.

'Stop mithering them,' her mother said. 'You're a flaming embarrassment is what you are.' She started dragging her daughter away.

'But I don't want them to think badly of me. I'm not what they think I am. There isn't a racialist bone in my body!'

Our table went silent. Ammi brought her knife and fork together on the plate. 'Can we go?' she asked, very quietly.

We dropped Becka off first and then went home.

'Lucky for her, her ammi was coming to take her,' Abba said, turning the key in the front door. 'Otherwise, only Allah knows what I would have done.'

'Yes, ji,' Ammi said.

'I was giving her a chance at the beginning. You have to let these people a chance to see their errors. But I was working up to giving her a big piece of my mind when, like I am saying, her ammi came.'

'Yes, ji.'

He'd been like this all the way home. Abba, it were like you were letting yourself be humiliated all over again. And it just fucked me off. I felt guilty, for taking you there and wanting the night to go really well. And I felt angry too, like I were sickening for something, like I were grieving the fact that I couldn't protect you like I had to.

'Anyway,' he said, exhausted. 'Time for bed. Goodnight. No milk tonight for me, Naushi.'

I watched him move down the hall, shrinking away.

'Couldn't you have just said summat? Told her to get lost? Instead of just sitting there?'

He turned round at the bottom of the stairs. 'What? You think I should lower myself to their level? Is that what you want your abba to be doing?'

'Couldn't you have just been normal?'

'Imtiaz, that is enough,' Ammi said. 'This is your abba you are speaking to.'

'How the hell do you handle the drunks in your taxi? Or do you lose your front there as well?'

'You are saying I should talk to these people like they are our equals?'

'Oh, no, course not. I mean, why should you stand up to anyone? You're only good for lording it over your own fuck-ing family.'

I'd gone too far – I knew it – and when Ammi came up to me I were waiting for the sting of her slap. But like these things usually are, it were still a surprise when it came, and God, Ammi, it hurt like hell.

That night I lay on my bed, eyes open. The phone kept on going – texts from B – but I read them without replying. I just remember staring into the black pool swirling out from the ceiling. It must've been about as late as it is right now before I finally got off to sleep. Ameen.

———

B, we just seem to be talking past each other the whole time. I sat down last night and I couldn't even write anything

I were feeling so wound up. I went downstairs, flicked through the TV, switched it off. But then I turned it on again because I thought I should make the effort. I never used to mind all that kind of stuff, when we used to sit and watch it together. I sat there trying my hardest to get interested in what were on, but it all seemed so bright and dead and pointless, and I got up to turn it off at the mains. I walked back through the house in darkness, touching the things you'd touched. The open CD case, the bag slung over the banister, the light switch. And then I came back upstairs and just waited it out for the dawn call, watching the sky slowly turn green and all the houses come forward through the light. If you look closely you can see it happen. I didn't want to spend the whole of today being 'under your feet'. That's why I went out. Not to masjid like I told you. I went to check out the vests from the Bradford brother Aaqil told me about. I rang him as I walked down to the trainport. He said he'd been waiting for me to call. He sounded like a freshie, his w's sounding like v's and the rest.

Bradford, man, it's like Paki Central. You couldn't move in the taxi place for seeing a brown face. His wife – a niqabi all in blue – showed me into the front room. It smelled of incense and cumin. He were sat cross-legged on a green mat with brown tassels. Fortyish? He had small round glasses on his big hairy face.

'A'salaam wai'lekum,' I said.

He rushed to get up and held me by the shoulders. 'Wai'lekum a'salaam, brother! Wai'lekum a'salaam! Mashallah, what proud brave soldiers our beloved Prophet, salli Allahu alayhi wa sallam, has given us.'

I felt my energy drain into the ground. It were going to be one of those meetings. His wife came back with cups of oversweet tea, and then he told her to leave us alone and not come in again, that men were discussing important matters. The house must've been on a bit of a hill because the door glided smoothly shut behind her. He smiled at me. He sempt a bit nervous, like he couldn't believe I were here, in his front room.

'The tea, brother? It is alright? Not too hot? Too cold?'

'It's fine. Thanks.'

'Good, good. That is good. The heating? Shall I put it up? It is getting cold, no?'

'I'm fine.'

'Acha. Something to eat, then? I can ask the wife to make something quicksmart.'

'Where are you from?' I asked. 'Back home.'

'Oh' – he sounded surprised – 'I am from a small village near 'Pindi. You have heard?'

I hadn't. 'What's it like where you're from?'

'Oh, so beautiful, brother. Even more now. It is only when you are far away that you understand.'

'Do you miss it?'

He nodded, and I nodded too, and then there were just this long quiet until he put his tea down and asked if he should be getting the vests.

'Yes. Yes, I suppose that's what I'm here for.'

Tucked back into a snug in the corner of the room, under some shelves of kids' photos, there were a metal chest with thick gold-encrusted corners. He slid away the big covering doily, and drew out a small brass key from his pyjamas. He had to rattle the key a lot to get the chest open. 'Here it is,' he said. He lifted up a thick waistcoat and held it against his chest. It were dark blue and made of heavy padded squares. Wires hung in loops out the bottom. It didn't look like much.

'Where's . . . ?'

'Oh yes.' He opened it out, exposing all the connectors and crocodile clips. Across the bottom there were all these little batteries, and where you might expect to see an inside pocket there were a plastic box where the detonator would go. 'Would you like to try, brother?'

I let him put it on me, hooking my arms through the holes. It were a bit on the short side and it didn't meet across my chest.

'The other one is bigger,' he said.

'I'll give this one to Charag, then. He's even skinnier than me.'

'As you wish, huzoor.'

I adjusted my shoulders until it sat right. I could feel the hard weight of the box against the left side of my chest. I felt like I'd grown ten inches. Like my chest had got bigger, too. I looked down at him. What was he? Nothing. But I'm a chosen soldier, full of the love of Allah (swt). I searched for some sort of switch.

'It's here, brother,' he said. He took hold of a short toggle poking out from the hem of the thing. 'When the blessed and magnificent time comes you only have to pull this hard. Like this.' I jumped back. 'No, no!' he said, begging forgiveness. 'It is not set up yet.'

'God, man. Give a guy a heart attack, why don't you?' He kept on apologising. 'Okay, okay. Take it easy. No harm done.'

It just felt like a normal waistcoat. With a jacket over the top, no one would ever know.

'So I can't take these with me today?'

'I will need time to set them up. The device needs some changes. It should not be taking long if I work all night.'

'Take your time. We have a few weeks yet. We need to wait for Aaqil.'

I ended up staying for dinner. When I got back, Becka were in the room folding baby clothes. Noor were playing at her feet. I think seeing the vests made it all more real for me. I tried to make an effort.

'How about we do something, yeah? Let's go somewhere.'

She didn't say nothing at first, just folding clothes and putting them in the basket. Then, 'Where?'

'I don't know. Let's take Noor out. We haven't been out together for ages.'

She shook her head. 'I'm tired.'

'Oh, come on, jaan.'

'Don't jaan me. If you really want to do something you could do worse than going out to work.'

'Come on. It'll be good to do something fun for a change.'

She looked up. The lines around her mouth set hard. They were new lines, as new as the ones around her eyes. She hadn't been sleeping. 'With what?' She pointed to the heater. 'There's about sixty-seven pence there. Is that going to get us very far?'

'This is getting really boring, B.'

She sighed, like she were telling herself to calm down. 'Seriously, Imz, have you thought any more about going back to work? We can't live off your dad's insurance forever. That taxi's been rotting there ever since you got back. If you're not planning on using it, just sell the thing and be done with it.'

I went behind her and circled my arms around her waist. I love holding you like that. The door went, and Charag came in. I moved to pick Noor up. Becka carried on with her folding.

'Back early?' I said.

'I was doing the afternoon shift.' He undid the top button of his yellow shirt. He stank of fish. 'Can I put the water on?'

When he came back from the kitchen he headed straight for the stairs. 'Arré, where are you going?' I asked.

'To have a bath, bhaiji.'

'But you know it takes at least half an hour for the water to heat up.'

'I will wait upstairs.'

He's been like this for a while now. Shy, cagey. Sometimes I think I ought to maybe follow him and see what he gets up to. 'Just sit down here. And I want to talk to you after your bath. Something important.'

'Like what?' Rebekah asked.

'Like men's talk,' I said, and winked at Charag.

After dinner, I managed to get Charag on his own while Becka ran Noor's bath. I told him to follow me into the kitchen and close the door behind him.

'I went to Bradford today,' and I began telling him about the brother who were helping us and what the vests were like. But all the while I were speaking he were glancing at the timer on the microwave, stealing a look at his watch. 'Is something the matter?' I said.

'Hm? Oh, sorry, bhaiji, but I said I would be meeting some friends tonight.'

'Friends?'

'People I work with only. I will be late.' He wriggled into a brown leather jacket I'd not seen before. 'Can we talk about this tomorrow?' But before I could answer, he were already out the back door. Ameen.

———

I hope you'll stay being a Muslima now I've gone, B. I've got a feeling you will. And I know you'll bring Noor up as one. It's my biggest wish for her. I want her to go back home at least once a year as well. They'll be plenty of time during the school holidays. That's what we agreed, remember? We talked about it on the morning you moved in. Or, actually, on the morning I spent lugging in your stuff while you sat being pregnant at the kitchen table.

'I can't help it. The doctor says I'm not to lift anything in my condition.'

My fingers slipped out from under the box, and it hit my knees before toppling to the floor. Something smashed. I reached for some water, gasping. The removal guy followed in, a cardboard box under each of his fleshy arms. 'Baby clothes, love.'

'By the stairs, please,' Becka said.

He offloaded the boxes, then asked if I were ready for another trip.

'Another?'

'There's still stuff in the loft that needs bringing,' Becka said.

I got to my feet, probably moaning. The removal guy laughed. 'This your first kid?'

'With her, yeah.'

'Funny,' said Becka.

It were your first night in your new home, and I remember how after the quiet, awkward dinner, Abba cleared his throat and stood up. He said he wanted you to know that you were his daughter now, and that your mother might disown you and I might leave you, but he would always stand by your side, and you'd always have a father in him. You just stood up and put your arms around his gut and pressed your cheek against his shoulder and said thank you. That night, in bed, I were thinking about that moment. I thought you were asleep, but then you heaved yourself up.

'What's up? The baby okay?'

'Bit parched, that's all. Fancy some hot chocolate?'

'Stay, stay. I'll get it,' and I pulled on my boxers and climbed out the bed and out the door, grabbing a T-shirt on the way. The tin in the cupboard were pretty much empty, so I put on some jeans drying on the radiator and left the house, checking I had my wallet.

Singh's only had some cheap shit, and I wanted Cadbury's at least, so I carried on to the end of the road and made for the top of the hill. But the Jet station didn't have any, and the only other place I could think of were the Metro, halfway to town. I pulled up my jacket collar, feeling it chafe against my stubble, and started walking quickly. I bought three large tins, then headed back, running now. I'd been gone over an hour by the time I got in and made for the kitchen. You were at the table, sipping.

'Where you been? There were some more in the cupboard.'

I said it didn't matter and put the tins I'd bought on the worktop. 'Feeling any better?'

'He's just playing silly beggars. Aren't you, baby? You

know, it's got to be a boy with all this kicking.' You sipped your drink. 'I'll be up as soon as he calms down. One of us might as well get a night's kip.'

'I'll stay,' and I pulled out a chair at the table and we stayed up most of the night, just talking. Ameen.

———

We went into town earlier today, me and Charag. It's time we started properly focusing. It'd been a sultry afternoon, full of warm wet air that sempt to make everyone walk half a step slower. Charag most of all. We'd checked out the cinema first (too many cameras), and we'd only rounded the corner when the rain started throwing down, this warm rain, the kind that you know'll stop in a few minutes as sharp as it came. We ducked into the doorway of a boarded-up music store. The graffiti on the plywood must've been recent – the rain were making it run. All around us people were pulling their coats up over their heads and rushing under the nearest bus shelter, shop awning. There were a blue estate parked on the road in front of us, and the rain drummed like gunfire on its roof. It reminded me of Afghanistan. I turned my back to the road, facing Charag instead.

'Is something the matter? Are you thinking of pulling out?'

'It's nothing like that. I'm just missing home only.'

I weren't convinced, still aren't, but I can understand him missing home. 'Okay, so, you choose, then.'

'Me?'

'Yeah. You. Why should I do all the thinking?'

Sighing, he looked out across the street. I followed his eyes. A couple of streets away, you could see the L of the Leadmill. 'What about there? It is a bar, yes?'

His English has come on, not calling bars hotels any more. I said we wouldn't get away with it. 'They can check you. Before they let you in.'

The Supertram went past, tiny blue sparks coming off the wires overhead. The destination were written along the side, first in English, then underneath in Panjabi and Urdu. Meadowhall. I took out my list again.

'It's very busy there,' he said, but I were already making for the tram stop. 'But it's Friday,' he called. 'Are we not going to prayers?'

I felt a flicker of reluctance, at having to go to prayers instead, but I forced the thoughts out. 'You're right. We should head back. As soon as it stops raining.' Charag looked confused, and I realised that I were stood in the middle of the road, and it had stopped raining a while ago.

———

After prayers, we went next door to the centre for our usual Friday-night game of pool. Neither of us felt like it, but we need to keep doing the ordinary things. Sometimes, though, I think people have already started to guess. Something a bit guarded in the way they look at me, like they'd heard of this new stronger Imtiaz. And that gives me a thrill, I have to admit. As I bent down to sink a stripe, I looked around me. The boys at the ping-pong table were giving me nervy side-long glances, and even the girls sunk into the corner beanbags were looking over.

The ball vibrated around the jaws of the pocket, refusing to fall. 'Everyone's looking at us.'

Charag looked around and behind himself. 'No one is looking at us, bhaiji.'

'You just don't notice these things.'

Later on, Fahim came up, all bouncy steps in his zebra shell suit and thick gold chain. I swear he measures his goatee out with a ruler. You'll remember him, B. I introduced him to you time ago, before you got pregnant. We'd gone to that Spar on your estate to get some lecky tokens for your mam. I were down by the chiller cabinet choosing a drink when he turned up, twirling the keys to his Golf on the end of his finger. We knocked shoulders. He asked me what I were doing here.

'Becka lives here, don't she? Just round the corner, like.'

There were the usual uncomfortable pause while he adjusted his brain to the fact that I had a white girlfriend. 'Sweet, sweet,' he said.

Becka joined us, taking care not to bend the pink meter tokens as she filed them into her purse. I introduced Fahim. 'His abba drives a taxi too. Our families go way back.'

'Ooh, so now I know where to go if I ever need some dirt on Imz.'

Fahim smiled, took a step back. He felt awkward, I could tell. And Becka, like she did every time she found herself in this stupid situation, just carried on making even more of an effort to reach out.

'Me mam's made enough to feed Switzerland tonight. Come over? It's all halal.' She leaned in, sharing a secret. 'We've got her well trained.'

'But I thought we were going out?' I said.

'We can do that whenever.'

'Do you hear that, Fam? It were her that wanted to go out in the first place.'

'A woman can change her mind, can't she?'

It were like a little act we felt we had to put on for some people. Falling into recognisable roles to make others feel at ease. I shook my head, as if to say, 'Women! You know how it is!' But of course he didn't know how it is. He were probably still downloading porn, burdened by his v-plates. I were in a world he had no experience of. He seemed to pick up on what I were thinking.

'I can't tonight. I'm on my way to meet my girlfriend.'

Becka perked up. 'Really?'

'Girlfriend?' I asked, trying not to sound doubtful.

'Yeah. Sophia. She's Italian as it happens. Her dad runs that pizza place in town. The one by the Roundhouse.'

'We should all get together sometime,' Becka said. 'I'd really like that.'

'She'll be busy working, won't she?' I were offering Fahim a way out, but he didn't take it.

'No, I think she'd like that. I'll ask her. Maybe we can get together next week or something?'

'I'd love that,' Becka said. 'I'll fix something up.'

She were off then, asking questions, taking an interest as if she really believed him ('How'd you meet?' 'Do your parents know?') And for every question he had an answer ('She's my sister's friend', 'I'm waiting to see how serious it gets first'). I watched Becka smiling at him, nodding, encouraging, making Fahim open up to her the way she does whenever she meets someone from my side of things. And usually that'd only make me proud, but back then, maybe because it were a guy, I started wondering if there something more going on, some secret communication. I looked from Fahim to Becka. I'd stopped hearing their words. I could only see their moving mouths, their smiling lips. This whoosh of jealousy flared inside me. I looked to the floor, and that saved me. Her feet. Her feet were pointing towards me. Whatever else she were doing, her feet were pointing towards me. That was where she wanted to be. Your feet don't lie. The relief were so strong it made me lightheaded.

I went to pay for my drink. When I came back, Fahim swung his keys into the palm of his hand.

'Imz, I best be off. Really great meeting you, Rebekah.'

'And you. And speak to Sophia. We'll set a date. Maybe next month.'

He said he would. We watched him go.

'He seems nice,' Becka said.

'I guess,' and I were beginning to think that maybe she were right, and I'd just read it wrong. Maybe he were telling the truth. But then, over her shoulder, right opposite where Fahim had been stood, there were a magazine rack, and the topmost magazine were some travel-guide called 'Sophie's Italy'. I put my arm around her shoulder to make sure she didn't catch sight of it. 'Come on. Let's go home.'

That were nearly two years ago now, but he hasn't changed. He were even wearing the same zebra shell suit at the centre today. I've changed, though, and I weren't ready to be so kind to him when he started getting cheeky this time around.

'Imz, ya chief.' He jumped up onto the pool table. 'What's with the look, man? You gone all fundamental since you went back home?'

'I'm just being respectful, pal. Traditional. Can you get off the table, please?'

'What? Oh, sure. But any more tra-dish and you'll be as much of a freshie as him.'

Charag looked up. He still misses the odd word and though he knew something had been said about him, he weren't sure what, or whether it were good or bad. He chose to smile, and that broke my heart a little.

'How's your sister?' I asked. 'Still getting dicked by that college gora?'

It worked. 'We're gunna sort it out,' he mumbled.

'You want to. Sharpish. Everyone's chatting about it.' He looked in pain, almost tearful. I relented. 'Just pray, and Allah, Subhana wa Ta'ala, will sort it out.' He nodded. 'How's your ammi and abba taking it?'

'Someone painted "shamed" across our gate the other night.'

'Yeah. I heard. Tough break.'

'We're gunna take a trip back home. You can tell everyone

that. One of my cousins is up for marrying her.' He snatched hold of my cue and took aim, but missed the easy pot.

In the car park, Fahim's abba – Sharaf Chacha – were waiting for him in his taxi.

'I wrote my Golf off,' Fahim explained.

His abba got out to greet me, making a real fuss. 'How proud your abba would be if he could see you now. Coming to mosque. Looking after your family. Very proud he would be.' He put his hands behind his back, his face now all solemn. 'I was very sad I could not make the funeral back home, beita. Very sad.'

'It's okay, uncleji. I understand.'

'I could not be leaving work for so long, you see. Raina Miah would have understood. I am sure of that. That man knew what hard work was.'

I nodded, but I wanted him to leave now. I didn't want to hear what were coming next.

'Every hour he would work. Every hour. Any why do we do it? For you all,' he answered, taking me, Charag and Fahim in with a long look. I listened for a little longer, but then made my excuses and hurried off. It had been reminding me too much of Abba. Whenever I had a go at him for working himself into the ground, he'd lay on the guilt trip ('But we are doing it all for you', 'It will all be worth it in the end') and we'd end up in a fight because I'd tell him to not kill himself for me. To not use me as an excuse. 'You will understand when you have children of your own,' he'd say. And maybe I do, maybe I do. Maybe I understand too much. We were meant to become part of these streets. They were meant to be ours as much as anyone's. That's what you said you worked for, came for. Were it worth it, Abba? Because I sure as hell don't know. I used to just slam the door and stand with my back to it wondering, What end? Whose end? When is this fucking end? Because what's the point, man? What's the point in dragging your life across entire continents if by the time it's worth it you're already at the end? Ameen.

———

It's the only way to live, Noor. To live your life like you're proud enough to die. Don't be trivial like everyone else. Or worry about trivial things like possessions. Your baba did and look where it got him. Sometimes he'd come home from doing the Friday-night shift and he'd just silently stand in the dark hall with a hand to his forehead.

'Arré, ji, have something to eat at least, please?' Ammi'd say, but Abba just went up to his room and closed the door behind him.

He'd always try to be back on form the next morning. I remember one time when he practically bounced down the stairs, ready to fall in love with the world all over again.

'How's my laadla today?' he said, cuffing the back of my head. I kept my eyes down, crunching through cereal. He sat opposite me, straight-backed as a king in his castle. 'And what has Ammi made today, hain? Arré, what is that I can smell?' Inside, I were shouting at him to stop this. 'While I am remembering,' he went on, trying to keep his voice casual, 'can you wipe a cloth over the back seat before I am having to leave today? Maybe use some disinfectant whatnot.'

Ammi nodded. She didn't need to ask for details. She'd seen it all before. She knew the routine. But I weren't going to let it slide, not again.

'Why? What happened?'

'Oh, nothing. Someone was being ill and accidentally brought up their food. That is all.'

'Right. It's just that when I went out and had a look it smelled more like piss.'

He frowned, but carried on eating.

'Abba, did someone take a leak in the back of our taxi?'

'Why are you worrying? It was nothing. Be a good boy and fetch me a glass of water.'

'Did you get their address? Where did you drop them off? Have you called the police?'

He made a weary sigh, like wondering why I were asking pointless questions.

'Abba, have you told the police?'

'Uff, what is the point in causing more trouble, hain? A little trouble is part of the job.'

I got up to dump my dishes in the sink. 'Yesterday they took a leak in your taxi, last month they put a brick through your window. Maybe next they'll just burn the thing. But never mind, eh? You just take it.'

It were horrible the way his eyes backed down, followed by his shoulders sagging. He looked across to Ammi, then bent back down to his food, chewing at it slowly. Really slowly. I wanted to go over and put my arm around him, and say that I'd sort it out because that were what sons were for and that he didn't have to worry. I didn't, though. I wish I had, but I didn't. I don't know if any of this is making sense, B, but sometimes I can't even work out what it is I were so ashamed of. I don't know whether I were ashamed of Abba because he were ashamed of himself, or whether I were ashamed of myself for being ashamed of Abba. Or maybe it were both together at the same time. It screws my head up sometimes. And it weren't just then, it were all the time. I felt it whenever family came round and someone would start boasting about their kids, or the size of their house, the donations they made back home. Afterwards Abba'd work harder, longer, more and more into the ground, like he thought that were all he had to do to join the others in talk about early retirement and summer houses in the suburbs of Lahore. But the worst time were always in that moment when he realised he were being pitied – because he only drove a taxi, because he had never managed to move away from this estate – and the shame would wash down over him, over his small eyes, and changing his cheery and beautiful face into a plain and disappointed one. Ammi, you know what I mean, don't you? You must've felt the same. It were horrible being witness to that. I swear down, your abba being made to feel ashamed is a terrifying thing to see. The way the child in him comes to the surface, so that all of a sudden it's like you've been turned inside out. The way all his adult strength is made to just crumble by a few well-placed words, and all you can do is gaze helplessly at him with a kind of horror, as if you're watching a tower collapsing.

—

I've just fished out one of your kurtas, Abba. The cream one with all the clever needlework around the collar. I've got it here stretched across my lap. Ammi wanted to lay you in the ground with it but everyone said it were too elaborate. Didn't you always say you'd wear this kurta to my graduation? That didn't quite go to plan, but maybe you could be proud of me now. Remember when I came home with my exam results and handed the paper over to you? You rushed to tear it open but then as your eyes went down the page your smile fell away.

'Never mind,' Ammi said. 'He tried his best.'

You put the paper down and picked up your keys.

'Abba . . .' I said.

You turned round and spoke in a disappointed voice. 'What is it, Imtiaz? Are you wanting to spend your whole life driving taxis like me? Do you not think of that? Do you not think of us?' And then you went out. But I did think about that kind of stuff, Abba. Swear down, I did. I didn't do it on purpose. You know, I reckon partly why I did so shit were because when I were supposed to be revising I'd just sit there with the books open and daydream. Everyone'd be stood up and clapping, and I'd make a little speech thanking my parents. And afterwards everyone would line up to congratulate you and Ammi. I'd write letters in my head and imagine them landing on the mat and you picking them up. Dear Mr and Mrs Raina, We are pleased to write to you to send you your son Imtiaz Raina's degree. We are pleased to say that he came first in his year in all subjects and was the highest scoring student we have ever had. But that were before I realised that none of that matters.

It took time to wring it out and clean myself, but I got there. I want to tell you all about that later, about what happened back home, about meeting Aaqil, but believe me it's a good job I did clean myself up before it were too late. Otherwise how would I answer Allah (swt) when Mahshar arrives and He asks me what I did while my people were being removed from the face of the Earth? Remember that, Noor. Remember that these material goods are just the things they try to dazzle you with so you won't notice what's really going on. And look where it got your baba. Heart attack while chasing some fare-dodger. You never saw him lying on the bed in his blue hospital gown. He looked so tired, you know. You looked so tired, Abba. Unshaven. Spent. The flesh on your upper arms all slack. Your stubble were grey, and there were spittle at the corners of your mouth that I kept on wiping away.

The night before you died I were there sat right next to you. There were a needle slid into your wrist with a red stopper at the end of it. I reached out for your hand and turned it over and ran my fingertips over your cracked palm. I put my own next to it, and I felt like crying. Ribbons of yellow headlights were sliding across the blinds, down the wall and over your face, and do you know what, Abba? Part of me wished that you wouldn't make it. Really. Then I wouldn't any more have to look at your hands and compare them to my own. But that were before. I don't wish you dead now. Honest I don't. I'd do anything to have you here with me right now, telling me to stay strong and that everything were going to be alright.

I placed Abba's hand back down on the bed and turned my face to the ceiling. The headlights were still failing down the wall. The machine were still beeping. When I looked again I noticed that Abba's gown had ridden up his thigh – his penis were poking out from the greying thatch of hair. But before I could walk round and sort it out the nurse came in, her shoes sounding new on the mopped white floor. She reached for the clipboard at the foot of Abba's bed. 'You stopping again tonight, Mr Raina?'

'Yes, fine, thank you.' I didn't want her to see Abba exposed to her like that. He didn't deserve that.

'Can I get you another blanket? Or we have an inflatable mattress in the staff-room you're welcome to use. It's a bit on the small side, mind.'

'I'm fine sitting here, thanks.'

She put the clipboard back. 'I'll just get you some fresh water, then.' She made to walk round to my side. She would've seen everything.

'Just leave it,' I flashed. 'It's fine.'

She looked spooked. 'Very well. Just call me if there's anything you need.'

I sorted out Abba's gown, then went out into the corridor to use the vending machine, but also to maybe smile at the nurse in an apologetic way. I didn't want her thinking bad of me. And she'd understand, surely. But she were on the phone to her boyfriend by the sounds of it. She were leaning on her desk, stroking the back of her calf with her foot. Her black hair were tied up in a messy top-knot, as if someone had struck oil in her head. She saw me walking up, frowned and went back to her conversation. I realised I had no money for the vendo, so I carried on into the toilets, waited a few minutes, flushed, then came back out. She were still on the phone, laughing now. Having a good old laugh about me. I could tell. I hurried back to Abba's ward and for a long while found myself standing at the end of his bed. Your feet weren't covered by the green blanket, Abba. I crouched down, circled my arms over them, then rested my forehead against your cold soles. Tears came. At first I brushed them away with my shoulders, but then there were no point. I could still hear the nurse's laughing voice down the corridor, which just sempt to make everything more unfair. I can hear her laughter now as well, in this room as I write this, filling it up as it did that corridor, while all around the dead talk to the dead. Ameen.

———

Another night. B, I felt like shit this evening. It were just one of those stupid arguments, weren't it? When we just keep on lashing out, knowing that a few kind words would save everything, yet never saying them. Pride, damnit. Your mother looked at me as she were hugging you goodbye, and it felt like I were being accused of something. And when she sent you upstairs to clean yourself up do you know what she said? She turned to me and said, 'Maybe it would do Rebekah some good to come home with me for a few days. Her and Noor. Just a bit of a break, you understand.'

She thought I were some monster she had to rescue her daughter from. 'Thanks for the offer, but, honestly, we're fine. Things are just a bit tight at the moment.'

She lowered her shoulder so her wicker bag yawned open. 'Let me loan you some. Enough to tide you over.'

'No – thanks, that's really kind, but I weren't hinting.'

'I know you weren't. And, please, pay it back whenever you can. There's no rush.'

'I said no,' and I wish I'd kept the blade out of my voice because it just sempt to confirm her suspicions of me.

She put down her bag and tidied her long pleated skirt around her knees. 'Imtiaz, my love, is everything all right with you?'

'Me? Yeah, fine, course.'

'It's just . . .' She looked awkward. 'I have noticed that you've started dressing very differently since you returned from Pakistan.' She put her hand on my hand. 'I'm just worried, my love. I think Rebekah is too.'

'There's nothing to worry about.'

'Is it drugs?' she asked.

'Is that what Becka said?'

'No. No, I promise you she hasn't said anything. You have my word on that.'

And that fucked me off, the way she were at pains to get that across to me, as if she thought I might do something to Becka. She'd clean forgotten the man who used to go to the shops for her, who picked her up from Bingo of a Tuesday and taxied her home and never took a penny for it. 'We're not having any problems,' I muttered like a kid.

She tilted her head, a smile on her face as if to say she weren't born yesterday. She put her arm across my back, and squeezed. 'Do you think this all might be a reaction to your father's death?'

I kept quiet. I didn't want to spoil things. It felt good to have someone put their arm around me for a while. See? I wanted to say. You can still touch me. The sky hasn't fallen in. The ground hasn't opened up.

That's when you came down, B, your face all clean and pink and hair skinned back. Theresa pulled on her brown leather gloves, finger by finger, and said she'd better get going or she'd miss the bus.

'It wouldn't kill you to visit your dear old mam once in a while, you know,' she said on the doorstep. 'You haven't been round for a cuppa since I don't know when. I'm beginning to forget what my granddaughter looks like.'

'Yeah,' I said, doing my best. 'You should go. It'd do you good to get out the house.'

Becka nodded. 'Maybe later in the week.'

'That's a date, then,' Theresa said. 'We'll hit the shops. Get you out of these baggy jumpers. Room enough for two under there.'

'Give over, Mother,' Becka said, laughing.

We on purpose waited until Theresa had rounded the corner, didn't we? We stayed standing there on the step looking down the street just so we could avoid going inside as long as possible. Where it would just be the two of us and the four walls. I for once were all for talking it through. I had things in my head ready to say. But when we did finally close the door all the words sempt to get shut outside and we just stared at each other. And then you said you were going to check on Noor.

—

You were asking me earlier where I'd been all evening, B. I weren't at masjid, like I said. At first I didn't have any real destination in mind, and left the house just to clear my head as much as anything else. I ended up in the park, by the lake. I watched the dark water for a while, waiting for the ducks, because I'm sure Ammi used to bring me to feed stale rotis to the ducks there. But the ducks never came. All that were in the park were a group of hooded-up kids on the creaking roundabout, passing around a plastic litre bottle of cider. I carried on out the town end of the park and walked all the way across to near the Novotel, to where Abba's old taxi base were. I thought if that's what it's going to take to stop you being so miserable, then I'll do it. A decent last few weeks together. Fahim's abba, Sharaf Chacha, were manning the phones behind the safety glass. He pulled off his headset and came round to me.

'Choté Miah! Welcome, welcome.'

I touched his feet. 'Salaam, Uncle.'

'Sit, please sit, my child.' The chairs were lined up along the window, showing their yellow stuffing – knife-slashed, fag-burnt. I explained that I wanted to come back on the road, as soon as possible,

'Alhamdulillah! Your abba would be so proud.'

He started flitting through his filing cabinet for some form I'd have to fill out.

'And I promise not to let you down this time, Uncle.'

'Hm?' he said, as a mucky brown file came flying over his shoulder. 'I am sure it is in here somewhere.'

The last time I'd gone taxiing were the day before we flew out to Pakistan to bury Abba. Ammi said it might do me some good to get out the house for a few hours. It didn't work, though. I remember having to stop at some traffic lights, and taking the time to look around me. It must've been around lunchtime because the High Street were all schoolkids and laughter, bubblegum and attitude. The usual scene, I thought, but then something happened and I started to see all the others. All the bereaved people hidden amongst them: the woman in the white sari quietly waiting her turn at the post office, the old man, tweed-jacketed, shopping alone for food. I'd never noticed them before. And it didn't seem fair somehow that the sun were still shining, the sky were still blue, and they were still trying to muddle on, buying stamps for letters to uncaring children, eating dinner on their lap, in front of the TV.

It were that same night, after packing for the trip home, that I had to go downstairs and stand still for a bit in the dark. Becka came down then, and said it were like I dealt with it mechanically. That it seemed like every time I felt it welling up inside me, I would just go through a process inside myself, step by step pushing it back down so it couldn't drag me under. Still now, I'm not always quick enough and it some-times catches me unawares and I find myself sleeping with an arm over my wet face to keep from waking the kid up. Times like that all I can do is wait it out, just sit and wait till I stop staring at the wall like some fuckwit and get on with things, just get on with what I've got to do. Becka asked if it were like a part of me had died with him. She said that must be the hardest thing. And I know you were meaning well, B, but I felt like shouting at you. It's not like that at all.

'Ah, here it is,' Sharaf Chacha said, blowing a layer of dust off the form. I said I'd bring it back the next day and walked out of there feeling pretty good about myself. Imagining Becka's face. I were daydreaming like that when I got to the corner of Division Street, down by where Charag works. In their window, the neon tubes of a giant burger were flashing lettuce-green, and getting brighter with every step I took towards it.

The two guys having a laugh behind the counter were blacker than even Charag. Proper freshies. Their yellow uniforms made them look like a joke. I looked about through the window but I couldn't see Charag anywhere. He must've left already. I were gunna leave as well, but then one of them saw me and for some reason I felt as if I had to go in then, out of politeness. The door buzzed. With a nod I went up to the steel counter, all the while feeling inside my pocket to see how much ready cash I actually had. 'Could I just have your smallest portion of chips, please?'

'Small chips. Any cheese, gravy, beans or mushy peas with that, sir?'

'No. But thanks.'

'Can I be interesting you in one of our Deal Makers, sir?'

'Just the chips, thanks.'

He were the one with the bad skin condition that Charag'd mentioned a few times. I couldn't remember his name but I know now it's Zuffar, and that the other one's Aalim. Aalim disappeared into the kitchen off to the side, bending under the frame he were so lanky. I heard a fryer begin to spit.

'Will be five minutes, sir,' Zuffar said. 'We are needing some new oil simply.'

'That's fine. I'm in no hurry. I don't mind waiting as long as it takes.' I sounded like some flid, needing to assure them that they had nothing to worry about, that I were on their side and not one of those who'd come in here and start giving them grief. He just looked at me, all wary.

He snatched the tea towel from his belt and wiped down the steel shelves behind him, where all the flat boxes were piled up. And then he moved to the kitchen entrance, leaning into the doorframe like a lot of freshies do: one hand on hip but with the wrist bent back on itself. I felt a strange sense of being abandoned.

'What next, then?' he asked. 'After the fireworks.'

'Then we just walked round the city,' Aalim said from somewhere out of my sight. 'But listen to this. Every girl we said Happy New Year to would give us a chuma. Right on the lips.'

'Really? Even the white ones?'

'Arré, only the white ones. Since when do our girls give us the time of day?'

They must've reckoned that I couldn't understand Panjabi.

'I had eleven kisses. Count them. E-leh-ven. Didn't I tell you to come? What was in Leicester?'

'Family, yaar. I had no choice.'

I heard the chip pan being shook, banged.

'Did Hero-Honda go?' Zuffar asked.

'Charag? No. Same as you. Family first.' There were a long silence, and then Aalim asked, 'Do you think he's asked about the room yet?'

Zuffar shrugged his heavy shoulders, then dropped his head back against the doorframe. 'I have no place to rest my head, for my room is full of dreams.'

'You know, if you put as much effort into your work as you do writing poems, you would have made enough to have gone back home a long time ago.'

'But what is time? Only the space between her words.'

I heard Aalim click his fingers twice. Sighing, Zuffar reached up to grab a white Styrofoam box. 'And about the room,' Aalim said, 'at least ask him for me, na? It's so cold in mine, yaar. And the roof is breaking more now. I'll pay. I'm not asking for charity.'

'I've told you. It's not up to him. It's his chacha's son's house.'

I wondered whether I ought to chime in here and say that I were the chacha's son and that of course he could stay, but then I realised what they probably thought about me, what they'd heard and said behind my back. Oh, him, Charag's cousin? That Raina Miah's son? Waste of space, that one.

Married to a gori. Doesn't work. Doesn't study. Gave his parents nothing but grief.

'Here you are, sir,' Zuffar said in English, coming back to the counter. 'Sorry about the wait.' Outside, the chips landed with an unhappy thud at the bottom of the cement-bin.

You didn't even notice me come in, did you, B? You were just bundled up in the corner of the settee with your feet tucked under yourself. Staring at the TV but not watching it by the look of you. Wish I could just switch off like that. Ammi used to say I were cursed with thinking too much. 'It's bad for you!' She'd say how at family parties, that even when it looked like I were having a laugh along with everyone else, my eyes never joined in. And she were right. I've always liked sitting in the corner of my life, watching in. It's amazing how much people give away just by the angle of their head or the position of their feet, a slight hesitation here, a tiny smile there that they think's gone unnoticed. And there's me, filing all the information, putting it all together with other little gestures and things they might've said or done – or not done – at other parties, other functions, and linking it all up so slowly I can build up a picture. But in a way, Ammi's right. It is a curse because I don't have a choice over it. And there are times when I wish I could just be like everyone else. There were days when I used to beg to ilahi to please rid me of this draining vigilance.

'You watching this?' I asked, reaching for the remote.

'Hm? Oh, sorry. Miles away. You just got back? Where you been?'

'Masjid. You watching this?'

'No, no. Switch over if you want.' You pushed off the settee, as if it were a load of effort to get to your feet. 'I'll heat up your dinner.'

'B?' You turned round, and saw the paper I were waving in my hand. 'It's the form so I can go back out taxiing again.'

It took her ages to smile, and even then it were one of those forced smiles. 'Great! That's really great.'

'At least say it like you mean it.'

'I do. I do. I'm just tired, that's all.'

I scrunched the form back into my pocket.

'Imz, don't be silly. You'll have to get another one.'

'I guess that's my problem, isn't it?'

She shook her head, as if to say she didn't have time for this any more, she didn't have time for us any more, and then she turned round to make for the door again.

'Yeah, you walk off,' I said. 'What do you care anyway.'

She stopped dead and turned on her heel. Her finger were

right up in my face. 'Don't you ever – don't you ever – say I don't care. I care loads, Imz. I care more than anyone but this – this is too much. You know? I can't do this any more. I really can't.'

'Do what? What the fuck are you on about?' She turned in dismay to the ceiling. 'Look, things'll get better. Now the money'll start coming in.'

'That's not . . .' She put her hand on my cheek. It were warm. 'You've changed, Imz. You've really changed. You've become nasty, this nasty cruel . . . When we sleep together, it's not the man I married.' I looked away. 'Why did you have to change? None of this would've happened if you hadn't changed. Why did you have to change?'

'Becka, please,' I said, gently releasing her hands from my kurta. 'I have changed. I know I have. But it's for the better. You'll see. Give it time.'

She padded off down the hallway and shut the kitchen door behind her. That weren't how it were meant to go. You were meant to be overjoyed that I were going back to work. I threw the remote into the settee but it bounced off and hit the floor, the batteries springing out across the carpet.

I went up to our room and I must've fallen asleep because the next thing I heard were the front door closing and feet on the stairs. 'Charag? That you?'

The door opened. He curled his head around the frame. 'Did you want me?'

I beckoned him in. 'How was work?'

'Good. Busy.'

'You were there all day?' That was too much. I'd not meant it to sound so obvious.

'I left early.'

Well, two can play at that. 'I went in to see you. I was in the area.'

'Oh?'

'Yeah. There were the one with the skin?'

'That's Zuffar. Our poet.'

'And the other? The really tall one?'

'Aalim. He's new. Six sisters, poor guy . . . I hope they did not ask you to pay.'

'How come you left early? That's not like you.'

He came and sat beside me, slowly, like he were giving himself time to think. 'I went to Meadowhall. To see if it would make a good place.'

'Right. And does it?'

He nodded. 'Very busy. And lots of glass.'

He were lying. I'm sure of it. 'Why didn't you say something? We could've gone together.'

He shrugged. 'Next time.'

It weren't good enough. 'This has got to stop, acha? This isn't a game. We can't just run around casing places out. We'll get caught. We have to be very careful. We have to be professionals.'

He said he'd take more care in future. 'Can I go and get changed now?'

'Yeah. Go on,' and I watched him go, not taking my eyes off him until he'd left the room and put the door to behind him. Ameen.

————

The flight to Lahore were long, dull, and I spent most of it with my forehead pressed to the rim of the window, staring out at the white walkways made by the clouds. Ammi sat next to me, and next to her an old niqabi who clucked her tongue in sympathy every time Ammi mentioned the boy's abba.

It were dawn when we landed, a gritty golden mist trembling in the air. The immigration hall were large, echoey, and save for the two queues of groggy passengers – nationals, non-nationals – there were just an old woman bent over in the corner. She kept one hand behind her back while she swept the floor with a charoo. The officer had his feet up on the counter, ankles crossed, as I approached with my passport.

With total boredom, he flicked through to my photo, looked to me, the photo, then back to me again.

'This is not you.'

''Scuse me?'

He shook his head. 'This is not you. I will have to keep you back.'

'But it's my passport.'

Ammi appeared, asking what were the matter.

'He says it's not me. He wants to keep me back.'

She looked straight at him. 'Eh, son-of-a-dog, we're here to bury his abba, not line your pockets. Put the stamp on.'

He sighed, stamped my visa and told us to move on.

'That is the only language they understand,' Ammi said. 'What is it? What are you looking at?'

I'd never heard Ammi speak like that. Not once in England had I ever seen her take someone on in that way.

As we left the hall and went to collect our baggage, the air-con fell away and for the first time I felt the force of the heat. My steps slowed. My neck burned. My arms itched. I could even feel sweat on my eyelids, sliding into my lashes. A man were coming towards us, a guard with a bright red diamond on his navy beret. His edges were slightly blurred, as if the heat had the power to thumb people into smudges. A couple of porters were ordered to wheel the coffin out, and while they ground out their beedis and did as they were told, the guard watched over them, all the time using the end of his lathi to get at an itch on his back. The porters trolleyed the coffin down the ramp and out the glass doors. Two men were waiting with a van.

'Your tauji and your cousin, Charag,' Ammi whispered across.

It were the first time I'd ever met either of them. Charag just looked like an updated version of his abba – clean-shaven to Tauji's frothy copperish beard. Hair oiled off into a quiff instead of wrapped in a loose turban. A shirt and wide trousers, and not his abba's lunghi. They were both thin-limbed and narrow-shouldered, though. Fragile-looking. We shook hands in respectful silence and Tauji gave me a supportive pat between my shoulder blades, and then we loaded Abba into the van. Me and Charag climbed into the back as well, sitting across from each other on the wheel arches, the coffin between us. I heard Ammi and Tauji getting in the front, and then we set off.

The journey were so bumpy we had to both keep a hand on Abba's coffin to keep it from sliding about.

'I am betting you don't have roads as rubbish as this in England. They are special for Pakistan only.'

I nodded, not taking my eyes off the coffin.

'It is good that you are doing this, bhaiji. It is good that you brought Chachaji home. And we are all happy that you have come.'

Later, I compared what Charag had said with Fahim and the others in Sheff. They'd mumbled sorry for my loss or something and then pretty much ran away. It had made children of them, where it hadn't of Charag or any of the other people back home – people younger than me – who'd later come by the house to give me their sympathies.

'Thanks. Thank you.'

He chuckled, nodded. 'Mention not,' he said, in English, and I made a mental note that saying thank you weren't the done thing over here.

I couldn't see much but I could hear the traffic and the horns and the quacking of scooters, all getting louder and louder as we moved through the city. But then as we drove out the other side and left the city behind, the sounds started to fall away, and it were now just the odd bicycle bell I heard.

'Home,' Charag said, as the van slowed, stopped, and then a few moments later Tauji opened the back door. I stepped outside, blinking in the sudden bright. My clothes were drenched and I stood there billowing my T-shirt.

'It's too fucking hot.'

Everyone else were heading for the entrance arch. I lagged

behind, making heavy work of avoiding the cow-pats, the half-buried bricks. When I did finally step under the arch, I thought maybe I'd come to the wrong place, or maybe there were something else happening as well as Abba's burial, because the whole of the dust-risen courtyard were full of faces I didn't recognise. A woman – Charag's sister, Qasoomah, as it turned out – tunnelled out of the crowd, calling out, 'Chachiji! Chachiji!' She fell against Ammi's breast and the two women cried out for Abba. After a time she pulled away and moved to me, and I feared she might start crying against my breast as well. But she just wiped her eyes and said that she'd waited to meet me for so long and how sad she were that it had to happen like this. I nodded, slowly, and felt this confused, guilty thing land on my heart, because I'd never in all my life given any of these people gathered here to meet me a moment's thought.

We lifted Abba out of the coffin, and everyone made way as me, Charag and Tauji carried him through on our shoulders and laid him out on the menjha. A thin white muslin kafan covered him, wrapped loose round his feet and head and tucked under his sides. I remember a warm current kept on picking at him so the sheet flapped tight against his nostrils. I folded back the cloth. He looked beautiful. His eyes were closed, his jaw shut. Someone pressed my shoulder. I turned round. It were Tauji, offering me the bowl of scented water. Rosewater, with petals, I remember. And the plastic bowl were dark blue but with a white surfish tinge got from overuse. The sponges were new and yellow. I took one and plunged it in, then started dabbing at Abba's face, across the forehead. Someone, I think it were Charag, eased the bowl from me and started washing down Abba's arm. The bowl got passed down from person to person, each taking a sponge and pressing down on Abba's gleaming skin. I think more sponges were called for, but I weren't really listening out. He were still shining and wet when we wrapped him in the white sheet again. The water clung through the material, spreading out like a wet ring from the bottom of a glass, showing up the lines on Abba's forehead. Everyone else had stopped, and Tauji told me I could as well, but I carried on washing him through the cotton, moving down to his eyes, his cheeks, the sides of his nose, his lips. And as I made my way down his face, applying the damp sponge, the sheet moulded itself around him. It were like he were coming up to the surface of a lake to try and greet me. Someone dropped a handkerchief into my lap. I hadn't realised I were crying. A sad-sounding song broke out from the women gathered at the back. I dropped the sponge and pushed the heels of my hands into my eyes.

We lifted Abba onto a properly carved wooden bench and

hefted him back up onto our shoulders. He felt so light, did my abba, as we carried him down the dirt track and to the far corner of the field where our family buries our dead. We could still hear the women back at the house singing.

'Wailing like cats. Where's that written?' I looked across. He were hunched forward like he were climbing a steep hill, his wrist held behind his back. About my height, but older than me. His beard were spare and spreading. He apologised. That were the first time I saw Aaqil.

The grave were already dug, set apart from the others and further back from the dirt track. Most of the graves were marked with headstones, bent this way and that like hopeless gossips. But you didn't need headstones to know where the dead slept. You just had to notice where the patches of darker-green grass were.

I cradled Abba's head, and then me and Charag started lowering him into the shallow ground. At one point we struggled, but Aaqil came forward and placed his hands underneath Abba's back and between us we managed it. Tauji led the prayers. As the son, I stood at the front, eyes cast down and fingers threaded together.

'At least Allah let him see his son get married first,' I heard someone say behind me. I'd hear that a lot during my first few days back home, and it always made me smile because

I'd remember Abba in his boxy suit, about ten years out of fashion, smiling from lobe to lobe while Becka and me signed the book.

Tauji were still praying, and others were joining in, their voices as if coming through the white glare in the sky. And then Charag motioned for me to throw in the first handful of dirt. I crouched down and took the warm soil in my palms and let it fall through my fingers and onto Abba. I did that twice more. We all spoke together: we created you from it, and return you into it, and from it we will raise you a second time. And it might sound like a wrong thing to feel at that moment but standing there as the final prayers were being said, with all these people gathered behind me, I felt really solid, rooted to my earth. I felt magnificent. Ameen.

———

Noor's teeth are playing up. Noor – your teeth are playing up. I were washing my face in the bathroom earlier tonight, thinking about what Charag might be up to, and then I heard Becka step across the landing and down the stairs. She had Noor in her arms. For a stupid second I thought she were running away and taking the kid with her. I finished up, draining the soapy water down the sink, and followed. The kitchen were all lit up at the end of the dark hallway. Inside, framed perfectly by the open door like some painting of mother with child, Becka were rocking Noor against her shoulder. I watched them for a while. I wondered if I really were ready to leave all this behind. Becka saw me.

'Sorry,' she said, as I walked in. 'Did she wake you?'

'Still got to pray yet.'

'It's her teeth. They're still giving her gyp.'

'I thought you'd taken her to the doctor's?'

I didn't mean for it to sound like I were picking fault, but you sempt to hear it that way. 'And when am I meant to do that, Imz? Hey? When I'm going round four supermarkets to try and save a few pennies? When I'm cleaning this pigsty? Perhaps when I'm scratting around in my purse so we don't all end up sat here in the dark? When exactly am I meant to find the time to get on a bus with her and traipse across town to the doctor's?'

I nodded, apologised. 'How about I take her in the taxi? Tomorrow?'

She didn't answer. She just took the milk bottle from on top of the microwave and tested it on her wrist.

'Here. Pass her here. I can do that. You get some sleep.'

She shook her head and left the room, reminding me to check the back door before I came up. You know, B, I know it might seem like I've abandoned you, but if you reached out and touched me you'd see that I'm really not that far.

—

Becka, you've once or twice asked me who this 'Aaqil' were that me and Charag sometimes talk about. He's a friend from the same village as us. Usually he were pretty serious-minded about everything, but sometimes, if he'd had a bhang lassi or something, he'd crack you up. He'd start trying to speak English – ingrezi – and end up sounding like a posh parrot. He'd hold his hands behind his back, tilt his chin up and say shit like, 'How do you do?' or 'I am a very punctual kind of fellow.'

It must've been only a few days after Abba's funeral when I met him again. He rocked up on his motorbike, roaring under the arch and parking up in the courtyard. I were laid out in a cross under the mossy ceiling fan hanging off the veranda. The fan were useless, only thickly churning around dead swampy air and sending it down to hug the breath out of me. Its brownish base were full of exposed wiring that flies whizzed in and out of. Except one fly, which I watched hover and rest, hover and rest. It took all my effort to turn my head towards the yard and the sound of the motorbike.

Aaqil strode over to Tauji and lazily bent to touch his feet, but like all the kids these days he could only be bothered to reach as far as the knees. Tauji put his iron bucket down, and then he and Aaqil spoke for a bit, once gesturing towards me. The buffaloes Tauji had been washing took the chance to nosy some more in the trough. They stuck their backsides in the air, and their hard wet fur shone like black metal. Aaqil started cutting a diagonal towards me. He wore sunglasses. Above them, his hair were parted in the middle and all high and bouncy like a theatre director's. His shirt pocket had three wavy blue lines sewn into it, like some water logo, and his flappy brown trousers ended a couple of inches above his ankles. He looked like he'd gone to a lot of effort. He looked like a twat. I sat up.

'We are going to the city,' he said, just like that. But I'd got used to this much at least. You didn't have to do thank-yous, and you didn't do hellos either, at least not with people from your own village.

I looked to Tauji, who'd been following behind, barefoot. 'Aaqil is one of ours. And he is right. All day stuck in this house is not good for you.'

'I'll ask Ammi.'

'What need to ask?' Tauji said. 'I have said, na? You two go.'

That were fine by me. Ammi were still in the back room with a few other women, mourning in silence. I found my trainers underneath the menjha.

Someone called, 'And where do you think you are going?' We looked up, making visors of our hands. It were Qasoomah. She were hanging our wet clothes out on the veranda. 'I am making food soon. You are not going anywhere.'

'Uff, Qasoo, they are going to the city only,' Tauji said, then turned to us. 'Go on, go.'

'But he has not eaten yet!'

'I will get him something in the city,' Aaqil said. 'A first-rate dhaba, bhainji.'

Qasoomah's high sweeping broad forehead tightened up and I understood why it were that some aunties were already worrying about where they'd find a boy for such an unpretty girl. 'Do not bhainji me, understand?' She looked to me, and her mouth shifted into a queasy smile. 'I am making your favourite, Imtiaz.'

I looked round, but Aaqil and Tauji had all of a sudden found something of great interest in the floor. 'Tomorrow?' I said weakly.

Her smile vanished. 'As you wish. But at least be taking Charag. He is in the next field only. I will call him.'

'I cannot be taking three on my Bullet.' Aaqil were always very proud that he owned a Bullet. 'The police are getting very strict these days.'

'We have a scooter, thank you very much,' Qasoomah said. 'A Bajaj.'

Tauji butted in. 'Enough tamasha. If you are going to the city, then go. Charag has work to do.'

At the edge of the village the road forked. I'd been to the same spot the day before, on the back of Charag's bicycle. That time we'd veered right, and Charag had told me that the road eventually led to the Indian border. This time, though, Aaqil hooked left, overtaking a man in a rainbow vest who were smacking his cows into line with a whippy stick. Soon we hit open road.

'Your sister does not like me,' he said, turning his head to the side. He had to shout over the grind of the engine. It took me a second to work out that he meant Qasoomah. 'She thinks I am trouble only.'

'She's just careful.'

'She does not want you being friends with me,' he said, meaning that he wanted to be friends with me. I felt a bit disarmed by that.

'She's had to run the house on her own. Ever since my Taiji passed away. It's made her hard.'

He nodded, and turned back to the road, niftily swerving round a large shallow crater. We began to pick up speed, and soon the minutes were flying past in a green and blue blur. There were nothing around, just the fields and the long clean sky. And this strip of road cutting through the middle. I'd never seen the world made that simple before. I closed my eyes. The warm grimy air caught onto my skin, covering my face and arms with a thin black talc.

Soon, the tarmac merged with the main trunk road into the city, and suddenly there were shops and exhausts and crowds, the odd roaming cow. The air turned gritty – I had to keep wiping my eyes – and the temperature sempt to have gone up a few degrees as well. Aaqil said something.

'What?' I shouted.

'Tuck your knees in,' and he tapped my knee just as we turned onto a thin lane with steaming pyramids of bricks piled on either side.

Outside a store called something like Ustaad Music Emporium, he slotted the bike into a space among a load of the same. All the bikes were parked at an angle on their rusting stands, like a line of dominoes frozen mid-fall. I saw my reflection in the shop window, between a couple of the harmoniums on display. I looked like an idiot tourist, freeing his sweaty jeans from where they'd gathered into his backside.

'You see that?' Aaqil said.

Off yonder, flat against the sky, were a pale-brown dome,

the tips of two red minarets either side. 'We going there?' I asked.

'It is our Badshahi Masjid.'

'Don't think I know that one.'

'You will have heard of it. It is world famous. Follow me.'

Next to the music shop, so sunk back into its concrete casing I didn't even notice it at first, were a little dhaba. A kid leaned across the counter, chin in hand and concentrating hard at the booming TV bolted high on the back wall. The steel shutter hung like a guillotine above him. Felled, and it would've sliced his back in two. We took a seat at one of the cheap square tables with the black plastic rim. Aaqil called the boy. Reluctantly, he unglued himself from the counter and mooched over to us. He never once took his eyes off the film, though.

Aaqil snapped his fingers. 'Eh, chotu, you here to work or watch TV?'

The kid looked at us, unimpressed.

Aaqil ordered plates and plates of food – fried murga, fish pakora, channa dhal, spiced goatmeat. 'And afterwards, pistachio ice-cream. Understand? Okay. Go. Double-quicktime. And make it tasty, acha?' he called after him. 'We have a valetiya here.' That means foreigner, B. I hated being called that.

When I suggested that he'd maybe ordered too much, he waved his hand, telling me not to talk such nonsense. 'I told your sister I would make sure you did not go hungry. I keep my promises.'

There were no humour in his voice. Carefully, he took off his sunglasses and hooked them into the open neck of his shirt. 'So, you are married? Bhainji did not come?'

'The baby's too young.'

'I see, I see. Boygirl?'

'Girl.'

He made a face, as if to say never mind. 'You married young, yes?'

'Not really. No point in waiting once you've found the right woman.'

He chuckled dirtily. 'She is from here? From Pakistan?'

He knew she weren't. The whole village knew she weren't. Everyone knew that I, Mubtasim Raina's eldest grandson, had married a white woman in England. 'No. She's from Meersbrook.'

He looked confused. 'Mesbru . . . ?'

'It's a hill station on the banks of the River Don. In Sheffield. Real old steel country, you know?'

He did not know. 'But she has reverted, yes?'

The rumours that must've flown round the village about that! Had she? Hadn't she? 'She has. Straight away. She's great like that.'

He nodded, and I could tell he were surprised. 'And you are working over there? In your country?'

'I've got a taxi.'

'New?'

'Fairly.'

'My motorcycle is brand new. A Bullet. As good as any you have in your country.' The food arrived. 'And I bet you will not have tasted chicken as good as this in your country either.'

'Right,' I sighed. It were all getting a bit boring, his bigging Pakistan up at every chance. I wanted to go home already. Aaqil tore a strip off the chicken and dangled it into his mouth. He mmm-ed and ahh-ed. I half-expected him to start rubbing his stomach.

'I am always coming here.'

He hadn't realised that the kid weren't out of earshot yet. The boy turned on the spot, his face a sly smile. 'Funny, Ustaad, I do not remember ever seeing you before.'

'Chup! What do you know, you stupid sisterfucking cunt?' And then Aaqil smiled at me in an embarrassed way, and I realised that it weren't that he were trying to put me down, but that he wanted to impress me. I lost some respect for him then, the way you do when you realise someone looks up to you. 'Eat, valetiya, eat,' he said.

'Don't call me that.'

'Call you what? Valetiya?'

'Just don't, okay?'

His eyes widened, as if dilated by some light he'd spotted inside me. 'But it is what you are, na? And it is no insult. Most men here are wanting to be a valetiya. You are lucky, no?' I must've had a proper face on because he said, 'Okay, okay. I am sorry.' He touched his ears. 'I will not call it you again. Now, eat, please. Before your sister is coming after me.'

During ice-cream, the kid came with two more cloudy bottles of Limca and refilled our chipped glasses. 'Food teekh-taakh?' he asked Aaqil, sounding like he didn't much care either way. 'Does the valetiya want anything else?'

Aaqil hit the kid upside the back of his head. 'Arré, saala, haven't your parents taught you to show some respect? Does he look younger than you? You call him bhaiji, understand?'

It became a kind of running joke while we were at the village. Whenever someone would call me a valetiya, Aaqil put on a show of correcting them, saying stuff like, Valetiya? Who? Him? No, no. Just light-skinned, that is all.

The kid went back to the counter, back to his channel-surfing.

'Thanks,' I said.

'What nonsense,' he replied, in English, which made me laugh.

Ameen.

———

We went to Meadowhall today, me and Charag. I've told him he needs to start paying more attention. I saved us a table in the middle of Oasis – the food hall – right under the huge screen that blasts out the latest store discounts. And I watched him, in his black jeans and green trackie top, making his way back with a tray of pizza. Briefly I lost him in the crowd, but there he was, winking cheerfully to some woman he'd nearly knocked over. He were never as confident when he first came over. The first time I brought him here to get some clothes for work he spent the whole time with his head down, not even meeting the salesgirl's eyes, as if he felt like some sort of barbarian in her presence.

'Pizza? Don't you get sick of eating that?'

He sat down, served out the jumbo-sized drinks. 'I guess,' he said, and bit greedily into a slice.

'I guess.' That were a new one. He's copying me. I guess I should be flattered.

'New clothes?' I pointed at his top.

He nodded, swallowed. 'They are the latest.'

'What happened to your London Jeans?'

He frowned. 'No one is wearing those . . . Don't you want?'

I pushed my plate towards him. 'Have it.'

The family next to us started getting into their coats, saying that if they got a move on they might just miss the traffic. When they'd gone, I leaned in, speaking quietly. 'Only took twenty minutes door to door – if the tram's on time. Say thirty, max. And I didn't count any cameras on the way. You?' I sounded fake, stupid even to myself. Trying too hard to bring him back on board.

He watched me over the top of his pizza. His chewing slowed.

'A Sunday like today. Maybe if you went over there, near the escalator – the stairs? – and I stayed in the middle. We'd have most of it covered.'

He put his slice down. 'Whatever you say is fine.'

'What's the matter?'

'Nothing.'

'I'm getting sick of your lies, Charag.'

But then a couple of girls blowing bubbles down their straws took the table next to us and we had to stop talking.

We didn't speak on the Supertram back into town, just standing up and gripping the red belts that looped down from the ceiling. At first it sempt full of the usual boring faces, but then I noticed someone looking straight at me. He were brown, mid-thirties maybe, sat a couple of rows from the back. I tried to ignore him, thinking I were imagining it. But, no, he were definitely staring at me. Not in a nasty way. More calm, the way someone might look at a tree, or a painting. Like he found me curious. Maybe he were a freshie, I thought. They sometimes stare when they meet another brown face. But he weren't a freshie. He weren't trying hard enough to fit in to be a freshie. I stood it for a while, even tried to stare him out, but when he didn't let up I moved to where he couldn't see me.

Charag got off at West Street – he'd been asked to do an extra shift. I said I were staying on, except, of course, I didn't stay on long. I got off at the next stop. There were a rap on one of the windows. It were the staring man. He smiled, then waved as the tram sailed up the hill. I were certain I'd seen him somewhere before. There were something familiar in that wide gap between his two front teeth. I couldn't place it, though. Maybe he knows something. Maybe he overheard something at the food hall. But no, no. We were careful. Fucking freak, I thought, and told myself to forget about it.

I turned back on myself, walking quickly until I saw Charag up ahead. Going to work, my arse. He's going to shop us in, I bet. He's lost his nerve. I followed him through town, over the flyway. I watched him draw out his phone and text the cops. He stopped to check himself out in a shop window, teasing his hair into place before moving on again. A girl? I thought. Is that all it was? And I hoped it was just a girl. That would've been so much more bearable than him betraying us all. He checked his watch, then broke into a jog. He turned up Division Street. I followed, running to catch him red-handed, shaking hands with some undercover officer. But I shouldn't have doubted him. He were only waving at his friends inside, and then he pushed open the door. A few seconds later the neon burger sign stuttered the window bright.

—

It were always like that with Charag. Even back home he'd be forever checking his hair in the scooter's mirror or worrying over some phantom spot on his forehead. There were one time when we were on our way to Murnalipur, where we rented some land. I were stood behind getting a backie on his bicycle.

'Why don't we take your scooter?' I asked once.

'You think petrol is growing on trees?'

On the way we stopped at the side of the sandy road, out-side a row of open-front shops. One sold steel girders for roofs, another tractor parts, the third were a dhaba. Along the top of the dhaba were a faded Coca-Cola board with a thick crack down its middle. The owners were all sat playing cards out front. Charag called out for a drink, and a youngish man in a stiff orange shirt that looked made from cardboard walked very lazily towards us. A few bottles lolled by his side, the necks gripped between his fat fingers. And a pair of jeans were slung over his shoulder.

'Kaise ho, Ustaadji?' he asked Charag. 'Murnalipur again?'

Charag nodded.

'I am thinking you must have a girl there to come visit, hain? Keeping you company at night. Am I right or am I right?'

'You should ask your sister that.'

The man laughed. 'Which one?' He stood all three bottles in his palm and held them out to us.

I chose Rosemilk, because no one ever chose Rosemilk and I felt sorry for it. The man popped off the bottle-tops. While we swigged, Charag told him to show me the jeans. They didn't look like anything special. Just typical stiff cheap denim.

'Turn them round,' Charag said. 'Show him the label.' Pépé Jeans, London. 'Just like you wear, hain na?'

I'd never heard of them. 'Yeah. Exactly.'

He beamed. 'I am saving up for these.'

The man said, 'And one day they will be yours, Ustaadji.' He folded them back over his shoulder, then took our empty bottles and went and stooped over the men playing cards.

'We paying?' I asked.

'He'll put it on our account,' Charag said, which I later worked out meant that they'd settle their debts at the end of the season, when the crops were harvested and sold off to the local government.

A gummy old woman made her way across the road then, between the large gaps in the passing traffic. Her black head-scarf made a perfect oval of her creased and shrivelled face. Charag touched her knees.

'Ah'daab, bibiji.'

She touched his head, wished him a long life.

'Off somewhere?' he asked.

'The bazaar. The grandson is only eating eggs in the morn-ing.'

Charag called over a kid sat on the stone steps of a house, wrapt up in some hand-held computer game. The kid came over, sluggishly, as if he knew he'd have to go run an errand.

'Go into the muhalla and bring bibiji some eggs, okay? And be quick.'

'Get them from Kaloo,' the woman called. 'And make sure they are desi ones or you will be going back.'

The kid went off, moaning.

'So disrespectful young people are these days,' the old woman said.

'He won't be long,' Charag said.

She didn't thank Charag or the boy. She just nodded, as if it had been no more or no less than she'd expected them to do. She turned to me. 'So, you are Munchiji's olaad?' Olaad means offspring, B, but it also means more than that. I suppose it means carrier of the flame. It's a nice word. I loved it when I'd be going round the village and people'd shout me over by calling, 'Mubtasim Ali's grandson!' or when they'd introduce me as 'Munchiji's great-grandson'. I were always so and so's grandson or such and such's nephew or whatever. I were never just me, on my own. No one ever called out, 'Hey, Imtiaz!' And I loved that. It were like for the first time I had an actual real past, with real people who'd lived real lives. Now I think that maybe when Noor takes her kids back home people'll call out to them, 'Arré, Imtiazji's grandson!' and then they'll sit in the shade of a banyan tree and listen open-mouthed to stories of the struggle that I, their baba, were part of.

'Has your heart settled here?' the woman asked.

I hadn't heard what she'd said at first – some truck had passed behind her spluttering brown smoke. She looked to Charag. 'Does he know the language?'

'I do,' I said, indignant.

'Well, has your heart settled here yet?'

'Ji. I like it here.'

She nearly laughed, as if it were the kind of earnest thing she'd expect a valetiya to come out with. 'You are married?' I said I were. 'Just one begum?' She chewed her bottom lip. I could see the plan coming together in her crafty head. 'Are you here for another? I have a grand-daughter. Very pretty girl. Skin as fair as milk.' I swear down, these people have some sort of radar for a British passport. 'You can have one wife for when you are in your own country and one for when you are coming home . . . What is so funny?' I were thinking of you, B, and the look on your face if I turned up on the doorstep with a second wife. 'Munchiji was having two wives,' the woman pointed out.

'Only because our first bibi passed away,' Charag said.

She turned on him. 'The details are not mattering.'

'Did you know him?' I asked, to switch the subject.

'Munchiji? Of course I was knowing. A very cheeky young man.' She pointed to the stone steps the kid had been sat on. 'All day sitting there playing cards, whistling at girls. Whistling at me,' she added, smiling. 'You will cause me nothing but shame, his abba would say. But then look what happened, hain? He surprised everyone when he became Munchi. We could not believe it.'

I were looking at the stone steps, picturing him. I must've looked pretty lost because the woman said,

'Arré, I am talking about Munchiji. Yes? Your abba's baba?' She turned to Charag, sighed. 'What do they care? Brought up in foreign lands, learning foreign ways.'

I hated it when they came out with shit like that. I were interested. I did care.

The kid came back shouldering a string bag made lumpy with eggs. He held it out to the woman. 'Eggs, bibiji.'

'Arré, am I looking to you like a coolie? Go on, take them to the house.' The kid's pointy shoulders slumped. He trudged off across the road. The woman followed. 'I am watching,' she called after him. 'Drop any and I will be speaking to that good-for-nothing abba of yours.'

Charag jumped back onto his bike. 'Tsk! Come on, yaar, it is getting late. What use just staring?'

I went with Charag a few times to Murnalipur. We'd head right when the road forked outside our village, riding further and further away from the city. It were a bitten-up, empty road.

The only thing to take any real notice of were the big white advertising billboard that Qasoomah had one time pointed out to me from the roof of our house – a woman with thick flyaway hair and a smile that got more crazed the closer it got to us. She were advertising PepsoDent toothpaste. Wintergreen flavour. The paint were peeling off in droopy sleeves but the thing were a bit of a landmark round those parts. People'd give directions by it: 'A kilometre after the tooth-woman . . .'

We were still some way off the billboard when we turned left through a big square arch with Murnalipur written in gold across its top. The entry gate were so impressive that I were expecting something a bit more than a single bumpy mud road and a bunch of low brick houses. It didn't even have a bazaar. Our busy village were a city compared to this place.

At a bend in the road, Charag turned onto one of the thin, humped paths of earth that ran through the field. The sun were hot on my face and the tall stalks kept on slicing at the backs of my legs. We made slow wobbly progress towards the concrete hut sat on its soily mound in the centre of the field.

'This all ours?'

'It better be. We pay enough for it.'

There were a large stone tub attached to the side of the hut, and a pipe jutting out of the tub spurted perfect clean water into a thick groove in the soil. From the groove, the water spread off along little channels out into the field, watering the land.

Charag rested his cycle against a tree and went about his work. He checked the water level in the motorised well, and made sure the black electrical boxes and their beards of wire hadn't been tampered with.

'Sometimes kids come in the night,' he said.

Then he got on his haunches and began sharpening his scythe against a rock. I went for a wander, first ducking into the hut. It were cool and shaded, but there weren't much room to stand about at the edge. A piece of blue tarpaulin were stretched across the great big well and held in check with small triangular boulders. Just as I were leaving, I spotted a couple of geckos padding quickly across the wall, as if racing to bagsy the corner. Behind the hut, a beaten-in menjha squatted under a leafy yellow tree. The weaves had lost their tightness and the ropes sagged in the middle. A magazine called 'Moviestar' lay open on the ground, its pages turning magically in the breeze. Next to that were a pile of large banana leaves, and a chipped mug half full with water, flies buzzing round. That were where Charag must've sat whenever the light went and he had to come here to keep the motor working by hand, or to just wait in case the light went off again. I remember the banana leaves because when I asked about them he said he used them to wipe his arse when he needed to go for a shit around here.

I picked up the magazine. It were over a year old and full of actresses wearing not very much.

'So this is what you do?'

He looked round, still sharpening his scythe. 'That isn't mine.'

'Whose is it, then?'

He smiled, turned back to his work.

'You've got a girl?'

He looked at me again, then nodded. 'Sometimes she is coming at night to see me.' I thought that were pretty unlikely. I didn't believe him.

I moved to the edge of the brown island and shielded my eyes to look out across the fields. The sun's rays spinned silver, prickling hot all over my skin. My shadow stretched longingly out in front of me, black enough to jump inside. There were movement off up ahead. I looked harder, closer, and saw a line of dark women crouched down in the grass, some with babies on their backs. I turned round to ask if they worked for us, but Charag had moved into the field as well, and all I could hear were the hack-hacking of his scythe. He hadn't gone far though, and I found him easily enough as I waded through the wheat. The stalks nearly came up to my waist, I remember.

'Careful you do not cut yourself,' he said.

He were hacking the wheat out at the base, making a pile, and then shuffling along to the next on his bare feet. It all just sempt so easy for him. Cutting and piling, cutting and piling. Like his limbs were just a simple extension of this land. I looked to my own arms and legs. Useless things. They didn't know the first thing about how to handle earth. I crouched down.

'Where do these go?'

'I'll store them in the hut for now. Tomorrow I'll bring the tractor and take them home.'

I turned my pyjamas up to my knees and rolled the sleeves of my T-shirt over my shoulders. Charag stared, wondering what the hell I were doing. I wrapped my arms around the first bundle.

'Arré! Leave them!'

''S fine. Sooner we finish, yeah?'

'But you're not meant to work.'

But that just made me more determined to heft the bundle up onto my shoulder. I started back towards the hut. I remember I had to keep on angling my head to see where I were going, and that stones pressed into the soles of my feet.

'There are some sacks in the hut. Bring them with you.' He went back to his hack-hacking. Ameen.

———

I've had time to think about it now, B, and maybe you're right. Maybe a few days' break at your mam's is just what you need. It'll give you a chance to put your feet up for a bit. Come back home all freshened up. I'm sorry if I sempt in a foul mood earlier. You'd not been picking your phone up all day and all I had were what you'd stuck on the fridge. I were worried sick. You should've seen how quick I were out my chair when I heard the door go. But it weren't you. It were only Charag.

I tried phoning you again, and left a voicemail, and it were not long after that when you rang to say you were at your mam's.

'Right. So do you want me to pick you up?'

No, you said, you were going to stay for a few days. You'd be in touch tomorrow. My hand were shaking when I closed my phone. I needed to talk to you, and that propelled me out the house. Charag followed, wanting to know what the matter were.

'Nothing. She's at her ammi's. I'm bringing her back.'

'Leave it until tomorrow, bhaiji. Or let me come with you, yes? Please?' But I were already starting up the taxi, pressing hard on the gas.

I waited outside your mam's a good few minutes. Working out what I wanted to say, the way I wanted to say it. And then I stepped out and knocked on the door. Your mam answered.

'Theresa,' I said, and I saw her straighten her spine, which fucked me off, her thinking I were the enemy.

'I don't think this is the right time, Imtiaz.'

I could hear Noor in the front room. I looked hard at Theresa, as if to tell her she had no business keeping my daughter from me. She lowered her eyelids and moved to the side. I picked up Noor, holding her to my chest, away from Theresa. 'Becka upstairs?'

'I really don't think this is a good idea. She's very tired. Please understand. I'll get her to call you tomorrow.'

I found her in her old room, sat on the edge of her bed. She looked up, like she'd made a face ready for meeting me. She weren't wearing her headscarf. Her hair looked greasy, with thin strands stuck across her forehead. Her big pale-pink sweater swamped her, and from the way her breasts drooped you could tell she weren't wearing a bra. She looked exhausted. I shut the door, not angrily, and went and sat next to her. It were time.

'This is your answer, is it? What happened to talking it through?'

'Leave it out,' she said in a tired voice.

'I've been in a bit of a world of my own lately. I know I have. But I'll make more of an effort from now on. Especially over the next few weeks. Promise.'

You looked away. 'Not yet.'

'Then when?'

'I don't know.'

'Soon?'

'I don't know.'

I looked to the floor, nodding. 'You still want me around?'

'Noor needs her father.'

'But do you? Want me around?'

There were a hesitation. 'Of course I want you around.'

I saw the hospital tag around your wrist. 'You been ill?'

She pushed her sleeve down over her hand and held it in place. 'It's nothing.'

'What happened?'

'Nothing. It was Noor. I had to take her in. She caught an infection.'

'Infection?'

'An ear thing. Don't go off on one. She's fine. It was nothing.'

'And that's where you've been all day?'

'That's where I've been all day.'

I saw a chance. 'I'm not surprised she caught summat. She should be at home. Think of what's best for her at least.'

'I do think of what's best for her. That's all I do.'

'I know you do,' I said, and then, more quietly, 'I know you do. And I do, too. I'm just doing what's best for her as well. One day you'll see that.' I brushed her damp hair away from her cheek. She didn't stop me. I kissed her neck.

'Imz, please don't.'

But she let me push her back onto the bed. I propped myself up on an elbow and slid my lips over hers. Her arms went around my neck. 'Knew you still loved me.'

'I've always loved you.' And swear down, B, that made my whole body come alive. I pushed your sweater up and took one of your breasts into my hand and into my mouth. I love your small hard pink nipples. My cock were curling out against my briefs. I looked up at you, wanting to catch your eye, smile, but you just lay there, looking away, letting me do what I wanted. That weren't what I wanted. I let my head fall onto your chest. How much we've both changed, B.

'I'm sorry,' I said.

'I know you are.'

I climbed off. She sat back up and tugged her sweater back down over her stomach.

'Just go. Please. Just go.'

'For crying out loud, B.'

'I can't do this right now.'

I pulled her to me, up close, pinning her hands down by her side. But the words, man, the stupid words just wouldn't come. I stared at her. She stared at me. She began to cry. I looked away. We were back to the start, back to sitting side by side on the edge of the bed.

She said, 'Please don't make me feel any worse than I already do. Please.'

'Just come home, then. I've said I'll change. I will.'

She shook her head, wiping tears. 'It's too much, Imz. Everything's too much of a mess. And I've tried to handle it, really I have, but I can't do it any more. I honestly, honestly—'

'Please, B. Be honest tomorrow, yeah? Just let me have this night. Come home tonight.'

'I'm sorry,' was all she said.

She put her hand on my knee and let it rest there for a while. And then she pushed up onto her feet and showed me to the door.

And maybe that were for the best. Maybe the reason Allah (swt) has willed this is to give me the time to talk more about what happened back home. About Aaqil and Faisal and Kashmir and Afghanistan and the rest. The more you know, the more I hope you'll understand, though I'm not sure that's always true. So maybe that's the reason why this had to happen. Right now, though, I just want to sleep. Ameen.

————

Everyone sempt to have a problem with Aaqil. Every time he came to call on me Qasoomah'd make some sort of remark. 'Is it me, or has the milk turned sour?' or, more directly, 'The devil's here.' Even Charag one time at Murnalipur stopped in his hacking and asked me if I thought all this hanging around with Aaqil were a good thing.

'He's lazy. He doesn't help his abba. He spends all day just going around on that motorcycle.'

But I didn't have a problem. Just because he weren't like them. Just because he had the guts to do his own thing. Nearly every other night we'd ride into the city, past the cricket stadium with its broken traffic lights and turn off down a road banked up on either side with the usual piles of bricks. We'd stop outside a dodgy-looking doctor's – Prithvi Practice, I remember – and climb the iron stairs to the room at the top.

The first time I went Aaqil introduced me to their ustaad, their teacher. His face were friendly, all fat cheeks that his squinty eyes disappeared into. The great thing about Ustaadji were that he always made you feel like your question were the first time ever that question had been asked, the first candle of the night. 'That is a very tough one,' he'd say, mulling it over, 'yes, a very good question indeed.'

The talks he gave were pretty short, less than an hour – some history and politics, mixed in with readings from the Qu'ran and advice on how to be a good Muslim. He kept it pretty mellow.

'He's from our village,' Aaqil whispered to me. 'Our mosque. All the best people are.'

'Right,' I said, and maybe my voice betrayed some impatience, because Aaqil turned his shrewd eyes on me, and I saw completely why some people were scared of him.

When Ustaadji left, the main business would begin. Out came the hookahs, the tobacco, the bhang. Someone would bring out a cassette player, turning up the volume when the qwaliya'an started. We took our pipes and sank into the thick ottomans arranged along the walls. Great curls of smoke rolled out into the middle of the room, hanging in the air and turning yellow under the light. It were one evening like that when I heard about the trip to Kashmir.

'Then we can see it with our own eyes,' Aaqil said, and pulled deep on his pipe. He held it in for a few seconds, then breathed out hard. 'We need to see it with our own eyes.'

A voice came over the top – one of Aaqil's friends. 'Can someone tell Gabar Singh that we are not going to the disputed areas? And if we are then to tell me now because, Inshallah, I am not ready to be dying just yet.'

'All of Kashmir is disputed,' Aaqil said.

'Arré, let it be, yaar.'

'Let what be? What about being loyal to the old wounds?'

Loyal to the old wounds. That struck me for some reason, and I were still thinking on it when someone asked if I were going too.

'Of course he's coming,' Aaqil said, throwing me a fresh packet of tobacco. 'It will be an adventure. It will be – how do you say . . .' He made his face long, ready to do his best English accent. 'It will be a jolly good time!'

Aaqil laughed, and so everyone else laughed as well. They wanted me to join them. I rearranged the coals in my pipe and pulled up on the smoke. The bacca were raspberry-flavoured – my new favourite – and I breathed out the smoke through the smile I could feel on my face.

We sempt to be back in our village in no time, riding past the roadside meat joints with their stacked tight cages of haughty chickens. I saw the owner opening a wire door and plunge his big hairy arm inside. There were squawking, violent flapping. We turned towards the farm and started bumping down the dirt track. The tall thick grass wagged in the dark fields either side. Mosquitoes swarmed in the giant triangle cast by the headlight.

'What did you mean? Be loyal to the old wounds?'

'What who were saying?'

'What did you mean?'

'Yes.'

The bhang hadn't worn off yet, or with Aaqil it were more likely that he didn't think it had worn off yet. I tried again, and this time he understood.

'I suppose I was meaning that we shouldn't forget.' He thumped his chest with his fist, but then the bike swerved. I were disappointed. I were expecting something deeper. The words had sempt so much more poetic than what hid behind them. At the house, I jumped off and gave him back his sunglasses.

We heard Qasoomah, deliberately loud. 'Arré, it looks like the loafer has finally remembered where his home is.'

Aaqil wished me luck, spinning round his Bullet and

roaring off until the drill of his bike retreated into the dark. The menjhe were all made and laid out in a line under the veranda, ready to be slept on. But no one were asleep yet. Ammi and Qasoomah sat at either end of the middle menjha, a wide steel tray of lentils between them. They were picking out the bad seeds, the small stones. A cool blue light were given out by the neon mosquito-trap – Charag had bought it the day we'd arrived and nailed it to the outside wall. It meant a slight smell of burning always undercut the air as insects got stunned and fried. In the mornings, Qasoomah would brush up the dead matter and tip it into the field at the back of the house. Just like that.

Charag waved at me from inside. He were lying on his back listening to the MP3 player we'd brought over for him. He still had on the loose turban he wore in the fields. He kept a bit of it trailing down his shoulder, using it to wipe the sweat off his face.

Tauji were sat on his menjha with his back at the wall. His dhoti were gathered up around his waist, making a valley between his thin thighs, and his long legs went wandering out into the light at the foot of his blanket. He swirled a peg of whiskey in one hand, ice cubes fizzing.

'Sit, beita, sit.' He collected up his feet. 'Come sit by me. Qasoo, bring the boy some food.'

'I ate already.'

Qasoomah picked a small stone from the lentil tray and threw it aside. 'Of course. Treats his home like a hotel. For sleep only. Spends all day out with that lefengah.'

I never pointed out to her that this weren't actually my home, but I liked knowing that she thought so. And I liked that she fell out with me, because you only fall out with the people you care about, don't you? I liked even more that everyone treated me as if this were my real home, as if England were just some place where I happened to be born.

'Bring him some hot milk at least,' Tauji said.

Qasoomah moved off to the mud oven, snatching up a brass pot along the way. She banged the pot down on the metal ring. 'Out at this time of the night.' It were barely eight o'clock. I were nearly twenty-two.

'You could've called me on my phone if you were that worried.'

'You see how he is talking back?' she said, as if I'd somehow proved her point.

Ammi sieved a handful of the lentil seeds through her palm, then cast a bad one to the ground. The bluish haze made it look as if she were haloed, with strange shadows falling out of the folds of her burqa. 'You are spending a lot of time with this Aaqil.' She looked up. 'Yes?'

'He's just a friend, Ammi. I can't spend all day stuck here.'

Qasoomah held out a small pot of frothy buffalo milk. She lifted my arm up for me. 'Hai, Allah, they are eating you alive. Why did you not put on your cream?'

I took my arm back. The bites weren't all that bad.

'What if one had gone into your eye, hain?'

'Aaqil gave me his sunglasses.'

'Aaqil gave me his sunglasses,' she mimicked.

'Uff, Qasoo. Stop picking on the boy and go and put some roti dhal together. Charag might have to go tonight. The doodhwallah was saying the light will go.'

'And how does he know? What is his job? Collecting milk or counting electricity?'

'Qasoo,' Tauji cautioned.

She went off in a huff, complaining that no one cared about her in this house.

'And then bed, acha? No watching those stupid dramas.' Tauji turned to us. 'All night she is up watching that show, that one with all those people – uff, what is it called?'

'My Crazy Heart,' Ammi supplied.

'With that stupid whore in those shorter than short clothes.'

'Sunita Bonita.'

'That shameful girl. No shame she has.'

'Tauji,' I said, 'she's only acting.'

'And that is better?'

Ammi got up from the menjha, dusted her hands. 'Imtiaz, help me carry this over there.'

'But all night Qasoo will watch,' Tauji carried on, the whiskey finding its voice. 'And at her age. She is what? Twenty-three now? Twenty-four?'

We laid out the lentils at the top of the yard so they'd toast a bit in the morning sun. 'She is still a child, bhaiji,' Ammi said, coming back to ease the bottle from his hand.

He let it be taken. 'What still a child? What were you like at her age?'

'Different times.'

'Nonsense.' He turned to me. 'Such a strong woman your ammi was. Always sat at the front of the class. Doing her work. Never making trouble. But if someone spoke to her in a shameful way, she would tell them off right there and never again would they bother her. I am telling you, even on the college bus she would sit with her friend only, not sitting with the boys like I am seeing every day now. I should know. I used to catch the same bus.'

'You went to college, Tauji?'

'Oh, for one year only, beita. But then the land caught an illness and there was too much work here. Your baba took me out.'

'But how come Abba went? I mean, Abba still went to college, didn't he?'

'Yes, oh yes, Rizwan was going the year after. All problems over by then. He was a very lucky man, your abba. Kismetwallah. Finishing college, diploma in his back pocket. And then his entry card for England came first time.'

'Imtiaz, you should sleep,' Ammi butted in, but I wanted to hear more. I wanted to hear about how lucky Abba was.

'You should have seen the line of men coming here,' Tauji went on. 'Everyone had a daughter for him to marry.' He looked to Ammi. 'Was it then that your abba came to visit too?'

'I do not remember,' Ammi said.

'Aw, Ammi, come on. You must do! It were your marriage.'

'Yes,' Tauji said, 'I am sure it was. Yes, I remember now. Your ammi's abba came and do you know what I was doing, Imtiaz? While they were discussing your ammi and abba's marriage do you know what I was doing? I was carrying sacks of grass back from the field and emptying them out into the trough. But I could hear everything. Oh yes. I could hear your ammi's abba saying that he had a beautiful well-behaved daughter who would be perfect for this house.'

'And did you know it was Ammi? I mean, did you know he was talking about the girl from the bus? From college?'

'Oh yes, I knew. I knew who he was talking about.'

I don't know why but I love hearing about Abba's and Ammi's past, before they even met each other.

'And then? What happened then?'

'And then? Well, my abba said yes, and your abba said yes and then it was just left to wait and see if your ammi would say yes and' – he raised his glass – 'she did!' He necked what were left of his whiskey, sending a shiver across his shoulders. 'She said yes. Can you believe it? She did not even spend long thinking about it. Straight question, straight answer. Like I am saying, Imtiaz, very strong woman your ammi is. Made of tough-tough stuff.' And then, more quietly, 'She said yes.'

It seems my abba were a bit of a don back in the day. 'And then?'

'And then nothing,' Ammi said.

'And then they married and left for England together, and I stayed here. With all this.' He looked around, sighed. As if in wonder at all the years that had gone. 'But everything is as Allah wishes, hain na? He is knowing best.'

'What use talking of the past?' Ammi said. 'What is left there? Now come on – phutaphut! Everyone to their menjhe.'

Tauji didn't move, and I just wanted to hear some more stories.

Ammi groaned. 'Is no one going to sleep in this house tonight? The beds are all made.'

Tauji laughed a little to himself, looking down at the hard cracked ground between his feet. 'Yes, the beds are all made.'

There were a long pause.

'Ammi, when you—' I began, twisting round, but she were walking away across the courtyard. She jiggled the bolt free and stepped into the room. The doors swung to a close in three long creaks. I turned to Tauji.

'Maybe it were for the best.'

His eyes froze on me, unsure. 'Kya?'

'You staying here. It weren't easy for Abba over there, you know. He had to take a lot of crap.'

'All us parents are doing that. You will learn that one day.'

'That's kinda what I mean, though. You don't get how hard it is for the kids. Growing up in England.'

'Really?' he said, as if I'd said something that amused him.

'Honestly, Tauji. We don't really know what we're about, I guess. Who we are, what we're here for.' But that weren't nothing like what I wanted to say. Even to me it just sounded like the usual crap I'd been hearing for years. I wanted to talk about why I felt fine rooting for Liverpool, in a quiet way, but not England. I wanted to talk about why I found myself defending Muslims against whites and whites against

Muslims. About why I loved Abba but had still wished him dead. But I couldn't think of how to say any of what I wanted. 'I mean, we're the ones stuck in the middle of everything. Like we're not sure whose side we're meant to be on, you know?'

Tauji made a scoffing noise. 'It must be very difficult for you. So difficult that you are having the luxury to sit around and be thinking such high-high thoughts.'

He were looking at me as if to say what the fuck did I know about anything, like what I'd said disgusted him. Going on like that when here in front of me were a man whose ribs I could see pressing out against his skin. The longer he looked at me, the more ashamed I felt.

'Go to sleep now. It is late,' and then he reached for the white tasselled blanket spread out over his feet and pulled it up over his head.

I stayed sat there a while, my knees hitched up and my arms wrapped around them. Rubbing my shins to reassure myself. I looked around for a clock, even though I knew the only ones were inside. I got up and went to the enamel latrine dug into the ground beside the buffalo trough. A high wall ran around it so no one could see in. I rolled up my pyjamas and set my feet either side of the basin, one arm stretched out to the brick face in front of me. My piss drummed hard against the bowl, splashing back onto my shins, and it were like all my strength were leaking out too, because suddenly I felt so very tired. I leaned forward and pressed my closed eyes to my fist. On the other side of the wall, I could hear the thin streams that carried the waste off into the fields start to gurgle and move. Afterwards, I soaped up my legs and washed them at the water pump. I were walking back to my menjha, re-tying the cord of my pyjamas, when the mosquito trap flickered off, and then the ceiling fan under the veranda came to a mournful stop. Off to my right, the yellow windows around the main bazaar all died, batch by batch. Some quickly came back to life, in houses that had trip-switch generators.

Charag came out of the house, yawning. 'Abba, the light's gone.'

'Are you going or are you wanting me to?' His voice sounded deeper, under the blanket.

Charag said he'd go.

'I'll come, too,' I said, but he had to get there quickly, and two on the bicycle would only slow him down.

Qasoomah came out of the kitchen, chased by a cloud of steam. She were dabbing her dupatta across her brow. 'This light tamasha is going to kill me one day.' She handed Charag his steel tiffin box, and he clipped it onto the back of his bike. At Murnalipur the well would've cut out, drying up the field, and he'd have to operate it by hand until the electricity came on again.

Tauji kicked off his blanket, sat up. Qasoomah brought him his flip-flops. He'd have to do the same job here, in the field at the back of the house. He got up to go.

'I can help,' I offered.

But he said there were no need. 'You stay. You have all your working out who you are to do.' I knew he were just ribbing me, having a joke, and that he didn't mean it hurtfully, but still . . .

Qasoomah took a fan from a rack on the wall. 'Come on, I will fan you to sleep.' I said I weren't tired. 'Why not?'

When I didn't answer, she twisted her hair into the nape of her neck and said she were going to sleep on the roof, where there'd at least be a little breeze coming off over the fields. I heard her slippers slapping against the concrete steps at the side of the house, and then the scrape of a menjha being dragged across the roof. And then silence, just me left alone in the centre of the courtyard. Ameen.

A weird thing happened today. I went to Meadowhall. I had to get out of the house, to be honest. The last couple of days have been too quiet, the silence pressing down on my head. Thought you would've called, B. And Charag's been working all hours, coming back at stupid o'clock. So this evening I just thought, fuck it, and drove down there. I stayed in the car park for the longest time, too scared to move, but then I told myself to not be so stupid. What would Aaqil think?

There were the usual boring noise in the food hall – girls, scanners, ATMs. Songs too, and one of them took me back a while. Maybe it were the song of that summer or something, but Noor hadn't been born long, I remember, and for the first time in forever we had some time alone in the house. You were wondering what to make for dinner, and I were just hanging around throwing magnets at the fridge.

'At least make yourself useful,' you said, looping around me to get back to the sink.

So I came up behind you, rubbing your arms. You let me slide round in front, running your hands under my T-shirt and up my chest, and I remember how the sun were warm on my arms as I lifted you up onto the table. It were the first time since the birth that you sempt to want me again.

Afterwards, you took your scarf from the floor and quickly twisted your hair into it.

'You're getting used to that,' I said, pulling up my jeans.

'You don't half get a bat on wearing it, though. 'Specially in this weather.'

The door handle turned. Becka hurried back to the sink, grabbing up carrots. I snatched out a newspaper from where it were wedged behind the radiator. Then Ammi came in, heaving the pram over the back step. She collapsed into the nearest chair, breathing so heavily the buttons on her rubber coat strained. She waved a hand, as if to say, 'Never again!'

Abba followed, humming to himself. 'Such a beautiful day, na?' Ammi cut her eyes at him. He chose to ignore it. 'And what have you two been up to, hain?'

'Hm? Oh, nothing.'

'Really?' And then he walked up to me and turned the newspaper the right way up and handed it back. I could see Becka out the corner of my eye, scrubbing carrots, trying not to laugh.

'Penny for them, eh?'

The chatter and mobiles and noise of the food hall whooshed back in. He were brown, clean-shaven. Thirties or thereabouts. His short hair were combed forward with too much gel. His white-shirt were half-sleeved and a walkie-talkie hung off the panel of his black trousers. His name badge said 'Tarun Wadia, Security'. He looked familiar.

I folded away my paper and stood up. 'What? A man can't even read a paper in peace any more?'

His put his arms up, surrendering. 'Not guilty, my friend, not guilty. I'm on my break.' He nodded at me. 'I've seen you down at the mosque, haven't I? Brightside way.'

I couldn't picture him at the mosque. 'Maybe. Probably.'

'Yeah, yeah, I have.' He held out his hand. 'Taz.'

It sometimes happens. You still get people who think if they spot another brown face they have to rejoice in the fact or something. He just carried on smiling and nodding. It were offputting.

'I have seen you before somewhere, haven't I?'

'Yeah, yeah. Like I said, the mosque.'

'Maybe.' But I knew that weren't it. His face, I knew that face from somewhere. It made no odds to him, though. He were still smiling and nodding. I felt obliged to say something. 'You work here?'

'Yeah, yeah.' He pointed to his badge. 'Security. Just started, actually. Only weekends, mind. Couldn't work here all fucking week. Getting enough of a belly on as it is.' He laughed.

Only weekends. My mind flashed forward to the Sunday me and Charag would come down, and I felt myself giving off all these tell-tale signs. 'Okay. Well, take it easy, yeah?'

He stalled me. 'Actually. I came over to give you these.' He pulled out a wad of paper, like bus tickets. 'Food tokens. I get free food for working here and, well, I don't need them.' I must've still looked confused. 'Because I noticed you weren't eating anything sat there. And, you know, what with your wife leaving and everything . . .' I met his gaze head on. 'People talk. You know how it is in our community.'

Always makes me wince, that word. 'She's not left. She's just looking after her mum for a few days. She's ill.'

'Hey, mate, I hear ya. Believe me, some days I reckon my missus is from a whole 'nother planet. She's only meant to be from fucking Huddersfield.' He laughed at his stupid joke, then urged the tokens on me again. 'Just take them. It'll make me feel better if nothing else. I'll have done my good deed for the day.'

'Thanks. But make sure you tell everyone else, yeah? That she's not left. She's just looking after her mother.' I could hear how my voice had trailed off, shading into embarrassment.

'You got it, bro.' He tapped his nose. 'I'll spread the word. You can rely on me. And there's plenty more where those tokens came from.'

Then it hit me. The gap-toothed smile. I pointed at him. 'You were the guy on the tram. The one who waved at me.'

He leaned back, hands in pockets, and laughed. 'Probably. I don't half get around.'

But no, no. It weren't just the tram. There were something else. Something that told me I'd seen him long before that. It were the stupidest thing but I kept on looking at his teeth and seeing them stained red. I had a memory of his red-stained teeth.

'Did I meet you in Pakistan?'

'Maybe. Nothing's impossible.'

'I thought I had. You were there last summer, weren't you?'

He looked at his wrist, though there were no watch there. 'Best get back or there'll have a search party after me.' He reached for my hand and shook it again. 'Keep in touch, Imtiaz, yeah? Keep in touch.' I watched him go, tipping his hat to people as he went. Ameen.

———

It were still dawn when Aaqil parked up in the van. We were going to Kashmir. The sun were just coming up over the roof, making the whole house dazzle, and the shadow over the courtyard began to shrink in response. By noon it would've shrivelled all the way back to the wall, only to break out again come the evening when we were gone.

Ammi passed Aaqil a paratha, while me and Charag loaded our cases into the back. Charag's were about twice the size of mine. When I asked him what he needed all that stuff for, he took a comb out of his back pocket and flicked his hair into what I guess he thought were a stylish quiff. 'I couldn't decide, bhaiji.' Aaqil banged the doors to a close.

'Go carefully, acha?' Ammi said. 'And telephone when you are arriving.'

Tauji stood behind her. 'They will be fine. They are not children any more.'

Qasoomah strode up, shouldering past Aaqil. The round tray in her hands held a few pieces of broken barfi, a bowl of plain yoghurt, and a bottle whose insides were streaked in amber – mustard oil, the sticky label read. She practically shovelled a heaped spoon of the yoghurt into mine and Charag's mouth. I'd just about gulped that down and she were already pushing the barfi past my lips. She drizzled the oil on the sandy ground, along the entrance arch, and gestured impatiently for us to step across it. We did. She hugged us both, on each shoulder, and then she left. Not saying a word to us the whole time. She'd done her duty. If we still insisted on gallivanting around like idiots then, well, that wasn't being her fault.

Before we'd even got out of our village a few other lads had joined us, and we had to swap seats because one of them complained he got travel-sick whenever he went in the back. We didn't believe him, but me and Charag moved to the back anyway. We kept on stopping to pick someone or other up, familiar faces from the times I'd gone with Aaqil to Ustaadji's. Soon enough, the talk turned to girls. One of them were shagging his teacher, which it turned out were pretty common. Another were hooked up with his landowner's daughter.

I'd managed to stay out of most of the talk, but then they started asking me what goriyan were like. Were it true what they'd heard? That they let you do anything, anywhere? That you could just stop them in the street and ask for it and they wouldn't say no?

It made me laugh. 'You've still got to put in the hours. Don't matter where you go in the world, you gotta put in the hours.'

Aaqil spoke from the front. 'Of course they are like that. You've seen the TV.'

'Others maybe, but not my Becka.'

A young guy called Faisal came in then. 'It is because he is old.'

He were one of the few that were new to me. He were a

friend of Aaqil's and he'd been waiting by a fruit cart about five or six gates down from our own village. His green back-pack kept on sliding down his sloping, relaxed shoulders, and he stood there making dust circles with his feet. When Aaqil honked the horn, he looked up and came running towards us, one hand on his topi to keep it in place. He were the youngest of us all.

'Arré, if not me then be at least listening to Ghalib.' Faisal made a show of clearing his throat and waiting for silence, and then he began to recite. 'How wearisome to find her there, a greater burden than a man could bear. The same old palace, all of emerald made, the same fruit tree to cast its shade. And – God preserve her from all harm – the same old houri on my arm. Come to your sense, brother, and take another. Take a new woman each returning spring, for last year's almanac is a useless thing.'

Some stamped their feet, others cried out, 'Wah! Wah!' or 'Kya baat hai!' as if we were in some twilit garden recital in the court of Shah Jehan and not instead being bumped about on the rusting wheel-arches of a Tata campervan. Faisal accepted the applause graciously, making his salaams to us all. He were a bit of a show-off, was Faisal. Loved his ghazals. He'd say them at night to some imaginary girl from his vil-lage, annoying the rest of us who wished he'd just shove out the light and let us get some sleep. Or maybe that's just my silly way of remembering him.

The trip up were a proper laugh. Aaqil kept us going with his impressions of our Ustaadji. Eyes half-closed, wobbling his head, this look of total calm on his face. 'If your heart is true, my child, then what need for false gods?' Aaqil could easily, naturally, take centre stage. He sempt made for it. Sure enough he started on me, with his frilly English accent. 'You have bamboozled me!' Even Charag joined in, which were a relief. I felt responsible for making sure he had a good time. He'd only come along in the first place because of me. He'd not wanted to leave Tauji, not when they were coming up to harvest time.

'Anything could happen,' he'd said. 'What if a lurgy is going round and we have to start early?'

But his sister had the biggest problem with me going. 'What? With that goondah? You are going to Kashmir with that lefengah Aaqil? Are you feeling alright?'

'Better than spending the next two months just hanging around here.' I wanted to defend Aaqil, but I wished I'd not said it like that. She looked hurt. 'I want to see more of the country.'

'Then pick up a scythe and go see the field. Find out what work really is.' There were a silence, and then she said, 'What business you have going to Kashmir, anyway? You do not watch the news?'

'Not business. And we're not going to that part, anyway.'

'I will not allow it. What ideas that shaitaan has been putting inside your head, I do not know, but I will not allow this.'

I turned to Ammi, but she were still distracted, grieving, and said I could do what I wanted. Tauji came on my side, though. 'You go. We do not want you thinking the whole of Pakistan is just this village, do we?' Qasoomah tried to protest, but Tauji shushed her. 'Charag will go with him. No arguments. Happy now?'

Qasoomah left for the kitchen, again taking out her anger on the cupboards. When I got back from the trip, she said all the fun had been emptied from the house while I were gone. And that surprised me. I'd never thought of myself as being one of those people who brightens up a home just by being there. 'Did you miss me, then?' I asked. I'd said it as a joke, but of course it's never a joke. It's always just so much fishing for affection. Her face turned serious and she said that of course she'd missed me. 'How can a sister not miss her brother?' Which caught me so off guard that I had to look away so she wouldn't see the smiles that had leapt into me. Ameen.

———

This must be the first time I've sat down to write and it's been daylight outside. It's not yet touching ten and other than going to masjid this evening my day's unbroken. Got the house to myself. I have to shut the window and curtains, though, and not just because of the kids having a kickabout. Prefer it like this. Curtains shut so the sunlight's kind of blotted out across them, and the door's locked even though no one's in. Like my own shaded little private cave. You know, I hadn't realised just how attached I've become to these pages. These notes, I suppose. Thoughts. I flicked through them last night in bed. Just reading with my elbows pressing down the duvet tight across my chest. Chewing at the top of my pen. Scribbling out a bit here, adding a bit there. Felt as if I ought to have been wearing glasses, or maybe one of those one-eyed jobs. Even right now I'm having to stop myself from reading back through what I've written. Keep myself going forward. Need to get to the end.

—

I'm not sure if you could call the place in Kashmir a camp. It's not as if we were in some desert with tents pitched up or anything. It were just a few rooms balanced on top of an isthriwallah's shop. He were an old friend of Ustaadji's. I'd see him every morning when I came down the metal stairs and joined the queue for the water pump. He'd be sat on his chair with his feet up, arms folded and his maroon fez pulled low over his eyes. He must've worked through the night, because there were always very neat and tall piles of ironed clothes tagged with names and tickets, all arranged on the counter so people could just come and collect their ironing without disturbing him.

It were dark when we arrived that first day. Ustaadji were already there, drinking tea with the isthriwallah. We piled out of the van, all grouchy and cramped up.

'Your rooms are upstairs,' were all that Ustaadji said, and then turned back to his friend.

The stairs weren't safe, wobbling all over the place, and you could only get up them by walking sideways, in slim file. Each iron step had lots of tiny raised ridges on it, as if someone had laid down grains of rice before pouring the metal over. From up top you could see the trench that ran along the back, with its smell of shit and its tiny stream of trickling black water. There were two rooms for all of us, each with four green mats rolled out on the ground. Aaqil slid his bag off his shoulder and took the central mat in the largest room. I hovered by the door, wondering which room were mine, but then Aaqil called my name and said I were sharing with him. Faisal and Charag took the other two mats, and the rest of them left for next door, complaining about why they had to have the smaller room. I went to the window, but I couldn't really see anything other than the shakily drawn outline of the mountains up ahead, and maybe a lake or a ditch somewhere in the valley far below.

I'm not sure what I felt when I laid down on my mat that first night, hands behind my head. I don't think I felt anything. I just saw it as an adventure, a few days of not answering to anyone. The whole point of the trip were meant to be to learn about our history in some of the places where it happened – a kind of field trip, I guess – but apart from that I thought I could do as I pretty much pleased.

Aaqil shoved out the light and said we'd better get to sleep if we didn't want to miss fajr. Just then my phone vibrated against my thigh and an envelope flashed in the corner of the screen.

'What are you doing?' Aaqil said.

'Message from Becka.'

Faisal made kissing noises. 'Missing you, darling.' I could hear Charag snickering too.

I switched the phone off. 'You'll learn one day.'

'Did you message back?' Aaqil asked.

'Yeah,' I said, but I hadn't. I hadn't messaged home for a while by then. Home just felt too far away.

In the morning, we went outside with our rough stiff towels

and joined the queue at the water pump. There were a system in place, where whoever were in the queue behind you would work the pump while you crouched down at the pipe and soaped your face and blew your nose. All the while I were queuing up, I watched how the men in front did it, how they crouched, washed, how long they took. I didn't want to embarrass myself. The man in front of me squatted down at the pipe and I went to pump the water for him. But no water came out. I gripped the rubbered end harder and jerked the long curved handle again. But still no water. There must've been a knack to it, but I'd been so busy watching how the men washed themselves, I'd not even looked at the ones pumping the water. The man looked at me, his hands cupped at the mouth of the dry pipe. I tried again. Nothing. I could feel the embarrassment heating up my scalp. I could hear the sniggers in the queue, people saying what more could you expect from a foreigner. I stood up, smeared away the sweat down my face, and walked off. Someone called after me, but I didn't turn back.

I didn't let that happen again. That night, when everyone were asleep, I went out and practised and practised until the water flew out of the pump every time. It were dark and cold but I didn't stop until I were satisfied I'd never make a fool of myself like that again. When I finally headed back inside, Ustaadji were at the bottom of the stairs. He'd been watching.

'Salaam, Ustaadji.'

He nodded, and let me pass.

—

Further down the hill, just where the mountain road started to bend round and disappear, there were a short low mossy wall. It were missing bricks, as if the local leaders had woken up one morning and decided to build a roadside barrier, but then got bored and forgot to finish the job. After washing up at the pump I'd sit on that wall and clean my teeth. If they were up early enough Aaqil or Faisal would join me, but usually I sat there on my own, gazing sleepily out over the valley while last night's dreams got chased away by the brushy end of a tooth-stick. It'd still be cool enough for me to wear the black shawl Qasoomah had packed. In fact, the air generally felt much cleaner than it did at home in Lahore, as if each morning it were freshly rinsed out. At that hour it were like a fine new damp green ash were clung to my face. The sun would still just be all orange water spread across the horizon, backlighting the mountains in a roseglow, and down in the city the first lorries would be making their silent way along the river road and out of Muzaffarabad. Behind me, one or two shops would start ratcheting up their steel shutters, and I'd hear weights clinking as the sweetmeat owner bullied his balances down off their shelves. Sometimes a couple of men – always the same two – came rounding the bend, hunched forward against the hill and rubbing their eyes. Blatantly they'd spent the night down in the city, probably with prossies, probably still high off bhang.

'All-night prayers again, bhaiji?' I'd ask, in bad Urdu.

'Of course! What else?'

'Very devout, you are.'

It were my favourite part of the day, with everything just starting to grumble and move. Sat on the wall with my knees hitched up, I felt like I were keeping an eye out for all who were asleep below. Not long after, the calls to prayer would rise out and even for those who weren't planning on attending masjid they acted as an alarm clock. Traffic started to thicken all over the city and horns would start to beep and I'd see guardsmen in hats like green dots struggling to control the flow over the bridges. More and more shutters would start going up, and the queue at the water pump would lengthen, and always someone would try to push in only to get slapped to the back of the queue, and always someone would point out to Charag that his abba didn't own the blasted pump, so could he kindly hurry the hell up? Usually at about then I'd bounce off the wall and leg it back to the house to grab my kufi before going down to masjid.

——

After morning prayers on the second day, Ustaadji knocked on our doors and told us to meet him outside. We found him perched up on the craggy boulders that made up the base of the wall. The day were a huge blue screen behind him, like he were up in the sky and we were sat there with our faces upturned and our hands in our laps, ready to catch whatever wisdom he'd think to throw at us.

He rubbed his hands, and reached deep behind the wall. He let out a little gasp then, and his short legs kicked out as he tried to keep his balance. Faisal, I remember, lurched forward and grabbed onto Ustaadji's ankles.

'Thank you, Faisal,' he said, righting himself. 'This wall has grown since I was last here.' He were holding a green plastic long sword, like a kid's toy. 'You have all heard of our Akbar, yes? The Shadow of God?' Only a few of us nodded. 'Well, be getting comfortable because today you will learn all about his rule. Once upon a time, many, many years ago, before even I was born . . .'

I got on my stomach to listen, feeling my elbows sink into the soft ground. Faisal laid down on the grass too, hands held across his chest and one knee pitched up. Aaqil didn't move, though. He stayed rod-straight and serious. Charag sempt to be the only one not paying attention, too busy tearing at the grass and watching the blades being blown from his palm.

About an hour into the story, Ustaadji's cheeks rounded out like golf-balls, like he were going to burst. 'And then the great Badshah Akbar, the Shadow of God, took out his sword!' He brandished the sword. 'And stood on the tower of the qi'lah in this very town, surrounded on all sides by his enemies, and said to his soldiers, "With this sword of justice I vow to return glory upon my religion and death upon the infidels!" '

He got so excited he were clapping his fat little heels in delight. We cheered and applauded, and the applause were for both the glorious story and the way he'd told it. Even a few of the locals who'd stopped to listen were joining in. But Aaqil weren't clapping, I noticed. His eyes had gone shrewd again, and when he turned towards me he didn't even seem to register that I were looking at him. He just slowly, scarily, turned his head back to the front.

There were another lesson in the evening, when the sky were more pink than blue, but this one were more around studying the Qu'ran. That sempt to put Aaqil in a better mood, because afterwards he borrowed an old black-and-white TV from the isthriwallah and we spent the rest of the evening watching some slapstick cable show. I remember laughing along even though most of the jokes didn't seem that funny to me really. Everyone else found them hilarious, especially Aaqil, but it were strange how we all laughed loudest whenever Aaqil laughed too.

His good mood didn't last long. He probably thought the story-telling session were just going to be a one-off thing to ease us into the more serious stuff. But it weren't. Every morning we'd get together at the wall and Ustaadji would start another yarn, about Aurangzeb or whoever this time. On around the third or fourth day, Aaqil finally spoke up.

'Ustaadji, can I respectfully ask that you stick to teaching the Qu'ran, please? I think that's what we're here for.'

Ustaadji looked around at everyone else. 'Is that what you're here for? Do you want scripture only? Hands up if you want scripture only.'

I put my hand up, and so did one or two of the more quiet ones, but no one else. I saw Aaqil glaring at Faisal, who were staring at the ground.

'I'm sorry, Aaqil,' Ustaadji said. 'But maybe a mixture of the two is better, yes?'

Aaqil sank back down. He looked furious. I could tell he wanted to leave, but it would've been too disrespectful. When the story were over, he strode off ahead of everyone else. He didn't even turn up for lunch that day, and when I took him some food he told me to put it on the floor and leave him alone.

———

In the evenings after the Qu'ran lessons, some of us caught a motor rickshaw down the hill road and into the town. Usually we went to a café called Jimmy's, where we'd sit under the green PUDA-branded umbrella at the rickety outdoor tables, tables with round legs like stacks of two-pence coins. Mostly we drank bhang lassis, trying to get high, but apart from a fuzziness at the edges, they never really did much for me, or Charag come to think of it.

Aaqil brought his drink down on the table, hard – some of it spilled over. 'What is this? School? Who cares about what happened three thousand years ago?'

'Arré, yaar,' Charag said, sounding anxious, 'can you see a PCO anywhere here? I left my phone behind.'

'Are we here to learn how to fight or not?' Aaqil kept his hand pressed against the table, so hard that his fingers bleached white. 'Tell me that, brothers, hain? Tell me that.'

I was only half-listening. I rose a little in my seat. 'Is that the old qi'lah? The one Ustaadji keeps talking about?'

Aaqil twisted round. 'Looks like it.'

Even from where I were sat I could see that it were only a couple of ruined towers and some blackish yellow walls, but it felt like I'd seen something from a book shimmer into life in front of me. 'Shall we go?'

Aaqil paused, the drink at his lips. 'What the hell for? It is empty only. Have some more lassi.'

'Charag?'

'Will there be a PCO there, do you think?'

'Uff! What is the matter with you?' Aaqil said. 'If you don't call home one day the sky will not be falling down.'

I said I'd meet them back at the room and set off for the fort. It were banked up on the other side of the river so I hailed down a rickshaw to get me over the bridge. The driver's gold-coloured shoes were covered in mud and snow, I remember, and I think that made me give him a bigger tip than I'd meant to. He dropped me off on the river road, beside a white board that read Welcome to Muzaffarabad's Famous Red Fort brought to you by Municipal Tourist Board of Azad Kashmir.

It were less red, more golden, really, or maybe that were just the way the sun were draped across it. Small trees sprouted out from the fort walls, reaching for the river. There were hardly no one about save a few women walking past with large gold hoops through their noses and baskets of bright cherries on their heads. I remember how the river kept hitting out at the side of the road and spraying a fine mist all the way across the tarmac and onto my sandals. Further along, I found the steps that led up to the walkway and into the first tower. I say tower, it were just a short stumpy thing and it didn't take much effort to climb the shallow stone steps with their worn middles. (How many feet over how many years?) I heaved myself through the trapdoor and up onto the roof. There were a horrible rotting smell, and then I saw the puddles of what looked like blackened cat vomit, full of tiny flashing white fish bones. Bile came up into my throat. I pushed it down, moved to the edge of the tower. With arms outstretched, I placed my hands on a turret either side of me, like a king over his kingdom. The river beneath me, the town in front, mountains beyond. There were a warm breeze all down my back.

I could see the emperors in all the years past stood where I were now, fighting off the Christians, the Sikhs, the Turks. Arrows arcing across the sky to meet their enemy. Cannons lining the fort, poking out. I could hear them firing, could hear the great noise of it all as we tried to defend ourselves. They were all around me. Soldiers in red turbans scrambling around for gunpowder. My archers were reaching over their shoulders for another arrow. A munshi hurried up those tower steps to tell me news of the situation at the other side of the qi'lah. I were there, with them all, leading the fight. 'Fire!' I shouted, and they did, and I heard the roar and saw the smoke blasted out as the cannons launched ball after ball. I turned to my archers. 'Ready, sepaiyo? Then aim! And fire!' And there were the thudding sound of a thousand tight cat-guts all being released and I watched as the arrows made their graceful flights over the river. I took out my telescope and could see their men on the far side of the water, clasping their chests, falling. 'We are winning, brothers! Hurry! Bring more men! Before they can regroup!'

It were only when I looked down and saw two women staring up at me from the road that I realised what I'd been doing. And suddenly the noise of war faded out, silence rushed back in. I took my hands – my telescope – away from my eye and smiled at the women, feeling like a total tit. They giggled, and one of them made the crazy sign, and then they carried on their way, still laughing.

I couldn't climb to the top of the other tower. It were in too much of a state. It still hadn't been repaired from the earthquake and the side facing the river were just a fallen spreading tree of rubble. That's the Municipal Tourist Board for you. Too busy lining their pockets. There were a couple of large sandy bricks at my feet. I bent to lift them up, and as I placed them back on the wall, I had this feeling I'd been there before.

I picked my way down the ruins and landed back on the road. The sun had clean vanished, and the dark river air had me rubbing the goosebumps on my arms. The bridge were too far back and there weren't a rickshaw around, so I walked up towards the limestone ghats, where I could see the river men bobbing on their boats. The road softened out. The mud sucked at my feet. I tried to ask if any of them could take me to Domel, but my Urdu's not good and they just looked at each other to see if maybe one of the others had under-stood. I tried in English but it made no difference. Finally, thankfully, one of them asked me in Panjabi where I wanted to go. He were tall, deep-browned. His long thin white beard were tied into a tiny knot at the bottom, and his dirty white ropes of hair were coiled into a bun on his head, held in check with a short comb. He were naked but for a dhoti tied up around his thighs. He were wet and shiny and looked like he were made of river.

He moored his narrow boat up on the step and invited me to step in. I hesitated at first. The rest of the river men had motor-boats. His were the only gondola. But the others had gone back to talking amongst themselves so I stepped inside the swaying boat, walked over to the other end and took a seat on the wooden slat, facing him. He used his foot to push off into the water, and I felt my stomach dip as we were freed from the green muddy lime. All the while across, he stood upright on the very tip of the boat, slicing his single oar through the water and switching sides every five strokes.

'You are not from Muzaffarabad?' He had a gruff voice.

I shook my head, but then figured he probably couldn't see me in the dark. 'I'm just visiting.'

'Good, good. Very good. Where from? America?'

I nearly said England, but caught myself. 'I mean, no. No. I'm from Lahore.'

He looked doubtful. 'You are not a ferengi?'

'I'm a Lahori.'

He thought that over and sempt to convince himself. 'I can see it now. It is in your eyes.'

I'd been expecting a wise man of the river. But he were just a fraud. 'Right.'

'The ferengis, they look but do not see. They are looking at me all the time, wanting to take a picture with me, but they do not see me, you understand? They are a blind people.'

I could feel this strange panic start to clutch at me. 'Why let them take a picture with you, then?'

'Rupeiya! Why else? I have to smile for them. You think I would let them touch me otherwise? I have heard they do not even use water to clean their arses after the toilet.' He wrinkled his nose. 'Believe me, beita, I am spitting on the ground after they have gone. Especially the Britishers.'

I looked away, to the glinting river holding the stars.

'I saw what those shaitaans did. Set brother against brother, carved us up. It all started with them. Inshallah, they will get what they deserve.'

And so he prattled on, all the way until we got to my stop and he zipped my notes into his battered Nike bum-bag and wished me well for the rest of my visit. I clambered up the ghat and started up the hill, taking in great lungfuls of air. I felt like turning round and launching a rock at him. I hated him for attacking my home, I hated myself for not defending it, but more for feeling that I should. Everything at that moment, the pot-holed road under my feet, the laughing moon in the sky, they were all against me, because none of them would let me be theirs. Ameen.

———

Third night in a row, B. I keep on dialling our landline from my mobile. Third night in a row I've gone to sleep to the sound of your voice. Ameen.

———

Last night, after Friday prayers, me and Charag were walk-ing across the car park when Fahim caught us up. He had his same old zebra trackies and he were just chatting on about his trip back home for his sister's wedding. He were trying to be casual about it but I could tell he were desperate for us to spread the word.

'Sure, sure,' I said, distracted. There were someone hanging around on the other side of the car park, near the trees. He were waving me over. It took a second to click that it were that Tarun bloke, the guard from Meadowhall. Charag and Fahim hadn't spotted him yet. I thought about just ignoring him, but he had given me those tokens, even if I had lost them since. It'd be rude to just walk off.

'Back in a sec.' I jogged across the concrete and found him leaning against the side of a white Transit van.

'I thought it was you.' He held out his hand. 'How you doing? Hope those tokens came in handy.'

'Yeah, yeah. Thanks. You just heading in?'

'Traffic were crazy. Who you with?'

'No one. Just my cousin.'

'Right, right. Anyways, I best get a move on, but, listen, I've got a shedload of those tokens going begging, so just pop down whenever if you want some, yeah? This weekend would be good.'

I didn't say nothing. I didn't like the way he were trying to order me around. But there were something about the way he stared at me, calm, unblinking. I said I'd do my best, and turned to go.

'Tell your cousin I said hello.'

I stopped, turned round, but he'd disappeared into the wood that led off the car park, and all I could hear were twigs snapping underfoot.

Charag and Fahim were waiting for me at the traffic lights.

'Been for a slash?' Fahim asked.

'Do you know him?' I asked Charag.

'Know who?'

'That guy just there?' I turned round, but the van had been in the way, so they wouldn't have seen him. 'Someone called Tarun? Some sort of security guy at Meadowhall?'

I shouldn't't've mentioned Meadowhall out in the open like that. I'm slipping.

Charag shrugged and turned to Fahim. 'How long have you been back?'

'Coupla weeks.'

'You did the right thing. Well done.' I patted Fahim's back absentmindedly. I were still trying to focus.

Fahim went quiet, his nostrils rising out. Then he said, 'You wanna look a bit closer to home.'

'What were that?'

'Before you go dissing others. Take a look in your own backyard.'

'Take a look at what?'

He said nothing.

'If you've got something to say, Fahim, you best just spit it out.'

He shook his head. 'Nope. Nothing to say at all.'

He turned onto his street, jogging away. I took a step towards him, shouting that he come back and tell me what the fuck he were on about. Charag pulled me back. 'Come on, bhaiji. He is causing trouble only.'

And I knew that's all he were doing. That he were only jealous of us and pissed off at his own family. But all the way home I couldn't get the thoughts out of my head.

'Have you heard anything?' I asked Charag, feeling embarrassed to ask it. 'Or noticed anything? About Rebekah?'

'Bhaiji, he is trying to taunt you. Don't listen to him.'

'So you don't think it could be true?'

He didn't really know what to say. Like he were just as embarrassed to be asked such questions as I were to ask them. 'I do not think bhabhiji would ever be wanting to shame you.'

I wanted to ask him what he were hiding from me. If he were just a fake like the rest of them. But I didn't. I didn't bring up what Fahim had said again either. But in a way it sempt to make sense. Why you've been so off with me, B. And all your mood swings lately. But I know that's just me thinking the worst. Ready to believe the worst. So I'm not going to think about it. It's not true and thinking about it will only distract me from the fight. So I'm not going to think about it. I'm going to just carry on telling my story. Easier, somehow.

—

Aaqil were getting more and more wound up with Ustaadji. He'd had enough of this soft-headed fool, he said one night. He were pacing round the room. Tiger in his cage. The rest of us were sat up in our sleeping bags, all eyes on him. He went to the window. 'This isn't what I expected,' he muttered.

'Not long now,' I said, but I don't think he heard me.

All at once he spun round and slapped on the light switch. 'We're going north.' He stared round at us all. He didn't blink once. 'North,' he said again. 'That's where we need to be.'

'North?' I said.

'I know someone. Abu Bhai.' Aaqil looked to Faisal, and I noticed Faisal give a little nod back, as if in confirmation of something or encouragement to carry on. 'He's leading the fight-back further north,' Aaqil went on. 'Against the Americans. We can help.' He came and crouched down beside us. 'We're like eunuchs here. With these lakes and his stories. But there' – he stood straight up again, taller than before – 'there we'll be men.'

'How much further north?' Charag asked, wary.

'Peshawar. Afghanistan maybe. Who cares? Wherever our brothers and sisters need us. Hain na, Imtiaz?' I nodded, slowly, not sure what it really meant, but excited by that not-knowing too. 'And you don't have to worry,' he said. 'I'm the eldest here. I'll take care of everything.'

He were waiting for an answer from me. I looked to Faisal, who said we should all go together, and then there were that secret look between him and Aaqil again.

'Imtiaz?' Aaqil shook my knee. 'What do you think? We need you as well. Come on, yaar, say yes?' And I did.

The next morning were when Aaqil finally lost it with Ustaadji. After another lesson spent listening to the battles of Jahendah Shah, Aaqil asked him why he were wasting every-one's time teaching us about the past.

'It's gone. Remember, yes, never forget, yes, but what about everything that is happening now? Everyone that is dying while you are making us listen to this?'

'The present is all around us,' Ustaadji said in his usual calm way. 'We are not blind. But our history,' he went on, his voice going dreamy, 'is too great a thing to risk to Providence. It is part of my job as His servant to keep it alive.'

'It is His job to keep it alive.' Aaqil pointed a finger to the sky. 'All power lies in Him. It is your job to explain to us what we can do to please Him.'

'And that is what I am doing, young Aaqil. If you listen, you will learn, and that will be enough.'

Aaqil turned to the group, as if asking how much more rubbish we were willing to take. 'So while we are here listening to your stories of kings and emperors, out there our brothers and sisters are being destroyed. Very good, Ustaadji. What a great teacher you are!' Aaqil gave him a round of applause. 'You are so busy gazing at the stars you cannot see how they are trampling all over our flowers. Allah would be proud.'

Everyone were buzzing, watching to see which way it'd go. Ustaadji kept his calm limp saddened look trained on Aaqil. But this time Aaqil refused to back down and he stood up and started quoting whole passages from the Qu'ran. Fluently, loudly.

Later that same night we were lounging about watching TV and talking about what had happened earlier. Then Aaqil came into the room and we started applauding. He took a bow, but then asked for quiet. He were waving a video cassette. 'Watch this.' The VCR suckered up the tape and there were the wheezing sound of it being fast-rewound, a sound I hadn't heard for so long it were like hearing my childhood streaming past.

The first man on the screen looked to be a sheikh and he praised Allah, Subhana wa Ta'ala, the Prophet, salli Allahu alayhi wa sallam, and thanked us for being part of the holy struggle, a struggle that will undoubtedly see us victorious. Then there were some piss-poor editing and halfway through his speech the tape cut forward to a small old woman in a threadbare brown headscarf. She were on her knees outside her fallen house, beating her chest and wailing to Allah. Behind her, a menjha were visible through the bombed hole in the wall, and next to the menjha a wooden bucket, its cargo of green and purple vegetables spilt across the floor. The camera panned over to a row of humped dead bodies wrapped in white sheets. Then the cameraman peeled back the cloth and what were left of a man's face were revealed. There were a crater where his cheek used to be. His jaw were horribly incomplete. The camera zoomed in. We all flinched, pulling our eyes away from the maggots wriggling under his face. The tape moved on – a man were pleading for a doctor as he carried his wife across his arms and through a muhalla where everyone else were running in the opposite direction. And after that a young-looking Jew in a big black hat were caught throwing wine over a passing, flinching, Palestinian woman.

Not everyone were staring up at the telly with the same commitment as Aaqil. Most of the guys in the room looked almost bored by it. Even their cusses sounded half-hearted. Some had turned away from the screen and started up their conversations again. They'd seen it all before, I suppose. We all had. It were nothing new. I could feel the same happening to me. I kept telling myself to concentrate.

Finally the screen faded to black and one or two started to leave.

But Aaqil said, 'Wait. Just wait. It has not finished.'

The laughter came first. These great savage whooping jeers behind the black screen, followed by gunfire. Slowly the screen lit up to show a gang of Americans in camouflage gear, swigging from brown bottles and toasting the handcuffed men in the back of their jeep. The camera closed in shakily and the only female soldier offered one of the prisoners a drink. He turned his face away, and the soldiers all laughed some more.

Everyone in the room were watching now. The tape flickered to black, then opened to a guy with shorn blond hair and heavy sunburnt shoulders. He had a sweatband round his forehead and were sitting half-out of his sleeping bag, making some sort of video diary with his mobile. Younger than me, he were one of those Americans that think they rule the world. Probably some track hero back home in Idaho or wherever. He were saying that he's missing y'all, his buds, but he's happy to report that he's seen some mighty fine brown ass round these parts that he'll be sure to give a good ole facial to before his leave this fall. And the way Aaqil's back stiffened up I just knew the subtitles had made everything sound even worse.

The next guy had the hungry face of someone who got bullied shitless at school but had now found someone else to bully in turn. He were pissed and his eyes were wide and mad with power. He were singing the Stars and Stripes anthem, and all the while he were singing he kept on stepping closer and closer to the camera like he were wanting to pick a fight with it. And then he stopped singing the anthem, speaking straight to camera instead. 'Burn, motherfuckers, burn.' He said it again, laughing this time. And then again. And then he were saying it over and over, loving the way the words sounded in his mouth, rolling them off and grinning his teeth out as he staggered on with his chant. He kept coming closer and closer to us until he were filling up the whole screen, like he were itching to just smash right through. 'Burn, burn motherfuckers, burn,' he said, his mad wide eyes not once moving from us.

He were clever, whoever put the vid together. That scene got replayed at the end two, three, four times at least. By the end of it there were this bright angry white flash searing through my head. I could feel everyone staring at me, because I were the valetiya, and in their eyes the American cunt were speaking for me. And there were no point in saying that I didn't want to be him. I just was. The same way I were my parents' child. When the video finally, mercifully, switched off, we just sat there in silence, listening to the tape reeling back to the beginning.

No one hardly spoke to me on the walk down into the valley afterwards. They didn't even want to look at me. Aaqil were taking long angry strides on up ahead, fists in and out of pockets. He didn't want to be seen with me. Faisal usually always chatted to me, but he were shunning me as well. Even Charag were only at my side because he felt he had to be.

'Those bhanchod bastards are needing a lesson, hain na?'

He were testing me, I knew. 'Yeah. Definitely. We shouldn't just stand by.'

'Has Aaqil spoken to you again? About going to see that friend in Peshawar?'

He hadn't, no, and that felt like a punch to the guts. I were already being left out of decisions. Excluded. And Charag would've known that Aaqil hadn't spoken to me. They were playing games with me.

'You don't have to worry about me. Pretty clear what you

all think.' Charag turned to me, unsure. 'The way they're all looking at me.'

He glanced around. 'The way who's looking at you?'

'And inside, everyone were gawping at me.'

He chuckled. 'Arré, yaar, it is in your mind only.'

But he had to say that. It were a different story once we got to Jimmy's and took our seats around the lamplit outdoor tables. No one called me over to sit with them. No one tried to pressure me into having a bhang lassi. Even the owner knew what I were, and took down my order last of all. I wished I were at home, lying next to Becka and Noor. I looked off up the road. A beggar with a useless left leg were hobbling away, rattling the coin-jar strung from his bandaged crutch. I watched him and I knew I'd played my part in that violence. I deserved this punishment, this freezing out.

Aaqil joined our table. 'Two, three days, and then we are driving north. Be ready, yes?'

I looked at him, trying to work out if this were some cruel trick.

'Remember? We were talking about it last night?'

'You want me to come?'

'Abu Bhai is expecting us. I've told him all about you.'

I think I beamed then. I weren't being left out. I hadn't disappointed him. It felt like I had an older brother.

'Why? You do not want to come?'

'He thinks you are all against him,' Charag said. 'That to you he is like them in the video. No one is asking him how he is any more.'

'That's a bit over the top—'

'What? You still want special treatment?'

'I never said anything about special—'

'I thought you are just like us now.'

'I am.'

'But it seems you still think of yourself as a valetiya.'

'But I don't.'

'Good. Because no one here thinks of you as different. You're not a valetiya any more, you understand? You're an apna. You're ours.'

There it was. I'd never thought a cheap rusty café called Jimmy's on an unmarked road in Muzaffarabad would be the spot where I learned that I weren't a lone man in this world. We were all of us here together.

Soon everyone started dropping their coins on the table and heading back to the house. But I carried on up the tarred road in the opposite direction. The old man couldn't have got far. I didn't know what I'd do once I found him. I just knew that I wanted to prove to myself that now I could look him in the face without feeling ashamed. That I were beginning to be forgiven.

Because that's what fighting is. You fight because you want to prove to yourself that you are worthy of forgiveness.

Before going home, I went back to the fort. The two bricks I'd laid that other day were still there, loose but still standing, which felt like an achievement, or a reward. I bunched the sleeves of my kurta up past my elbows and squatted down beside the rubble. I picked up a big dusty yellow brick and fixed it on the wall next to the previous two. And then I took up another and set that one next to them. Then two more on top of that, and I kept on returning to the rubble and digging out a brick and carrying it along the wall and placing it back where it belonged. And it felt good to be doing that. The way the muscles in my arms tightened with the weight of each brick. The way my spine stretched and clicked as I straightened up, as if it were being asked to work for the first time in its life. I felt like I were paying my dues.

Maybe an hour passed like that, maybe two, I don't remember, but over the river and across the town the night were starting to lighten. My arms and face were covered in chalky dust. It were time to leave. I looked at what I'd achieved. The rubble were still like a mountain, and the tower looked more or less the same as when I'd arrived. No one tomorrow would notice anything different about it, that it were a little higher now, a little less broken.

I walked all the way back to the house and when I got there it were an awkward job trying to work the pump and clean myself up at the same time. The front of my kurta were getting drenched and my feet kept slipping on the slick stone floor. But then the pump sempt to pick up pace on its own and the water started to gush. I actually thought it were Allah's doing, but then I washed the soap off my eyes and saw Ustaadji working the pump for me. A green plastic bottle were in his hand. He must've been for a shit over the trench behind the house. Silently, I washed all the grit from my arms and then rolled back down my sleeves.

'You are up early,' he said.

I nodded. 'Couldn't sleep.'

'Acha, acha. That is understandable. It cannot be easy trying to sleep when your bed is made of bricks.'

I didn't understand. He pulled round the hem of my kurta – my back were covered in yellow brick dust. He invited me to walk with him. 'I hear stories that you are all moving on soon. To the North, yes?'

'Not all of us. But some of us are.'

'Acha, acha. To join the fight?'

'To see what's happening with our own eyes.'

'I see.'

We'd reached the low mossy wall just before the path bent

round the hill. Neither of us sat down, though. Ustaadji held his wrist behind his back, the bottle still in one hand, and breathed in the green morning air. It were still dark but the day were starting to ease through. I raised one foot up onto the wall and leaned with my elbows crossed over my knee. The way I'd noticed the local men doing whenever they gathered there for an evening smoke. They'd have their kangris under their shawls to keep warm, those little clay pots of fire that from a distance made it look as if their hearts were giving off a strange light.

'You don't approve?' I asked.

'Hm?'

'Of the struggle?'

'Oh, no, no. It is nothing like that. The struggle is fair. And it is our duty to fight back, yes.'

That surprised me. I'd always thought Ustaadji were against all that. Maybe because I'd never heard him speaking off like Aaqil. Ustaadji sempt too calm, too much into laughter. Must be what age does.

'I only wonder if you are going for the right reasons, Imtiaz.' He turned to me. 'Is it because you are being called by Allah, Subhana wa Ta'ala, or because you feel you are owing your brothers and sisters something?'

I thought of what Aaqil had said about me being one of

them. 'But it's the same thing. Me feeling this way is just Allah's way of calling me.'

A strip of yellow had appeared on the horizon, and the first low calls to prayer began to circle around the valley. We returned to the pump, where I worked the lever while Ustaadji completed his wudu. He took more care than I did, making sure he washed right up to the elbows, and all the way down to where his beard started, and all around his ankles. Afterwards, I turned to go inside. He called me back.

'Go fetch your kufi. We will offer salat out here.'

When I got back Ustaadji were at the wall. I stood behind him, securing my kufi on my head. He turned round and asked me to step forward.

'Ustaadji?'

He applied his hand to my back and pushed me on in front of him. 'If you are insisting on walking down that road then it will be with Him in your heart. Come on. Begin.'

I cleared my throat, turned to Ustaadji one final time. He urged me on. I nodded, closed my eyes, and began silently mouthing the niyyah. The colours were bright behind my eyes. I raised my hands up to my shoulders and gave voice to my prayer. The sound were weak and tentative even to me.

'More,' Ustaadji said.

I forced my voice louder.

'More! This is Him you are praising, yes?'

Louder still, and louder more until I couldn't quite believe how full and clean and fresh the sound coming out of me was. It were billowing around the old valley, breaking free in a way that pleased me so much I could feel the corners of my mouth twitch into a smile.

At some point between me pressing my forehead to the ground and rising back up, I noticed all the long pale shadows slanting off to my side, hands raised and faces upcast. The others had joined us. And I could hear the footsteps of more joining still. And I were leading them all. It spurred me on. I could feel the words growing in my stomach, tiny seeds budding, sprouting greenly out of my mouth. And then, at the start of the third raka'ah, other voices joined in. I could pick out Aaqil's loud boom straight away, and then Faisal's softer sounds, and, later, Charag's flatly spoken words. And soon we were all as one great boiling voice washing over the valley. Magic were spilling over me. The whole world were on fire, trembling with the force of us all on the crest of that hill. At that moment I knew no one would be able to beat us. No one could beat a force this straight and bright. I turned to my right shoulder, my left, then finally opened my eyes. The sun were a warm blessing on my face, and far away in the distance the snow were starting to fall. But the mountain air were a dreamy green, as if Allah Himself had chosen to lean down from on high and breathe upon this day. Ameen.

———

I rang Charag's work yesterday evening, but they said he'd called to say he weren't coming in. It didn't surprise me. Haven't I said he were up to something? But still, I tried to stop myself from thinking the worst. Maybe he'd just met a girl or something. That could be it. It didn't have to follow that he were going to betray me.

It were touching midnight when he got in and hung his brown bomber jacket up. 'I didn't think you would still be up, bhaiji,' he said, coming into the kitchen. He took an apple from the bowl and jumped up onto the worktop.

'How was work?'

He nodded. 'Okay, okay.'

Liar. Liar, liar, liar. But I kept my cool. 'You're doing a lot of overtime these days, aren't you? Sounds to me like they're working you too hard. Taking advantage. I should have a word.'

He blinked twice, I noticed. 'I don't mind. I need the work. We still have Qasoomah's wedding to pay for. What have you been doing today?'

Notice that? Him changing the subject. 'Your bhabhi came round with Noor. They brought the apples.'

He bit out another chunk. 'How is she?'

'She's okay. Crying a lot.'

He looked up. 'What's happened?'

'Hm? Oh, nothing. It's just her teeth again.'

He frowned. 'You mean Noor.' He shook his head, slid down off the worktop. 'Bedtime,' he sighed.

'Listen.' I waited for him to turn round. 'Just – I just wanted to ask if everything was okay?'

It were as if my concern were funny to him. 'Everything is fine.'

'You've not lost your faith, have you? Because if you have, you know, we can do something about it. Maybe talk to Abu Bhai?' He said there were no need. 'Then why have you been lying to me?'

'Lying? Me? About what?'

I made an impatient noise. 'Don't treat me like an idiot, Charag. Just don't. Where've you been all these nights?'

A tiny laugh came out of him, crinkling with nervous edges. 'It's nothing, bhaiji. Honestly. I was only going to the shopping centre. To see how easy it would be.' I stayed silent. He carried on. 'You are doing so much to prepare, and' – he shrugged – 'I thought I would be doing something also.'

I wanted to believe him. 'I don't want you going there again without me. You understand?' He nodded, apologised. 'In fact, we'll go on Sunday. Together.'

'Sunday?'

'But in the morning. Keep on going at night and they'll get suss.'

He did the little wobble of the head that men back home do to show they agree, and then he turned to go. Again I called him back.

I took a piece of paper from the knife and fork drawer. 'It's the prayer I told you about. The one we need to say right at the end.' He looked right at me, his mouth a little open. 'I printed it off the net. It's in Urdu for you as well.' I pointed at the sheet. 'At the bottom.'

'Thank you,' he said quietly.

'I've memorised it. You need to as well.'

He said he would, and shoved it into his back pocket.

—

Thinking back, maybe the signs were always there with Charag. He hadn't really supported Faisal when he'd decided to become a shahid. He were sometimes missing prayers too, especially the dawn one. Still is, matter of fact. And the only reason he'd left Kashmir and come north with us in the first place were because I were going and his abba had told him to not leave my side. But at the time, as we said our goodbyes to Ustaadji and the others and started driving down the hillside and out of Muzaffarabad, I were just too excited to pay much notice to him.

—

We took the same campervan north, but there were a lot more room in the back now it were just me, Charag and Faisal. Aaqil were driving. We'd set off at night and I spent most of the trip with my head on a messy pile of orange bedding, coming in and out of sleep. I remember the moon tailing us in the grubby back window, and seeing Faisal and Charag playing cards. I remember it were cold and that I had my arms crossed and hands tucked into my armpits. I've got a hazy memory of Charag looming as he draped a blanket over me, and of Aaqil wrapping more heavy-duty brown tape around the radio on the dashboard. And as we drove longer into the night, I remember the faraway sounds of Faisal singing some old movie songs, full of the usual plaints, the usual complaints, and I remember Aaqil telling him to not be such a miserable bhanchod and couldn't he sing something a bit more cheery instead?

Faisal shook me awake – the sun is coming up, he said – and the four of us got out and knelt by the roadside ditch and prayed as the thick morning light turned all those wheat fields into gold. After that, I slept and slept and only woke again when I heard voices outside. Someone were shouting. I sat up. The front door were open and in the wing mirror I could see Aaqil. He looked frantic. He were jabbing at his mobile. Then a big brown hand grabbed hold of his jaw, squeezing. Bandits, I thought. Dacoits, even. I started edging away, stretching for my phone. I don't know why. Who did I think I could call? Who were going to help me here? I couldn't even see Charag or Faisal. They could've been killed. My legs were shaking, and I stepped right back into the hot metal floor. I swallowed the scream, lurched forward. The van shook. I stood still, begging to God to please not let it end like this. I thought I'd got away with it. But then the back door swung open and a man stood there. He had a rifle.

'No!' I said, in English, moving my hands in front of my face. 'Please no!'

He were shouting, but I didn't understand, and then he reached deep into the van and dragged me out by the collar. I tripped up landing on the tarmac, but he just pulled me to my feet and pushed me towards the others. He were still shouting, but it weren't Urdu or Panjabi. His red shawl were wrapped over his head and tight across his nose and mouth. I could only see his yellow eyes, and the long feminine eyebrows peaking down on them.

Charag and Faisal were stood next to me, silent and bent forward against the tilt of the van, as if we were keeping the thing from toppling over. Aaqil were still trying to get through on his phone, all the while saying, 'Abu Bhai? You are knowing Abu Bhai?'

But the name sempt to mean nothing to the man and he started patting at our clothes. He found Faisal's wallet and pocketed the notes.

I kept my head down. I didn't know where we were. I could hear market-sellers in the distance and trucks passing behind us. No one stopped to help.

He found my wallet too and, inside it, my UK driving licence. He came right up to me then, and grabbed my hair and jerked my head back. I gasped. He said something vicious-sounding into my ear. He had his rifle in his hand. I forgot how to breathe. Everything became kind of erratic, my thoughts racing ahead of each other. I could hear my chest heaving. Tears pricked my eyes. I started thinking of Noor.

'Hello? Hello?' It were Aaqil. 'Abu Bhai? It's me.' He spoke manically, with one finger in his ear. We were being stopped at the border. This man wouldn't let us through. He thinks we are spies or something. Aaqil held the phone out to the man, urging him to take it. He did, and moved away from us.

Charag whispered across that it'd be alright. I were fine, I said, glancing up. It were then that I saw the guy's accomplice for the first time. He were sat casually on a large boulder near the roadside, his rifle between his knees. Not yards from us. He were eating something.

'I told you they would be fine,' he said. 'Look at them. They're kids only. Babies. No good to us.' He wiped his mouth with a large leaf and then started attacking his teeth with a toothpick. He must've been eating paan. His gappy teeth were stained red.

The violent one gave Aaqil his phone back and said we could go.

'Not so brave now, is he?' Faisal said, fists on hips. 'Now he knows who we are.'

Charag pushed Faisal in the back. 'Just get in the van.'

'But what about my money?'

'Just go.'

Aaqil started the van up again, and we edged into the line of slow-moving trucks. No one said anything at first, but then Aaqil twisted round. 'That was exciting, hain na?' We gave him a look. He frowned, turned back to the front.

While I were sleeping Aaqil had got a phone call from this Abu Bhai telling him to forget Peshawar and to come straight through.

'Straight through to where?'

'Afghanistan. Torkham.'

'But I thought—'

'Uff, you were the one wanting to come here,' Charag said. 'No point complaining now.'

'I'm not complaining.'

A thick arrow of people were massed on the other side of the border, luggage in hand, waving papers. Aaqil dialled Abu Bhai again and passed the phone to the guard. Eventually we got waved to one side and allowed through. All three of us in the back were stood up, hunched against the roof, faces pushed out between the gaps in the seats. The road were rammed. There were a few buildings here and there – a shop selling radios, a motorcycle garage – but mostly it were just a slim rangy road with some spiky grey mountains at the end. Then I noticed something strange. All the people around, the hundreds of people walking up and down the hot road or standing in lazy groups, they were all men – men or boys.

Aaqil parked up. 'I'll find out where we are going,' and he got out to speak to some men smoking nearby. The rest of us got out too – it were baking inside – and retreated to the bright black shadow of the van. It made little odds. The sun refused to let us hide and under my turban my scalp seeped.

A boy in torn long blue robes were looking at me. He were crouched down at the side of the road, cleaning his teeth with a stick and spitting into the sand. I were expecting him to come begging, but he didn't. He just spat again into the small frothy puddle of dirt he'd made, then got up and walked off. I think that were the first time I'd been on a busy street and no one had hassled me for money. Maybe it were my own grey robes and loose turban, my beard and way of standing, but whatever it were no one sempt to take me for a valetiya. I'd changed.

___

The roads were even worse than at home in Pakistan and we had to shut the windows to keep out the dust clouding off the wheels. We drove for what sempt like miles out of town. Faisal said we must've missed a turning somewhere, but just then this little collection of stone houses sprouted high above us. The track leading up to the village had been left unfinished, just a strip of small loose stones and potholes. Aaqil shunted into a lower gear. It took all his effort to keep the van on course.

The climb were steep and lined on both sides with weedy-looking trees carrying weighty red fruit. We passed a burnt-out oil tanker laid on its side – a few kids in bright clothes were using it as a playground. The road didn't end so much as just kind of widen and fritter out as it merged into the village courtyard. There can't have been more than thirty or forty houses squatted about. Up ahead, the mountains sempt closer than ever, like rotten teeth, as if the whole dry gritty valley had its mouth open thirstily towards Allah (swt). There were a couple of water-pumps at the top end of the courtyard, and at one of them two women in full burqa stood chatting, fat brass pots tucked into the scoops of their hips. When they turned and saw us strangers they went indoors, leaving the courtyard empty. There were a few jeeps parked up around the place, all open-top, with busted sunk-in black seats. And even though only one of the houses had a satellite dish, green and red wires sagged and criss-crossed from house to house until it sempt like pretty much everyone were getting free cable. I could hear a television playing dimly somewhere.

The kids we'd passed on the way up came and stared at us in a bored way, waiting to see if we'd provide any entertainment or if they should go back to their tanker.

'Oi, which is Abu Bhai's house?' Aaqil asked in faltering Pashto.

They all pointed at different houses.

'Fucking kids,' he muttered.

A pair of wooden blue double doors swung open in the house with the satellite dish, and a man unfolded himself and came striding proud and tall towards us. Soon enough I'd get to noticing that he always walked like that, chin up and his hard round gut pushed out, as if someone were trying to winch him back. And he always spoke unnecessarily loud, like he had earplugs in.

'You made it, then!'

'That's Abu Bhai,' Aaqil said, then went to meet him halfway. They each put their right hand on the other's chest, then leaned in and touched shoulders. The rest of us looked at each other, wondering if we were meant to do the same or if that were just a special greeting for certain people and, if so, might he be offended if we tried it too. We settled for shaking hands.

'Well done, very well done,' Abu Bhai said. His smile were like a gash in his beard, a beard that were beginning to grey and climbed all the way over the tops of his cheeks. 'No problems?'

'Only nearly getting killed at the border,' Charag said.

'Oh yes. Ritu.' He laughed. 'He can be a little hot-headed.'

'A little?' Charag exclaimed, but Aaqil threw him a look.

We had to duck to enter the house, but inside there were easy enough room to stand up straight. The light came in through the barred windows and made a kind of striped welcome mat across the doorway. There were one settee and it were backed against the wall and decked out in quilted red and gold covers. Round tasselled cushions had been placed tidily across the top of it. The floor had been swept. Somehow, I hadn't expected them to be houseproud. It were hotter inside than out, though, the air thick and juicy. Even the walls were warm. I might have been panting too, because we were ushered to the centre of the settee, opposite the electric fan mounted on the wall. It made a noise like chattering teeth every time it went round, but the breeze it gave off were hot, and only made my scalp itch even more. A door off to our left led to another room. A TV and computer on a low table. A couple of brown nails hammered wonkily into the wall – a Hajj calendar, a green towel.

Abu Bhai spoke. 'How is my dear friend, hain? I hope you are looking after him?'

'He's fine,' Aaqil said. 'The same.'

'Has he bought a tractor yet? Every time I visit I am telling him, "Tanwer, buy a tractor. I will give you the money myself." '

'Since when is Abba listening to anyone?' and I thought I heard some bitterness come into Aaqil's voice.

A man came in with a round steel tray of biscuits and mint tea, all covered with a white handkerchief. He did his salaams, and as he passed us our cups I saw the rifle swinging across his back. I felt a short sharp mad thrill. He sprinkled some salt over the biscuits, then left, the tray dangling by his thigh and knocking against the butt of his rifle.

Faisal looked glumly at the salty biscuits.

'This is a snack only,' Abu Bhai said, waving away the flies. 'I have asked for some chickens to be bled for tonight.'

The biscuits were soft and damp and fell apart as soon as I laid them on my tongue and pressed them against the roof of my mouth.

'Which is the valetiya?'

I swallowed down the buttery mulch, raised my finger. 'Me, huzoor.'

'As I thought. You have had enough of eating the bread of the enemy, hain? Washing it down with your brothers' blood?'

'I'm here to learn,' I said, but the words didn't sound made for my mouth, and I worried they'd pick up on that.

'Well.' He took a sip of his tea. 'That is very easy to say. But would it not be easier, my friend, to have stayed at home in your own country?' Aaqil tried to speak up for me, but Abu Bhai warded him off with a raised hand. 'You have been watching the humiliations for so long, after all.'

He were testing me, I knew. He'd never have let me through the door if Aaqil hadn't already convinced him I were for real, but still it cut deep. But that's the thing about leaders, I suppose, people who know you're desperate for their approval: they know exactly where it hurts. 'I'm here to protect my people.' I met his gaze head on. 'I'm a Muslim.'

'Deobandi?'

I knew I were, but for some reason I hesitated.

Abu Bhai laughed. 'He does not even know what he is!'

'We're Deobandi,' Charag confirmed.

'You should be telling him that!'

'I know what I am,' I said over him. Abu Bhai quit laughing, but kept his amused face on. I told him, 'I can take the struggle back. You should be thanking Allah, Subhana wa Ta'ala, that He has seen fit to bring me to you.'

No one spoke for the longest beat, waiting to see which way the thing would turn. Then Abu Bhai put his hands on his knees and pushed up onto his feet. He had to go and supervise the killing of the chickens. The door shut behind him, and there were this almighty release of laughter in the room. Aaqil, Faisal, Charag, they were all climbing on top of me, like team-mates after a goal. My head got rubbed, my back patted, my shoulder squeezed. Kya line mari, I remember Aaqil saying, just like a filmi hero. Ameen.

This afternoon, I were rushing to the tram stop, checking the time on my phone. I'd let myself get held up at the mosque, making enquiries about Charag. Whether he were still attending. If anyone knew what he got up to. It drew a blank, but I know something's not right. I can feel it.

'He seems like a good kid.'

I stopped, but I didn't have to turn round. I knew it were him. 'Who?'

'Charag. The one you're mumbling on about. He seems like a good kid.'

'What would you know?'

'Oh, just what I've heard, I guess.'

I turned slowly towards him. Charag. His name. I tried to think if I'd mentioned it that time at the mosque car park. Tarun were smiling at me, like he were egging me on to ask him. He knew what he were doing. I weren't going to give him the satisfaction. He looked about and around me.

'Some fast pace you had going on there. Who you running away from?'

'Don't believe in running away. What's the point? Allah sees everything, don't he?'

'So I hear,' and there were something mocking in the way he spoke. I turned to carry on my way. 'You off?'

'Yeah. Becka's bringing Noor over and . . .' I stopped. I didn't have to explain anything to him. 'I'll see you around.'

'Sure, mate. My regards to your missus.'

I paused, then carried on away from him. All the way home my mind were flaring. He knew. Him and Charag, they were going to stop me. Everyone knew. I spent the whole of the tram ride looking at the passengers from under my eyes. Searching for signs for which of them knew. They were looking at me as well, nudging each other. It freaked one girl out enough to have her charging off at the next stop. Yeah, run now, I thought, as she smiled and kissed her boyfriend off the tram, but where you going to run to when Allah comes after you?

I'd only been back a few minutes when Becka turned up. I locked the door behind her.

'What's up with that?' She found it funny. 'You expecting the bailiffs?'

I didn't say anything then, but when she came back later to pick Noor up, I asked her if she'd noticed anything weird about Charag lately.

'Weird? Like what weird?'

'Anything.'

She buckled Noor up in the pram. 'Does he still sometimes eat baked beans with his roti? I always found that pretty weird.'

'No, I mean . . .' But I didn't know what I meant. 'Is he seeing anyone? A girl?'

She yanked the pram-cover down. 'How the hell should I know? I'm not his keeper.'

And then I remembered Tarun, and what Fahim had said about looking in my own back yard. 'Do you know someone called Tarun?'

I watched her close, but she didn't give anything away. 'Who?'

'Tarun. Tarun . . .' His name badge came into focus. 'Tarun Wadia.'

'Don't think so. Why?'

'Don't know. You tell me. Maybe you're the one seeing someone.'

She stood up. 'Imz, what is this?'

There were all these thoughts coming into my head from all corners, but I couldn't link them up. 'Nothing. Nothing. I'm sorry. I'm not thinking straight.'

'Too right, you're not.' I kept quiet. She softened. 'Call me if you need to?'

I sighed. 'Not if I want to? Only if I need to?'

She swivelled the pram round and pushed off down the hallway and out the door.

I sat in the armchair with my head in my hands. I were still sat like that when Charag came whistling though the door in his stupid yellow hat.

'Charag?' I rushed to the hallway. 'That guy. How does he know your name? How the fuck does he know your name?'

'Kya? What's the matter? Whose name?'

'That guy. The security guard. The guy from the car park the other day. What's his name? Tell me his name.'

His eyes moved around the floor. 'Tarun?' he said, all tentative.

'How'd you know that?' I practically had him trapped against the wall. 'Did you read it off his name badge?'

'Maybe. Why? What's happened?'

'But you can't read English, can you? So you couldn't've. And I didn't think you'd even met him? So why are you lying to me? Why have you been lying to me all along?'

'I haven't.' His voice turned hard. He freed himself. 'Don't ever call me a liar. And it was you who told me this Tarun's name.'

'And you just happened to remember it, did you? From that one time I mentioned it? Pretty good memory you've got.'

'Fahim was there, too.'

I scrolled down to Fahim's number. He answered. I said I needed to contact that guy I met at the mosque car park that time, the one I'd told them about after, but I couldn't remember his name. Had I mentioned it to him? Yeah, I know, shit for brains, that's me. He thought hard, then came back with 'Tarun'.

'But don't ask me the dude's surname. Did I even meet him?'

'Tarun? Sure? You sure? How'd you know?'

'You mentioned it a couple of times. Kept on asking if we knew this guy, whoever he were. If I'm honest, blood, you looked pretty freaked out by it. Is everything alright?'

I switched the phone off. They're lying to me. They're all lying. I turned round, and Charag looked worried as all hell. Ameen.

If they really are on to me then I need to get the rest of everything down quick. I tell you, B, I thought of you when I were over there in Afghanistan. I might not have rang as much as I should of, but I definitely always thought about you. Especially Noor, and especially at night, when I'd be on the roof wrapped in an itchy blanket. The nights would feel so cold over there, like the cold wanted to settle in my bones and make me its home. It's funny, it might've been the most isolated place I've ever been, but I don't think I've ever felt more connected to the world. Not in the packed streets of Sheff or at uni, not in England really, where I always felt that even though there were all the rush and noise you could want, I weren't actually ever bumping up against life, instead just constantly moving out of its way. It weren't like that back home, not when I were stood on the roof of Abu Bhai's house, folded and folded again into the great black night. There could've been someone stood two feet in front of me and I wouldn't have seen them. Sometimes I'd hear Abu Bhai puffing up the stairs, step by slow step, and he'd come up onto the roof with his clay kangri burning in his hand. He'd round the satellite dish and come closer and closer to me, and the fiery light would reveal more and more of his face, pushing at the shadows until they slipped down his neck and off his shoulder, like a gown left hanging across his arm.

'Here again? Waiting for fajr, hain?'

'Yes, Uncle.'

'Good, good. Very good.'

He put the kangri on the sandy wall that ran round the roof. He looked up.

'Can you see them like this in your country, too?'

I smiled in the dark. Your country. There really were no point in fighting that particular battle. But it didn't seem to matter any more. I'd found my people.

'How many there are, hain?'

He meant the stars. And it were true. It were like an awe-some carpet of differently twinkling points. 'They're usually hidden behind clouds in my country.'

'Or maybe the people are too blind to see them.' He sounded pleased with himself, like he did whenever he said something he thought were really clever and deep. 'My ammi used to be telling me that they are all His eyes. That this is His way of watching us at all times. That was how she got me to behave.'

'That's a lot of eyes He's got.'

'There are a lot of people He is needing to watch. And, anyway, no one is coming up with a better reason of what they are.'

I turned to him. 'Well, they're like our sun, aren't they? They're just like, you know, the sun.'

And I explained one of the only things that really grabbed my imagination at school. That each one of those stars were built of the same stuff as our sun and how some of them had planets going round them too, and that it were probably likely that there were other people out there somewhere, maybe just like us. But the more I spoke the less it looked like he were believing me, until finally he laughed.

'Very good joke. I must tell the others tomorrow.' He looked proud that he'd not let himself be sucked in.

I left it. Maybe it were just a trick of the light burning on the wall, but I thought I'd suddenly seen the child in him. 'But, Abu Bhai, tell me about shooting stars, then? When stars fall from the sky? How do you explain them?'

He slowly turned his face towards me. 'Why, Imtiaz, how little you must think of Him. Do you not think that He too might shed a tear for His children?'

—

About every other day we'd drive down to the main street in Torkham for food. Most of the small shops and huts were still standing, but all the tall ones were wrecked. There were a huge building opposite where we parked, and one side of it were just this waterfall of sandstone bricks, crashing down into a pool of stone and dust. Maybe it used to be a TV station or something because one day I saw kids digging about in the rubble and finding bits of radio equipment – a headset, a microphone. They put them on and started playing at being presenters. I were about to say that shouldn't someone move those kids on, that it's dangerous to play there, when I saw the Americans. Two of them, in army gear and wraparound shades that made them look like overgrown insects in camouflage. They were frisking someone. I looked closer. It were only an old man. He even had a walking stick. They made him put his arms up, and when he couldn't lift them any higher they pushed them up for him. They made him take his shoes off.

I'd seen a lot of stuff like that by then. The first time, I'd told the others that we should do something. 'He's got his rights.' And as soon as I'd said that I knew how stupid it sounded. The kind of thing a foreigner would say. Aaqil and Faisal had glanced at each other, smiling.

My eyes moved from the Americans with the old man to the comb-seller winding his way through the crowd, his tray held high like a waiter in a posh restaurant. Every now and then he shouted out, 'Quality!' in English. No one could ever find a comb in Abu Bhai's house, so I slid down from the jeep, calling for the man. With a bit of a flourish, he lowered the tray from his shoulder. They were pocket combs, all different colours and fanned out in a spiral. He said something in Pashto, but when I just looked on, he peered at me more closely. He spotted my foreignness then and laughed to himself, as if wondering how he could've missed it the first time round.

'Hello, sahib.' For a horrible second I thought he were going to salute.

'A comb,' I said.

'Red? Blue? Shiny-green?' He held up a yellow one with

most of its teeth missing. 'Like sun,' he said, grinning, point-ing. I followed his finger, bronze in the sunlight. I could feel my tunic soaking and shrinking against my back. My head were starting to throb.

Around me the crowds starting moving into the middle of the street as the Americans bullied their way onto the roadside. They parked outside what were either a chemist or a doctor's. Just a small stone shack with the shutter up and bottles and packets and tubes laid out on blankets along the ground. A man in a tight kufi full of tiny glinting mirrors ducked out of the hut and picked his way through the bottles and whatnot, his arms held out to his visitors. The soldier in the passenger seat lifted his gun off over his head and got out to meet the doctor. They unhooked the tarpaulin and began unloading the medicines into the hut. Each box had a wrinkled piece of pink paper stuck to it.

I found myself staring, properly staring at them, and then the soldier saw me too. He said something to his com-rade, then walked round, stopping right in front of me. In the smooth black lenses of his shades, my warped reflection stared back. But then he pushed his glasses up onto his helmet, and that sempt to knock me a bit, as if he'd suddenly become a proper person. He had thick blond eyebrows, I remember, and sun-lotion under his eyes and a tiny battered cross at his throat. He said something in stilted Pashto. I think I panicked a little, but I had enough sense to know that I weren't to look towards Aaqil and the others. Instead I looked to the comb-seller, who came alive. 'Ferengis,' he said, pointing from me to the soldier, and then he stood back and smiled his toothless smile as if he expected us to greet each other like long-lost friends or something.

'You're from the US?' It's only now that I wonder whether if I'd been white he would instead have asked, 'You're American?'

'England.'

'Right. Long way from home.'

'I'm visiting family.'

'Dangerous time to visit. Where are they? Your family?'

'Around. Shopping. I just wanted a comb.' And remembering that, I threw I don't know how many puls into the tray and picked up the yellow one. The old man went off, chuntering out his sales pitch again. Reluctantly, I turned back to the soldier. The throbbing in my head were getting louder. 'Okay, then. I've got to go.'

'Sir' – he stepped closer – 'it's strange to meet a non-resident in this town. Are you sure everything is okay? We're here to help.'

'Everything's fine. Thanks.'

He were silent, and then he said, 'Can you tell me when you arrived?'

'Not long ago. Days. Maybe weeks?'

'Can you give me a date?'

'A date?'

'The date you arrived in the province?'

'Province?'

'Sir, is everything okay?'

His eyes, they kept on changing. They were bloodshot and mad. But then I blinked and they were normal. Blinked again and they were mad.

'Can I get you some water, sir?'

My fingers tensed and twitched.

'Sir? Sir?'

Abu Bhai appeared at my side, pulling himself up to his full great height. 'What is the matter?' he asked me in Panjabi.

'Nothing,' I said tightly. 'Nothing's the matter.'

I closed my eyes. I could feel the heat on my eyelids. Please keep it together, I told myself. I looked again. His eyes were blue. I blinked. They stayed blue.

'This is?' the soldier asked.

'This is my tauji, my uncle.' I said it very slowly so Abu Bhai might understand. He did, and threw his arm across my shoulders.

The American driving the jeep leaned out of the window and asked if they had a situation. 'No,' the soldier replied, 'no situation,' and then turned back to me. 'Can I just get your name, sir?'

Abu Bhai, hearing the word name, came in magnificently. 'He is Ahmed Dustoor Khan, son of Akbar Dustoor Khan, grandson of late Mahsood Dustoor Khan.'

The soldier looked doubtful, and started to ask something else when his friend said, 'Mark, we need to get moving.'

'Right,' the soldier – Mark – said. He nodded at me, at Abu Bhai, and then pulled down his shades and jogged back to his vehicle.

Back on the road, the scrape and munch of the gears played over our black mood. I quietly asked Aaqil if we could go find the old man, but he just looked at me like I'd gone crazy and told me not to talk rubbish. Ameen.

———

In the evenings, when the training were done, we'd drink cane juice out of steel glasses and watch one of the Islamic channels on cable, or something from Abu Bhai's video collection. Others would join us, sitting cross-legged on the floor with their rifles pointing up. Sometimes it got so packed inside we had to turn the TV round so the kids looking in through the windows could watch as well.

Things'd start off with the usual complaints about how much it cost to bribe the border police, or how little the children helped with the land, but then an image of one of our brothers would flicker up on the screen – on a dog lead – and everyone would fall silent, as if in respect for the man and his shame. Aaqil would get to his feet.

'Everywhere we are looking it is Muslim blood.' He looked round like he were daring someone to challenge him. 'Here in Afghanistan it is Muslim blood, in Iraq it is Muslim blood, in Kashmir it is Muslim blood, Palestine is Muslim blood, Bosnia is Muslim blood, Cyprus is Muslim blood, Somalia is Muslim blood. Everywhere it is Muslim blood but they say they are for peace? They turn the land to dust and call this peace?'

It were like he were speaking directly to me. When he'd finish, though, there'd just be a load of curious faces staring back at him, and Abu Bhai would have to get to his feet and translate.

One night, when I got up my courage and spoke about the role of Muslims in the West, no one laughed. No one called me ridiculous. They just ran with my point, expanded on it, and afterwards Aaqil clasped my shoulder and said I should speak up more in future. I think it were straight after that meeting, outside emptying the sand from our flip-flops, that someone asked me whereabouts in England I were from. And I remember how it took ages for Sheffield to float up into my head, as if I'd had to first remember a whole other person, a whole other life.

—

The red field at the back of the house were where everyone dumped their rubbish – clay pots, broken hookahs, wheel-less motorbikes. The field stretched all the way to the mountains. I've never seen nothing like it, not on that scale. Standing on the bank, it felt like the whole country had been brought to ground.

I didn't go all the way to the mountains, just far enough so that I could fit our house inside the O of my thumb and finger. The first time I went down, I had to spend ages clearing a spot in all the rubbish to sit in. And I would just sit there, thinking. Every evening. The mountains like old friends sat with me. I weren't thinking about anything deep. Just taking it all in, really. That I were here, sitting here on this earth. And that there was the sky. And there were the mountains. There, the stars. Simple stuff, I guess, but it were like I were thinking about it for the first time in my life. Sometimes Moti Lal would join me. I met him one evening, when I saw some movement in all the tin cans up ahead. Suddenly this pointy brown whiskery face poked up through the rubbish. I think it were a gerbil. He took no notice of me though, just went on his business like I weren't even there. It were his patch, blatantly. His territory. I called him Moti – which means fat – because he were so thin. One time I even sneaked some food down with me and when he finally bothered to turn up I tore the chapatti into strips and scattered it round for him. But Moti Lal had one sniff and decided not to bother. And I swear he looked at me as he moved off, appalled at my taste. There were bats, too, as well as gerbils. There must've been a secret cave up in the mountains where they lived. They'd fly out and swoop down the sky in a tight black V, growing louder and louder as they clapped the coming night.

I started performing isha'a while I were down there, alone. Night after night I'd fold out onto my knees and raise my hands to my shoulders. By now the words came easily, stepping clean out of my mouth. And as I prayed, I could see all the brothers around the world just like me, humbling ourselves before Allah (swt), or working the land of His earth, bending and lifting, bending and lifting. Like we were all working in one rhythm in service to Him. I'd never felt like that before. I'd been back home for a few months by then, but there sempt to have been years turning in that summer.

On my way back, picking through the rubble, I noticed everything, as if Allah (swt) had given me new eyes. And all the things I felt were connecting up and falling into my hand, the lines on my palms leading me on.

No one ever said a word to me when I got back to the house. They understood, or thought they understood, and we'd all just squat down in a circle around the food. By then I'd taught myself to sit on the flats of my feet like all the others, without falling back. We'd take a roti each from the pile, tear off the top and shovel it through the large vat of dhal placed in the middle, our guns resting in the corner.

—

Sometimes, if the afternoon got too hot to be either indoors or out, me, Faisal and Aaqil would climb up into the mountains to hide in one of the long dark caves. Charag never came with us. 'Too hot to walk all that way, yaar.' But it weren't that far, and an hour or so after leaving the house the three of us'd be making our careful way down the smooth cave stones, the porthole of sky shrinking to a close. As if to prove some sort of point, Aaqil always went further down than me or Faisal, but soon enough we'd all have our own separate ledge and we'd kick off our chappals and squat down. The stone'd be nicely cold under my feet and I'd lean forward to peer down into the bluey dark. There were still miles to the bottom, but I swear I could see the banks and banks of lapis lazuli buried underneath. The light it gave off were so strong it rose right up through the dark, straight past me and all the way up to the skyhole, making a golden dance of everything that came in its way. We spent the time there doing the usual things: listening to our echoes, dodging the stones we launched at each other, then counting out the seconds until the pebbles hit bottom. But mostly we just laid down, hands behind our heads, and slept until the heat passed over.

I loved those afternoons. The silence were like a pact between us. And the whole time we were messing about in the cave we weren't soldiers or fighters. Not chosen, not responsible, not anything. Just a few friends laughing the day on. And it weren't just us that ran to the caves to escape the heat. Loads of men, young and old, from all the local villages would climb the track looking for an empty cave where they could play cards, have a smoke. Afterwards, once the heat dwindled to a haze, you'd see people heading back down the mountain, leaving behind circles of cigarette butts. Not everyone left straight away, though. Usually one of the kids brought along a grey rubber football and would say how about a quick game, village versus village. Aaqil and Faisal never stayed – they thought it were childish – but I didn't care, and added my topi to the pile that made up one of the goalposts.

It were one afternoon coming back from a game that I heard this loud flat zinging sound. I stopped, looked up. Nothing. The kids were still on their tree-swing, the birds were still in their trees. Must be a jeep backfiring. But as I got to the house I could hear laughter from somewhere round the back. I found them all stood on top of the banking above the field of rubble. Faisal were reloading a rifle broken open across his arm. Over his shoulder, I could see brown glass bottles secured in the rubbish up ahead, the targets zig-zagging through the field. Faisal locked the gun and hauled it up. He bit his lip and took aim.

'Stop!' Abu Bhai said. 'Again, are you trying to shoot the sky? Where are you looking, hain? Can someone show him, please?'

A man came forward and started manhandling Faisal into place. He moved his legs round until he were standing side on. He dug the rifle butt into Faisal's armpit. Roughly, he pushed up his elbows and cocked his head to one side. The man stepped away.

'Am I okay to shoot now?' Faisal asked woodenly, afraid to move.

'Yes, yes,' Abu Bhai said. 'Do you want an invitation?'

I covered my ears, along with everyone else. The blast were muffled but I still felt myself jolted back a step. Up ahead, some of the rubble got disturbed, but that were about it. A low laugh went through the crowd. Abu Bhai shook his head. Faisal held the gun out – to me – and went to the back of the queue with his head down and in a bit of a mardy sulk.

I tried to pass the gun onto Aaqil, but he wouldn't take it and then Abu Bhai told me to get on with it and that I couldn't be any worse than that idiot. He passed me some cotton wool for my ears. I moved to the edge of the bank and stretched my hand under the sleek warm heavy barrel. I took the rough brown butt of the gun tight in my grip and hefted it up into my shoulder. I stood sideways on. There were a minute or so when I didn't do anything, just the barrel bobbing up and down slightly in my hand.

'Be keeping it steady,' Aaqil advised. 'Don't be nervous.'

But I weren't nervous. It were something else. I felt how commanding my position were. It were like I were ripping free, like my skin were tearing apart to reveal a new and stronger man. The thought flashed into my mind that if I wanted to I could just suddenly turn round and shoot them all dead. Every single one of them. I had a horrible feeling I were going to smile.

'Take as much time as you need,' Abu Bhai said.

My cheek were hot on the black metal. I closed one eye and trained my gaze down the strong line of the gun and towards all those bottles weaving away into the distance, like the footprints of some boy called Imz that I used to know from Sheffield. I could see him trying desperately to run free. I moved my finger onto the trigger and slowly pressed down. I remember how my shoulder were knocked back with the force of the shot, and then I remember hearing Aaqil cheer, but most of all I remember watching the slow ropes feeding out at the end of the barrel, like two plaits of smoke twisting and disappearing around one another. Ameen.

He came round this evening, did Tarun. I opened the door and there he were, bold as fuck with his floppy big smile from ear to ear.

'Alright, there? Haven't seen you for a few days so – you know – thought I'd pop by. See if you're still alive,' he added, with a smile.

'Course I'm still alive.'

He raised his eyebrows. 'It's just a figure of speech, mate. My my, aren't we all on edge?'

I didn't ask him how he knew where I lived. He would've had some answer lined up ready.

'Don't mind, do you?' and he stepped straight past me, filling up the hall like he owned the place.

As I shut the door, I could feel the sweat slipping between my palm and the lock.

''Cos, you know, we have to look after each other, don't we?' He turned round. 'Power to the Muslims and all that.'

'The front room's just' – I moved past him – 'just through here.'

He didn't even take his shoes off. I wiped my hands on the hem of my kurta.

'A drink? Can I get you a drink?'

'You alright, mate? You seem a bit on the nervous side of things.'

'No, no, it's nothing like that.' Laughing a little. 'It's just my daughter's visiting and, you know, I want to make sure everything's alright.'

'Say no more, my friend, say no more. Don't want to be giving the missus cause for complaint. You do right. Mine's the same. Eyes like a hawk.' He sat himself down on the settee and stretched an arm out along its back, making himself right at home. 'But, yeah, I'd love one, thanks.'

'Hm?'

'A drink?'

'Oh, right, course.' And I went down the hall, telling myself just to keep it fucking together. I were banging cupboards, looking for a clean mug, but then I thought fuck it, he can have a dirty one. If nothing else, it'd make me feel better.

'I were speaking to a few of the guys down at the mosque.' He took the mug from me.

'Oh yeah?' I said, my voice travelling up the scale.

'They say you've got really into your religion since you came back. From Pakistan.'

I took the armchair opposite and trapped my hands under my thighs. 'No more than anyone else.'

'I'm all for it, myself. Already got the kids reading namaz.'

'You've got kids?'

'Three. Ayesha, Jamal and Little Mo. Seven, six and two.'

That were exactly what I'd always wanted. Two boys and a girl. 'That's nice. That's good.'

'It were the wife's idea if I'm honest. She were dead keen the kids grow up to be proper Muslims. It's like that's her life's work.'

'They should know what's going on in the world. Your kids.'

He took a sip of his drink, eyeing me from over the rim. 'What do you think of what's going on in the world?'

'Me?' I shrugged. 'I don't think anything.'

'You just let Allah do your thinking for you?'

Charag came clomping down the stairs and into the room. He were late for work. 'Have you seen my top, bhaiji? I can't find my top.' I were watching but the two of them didn't even so much as glance at each other. Tarun just kept on silently sipping his drink, while Charag checked under the table. If it were all an act, it were a pretty convincing one.

The doorbell went. I let Becka in, helping her reverse the pram over the step. 'You alright?' she asked. 'You look stressed.'

I took Noor out of the pram and carried her into the front room. Becka followed. Just as we walked in, Charag got really self-conscious and covered his chest with his arms.

'He's lost his uniform,' I explained.

'Maybe he should try the washer,' Becka said, and Charag went off to have a look.

I were about to make the introductions, but Tarun just carried on sipping his drink, head turned away, like he had no interest in being introduced to anyone. He were being pretty rude, actually. But there were something more going on.

Something weren't right. I looked down. Becka's feet were pointing towards the door. She wanted to get out of the house. But I couldn't work out why, and that made my head start to beat and pulse. It became an effort to stay standing. I felt sick.

'Anyway,' Becka said, 'I guess I'll just finish making up her feed, and then I'll leave you lot to it.' She took the baby-bag from the pram and carried on down the hall.

Tarun put his mug down and said he'd better make a move as well. 'Got a date with the missus and a garden centre.' He rolled his eyes. 'But come down and visit soon, yeah? I'm there every Sunday, without fail. And if you don't come' – he pointed a finger at me – 'well, I know where you live, don't I?'

I were still carrying Noor as I followed him to the front door. 'Listen, you don't have to go. You can stick around if you want. I'd like that.'

He smiled, like what I were saying weren't surprising him one bit. It were surprising me, though.

'Next time bring your kids, yeah? I'd really like that. And your wife. Seriously. I really mean it. I'd really like that.'

He'd think about it. He left.

I came back into the room and put Noor down on the floor. I noticed Tarun's mug then, on the side table, full still. Becka came back in, putting on her coat. 'She should be fine until she gets back, but the formula's all made up if you need it.' She zipped up her coat. 'What time you planning on dropping her off?'

'B,' I said, and turned to face her, 'is there anything you want to tell me?'

'Like what?'

'Anything.'

'This could be a long conversation.'

Maybe I did have it all wrong. I still don't know. I shook my head. 'Forget it.'

The front door banged shut then, and out the rainy window we saw Charag passing through the gate. He were hunkering down against the weather. He'd found his yellow uniform.

'He could've come in and thanked you at least.'

'Doesn't matter,' she said, and pulled the hood up over her head. Ameen.

———

We kept the practice range up in the field behind Abu Bhai's house. Not that we ever planned on going out and fighting with the guns. It just brought us closer together. We sent Faisal running out to put new bottles in once we'd smashed through all the old ones. He'd hold on to his topi – he sempt to always be having one hand fixed on his topi – and pick his way through the rubbish with a new set of empties clinking in a little blue crate by his side. He had a way of running, kind of jumping from side to side like a man three times his age, that made us crease up. When he turned round to come back, we'd have our guns trained on him, and he'd freeze.

It were one morning that first week with the rifle range when I heard a few of the local kids running up the track shouting, 'The murderers are coming!' The electricity were out, I remember, because I were struggling to plug in the generator and just happened to look out the window and see them. It weren't a jeep this time, but a proper Humvee. I slid open the iron bolt and ducked outside. All around I could sense female eyes crowded at the gauzed windows, and then the men began to appear at doorways, fanning themselves with the untucked ends of their turbans. We watched the Americans blundering up the last difficult part of the climb. In the passenger seat, his hand out gripping the roof, were the same guy I'd met that time outside the doctor's, and it were him who got out while the other two stayed put. Abu Bhai strode forward, telling me to follow and translate. The soldier – Mark, I remembered – had switched his helmet for a green cloth cap, and his shades rested up on the beak. His thick reddish stubble were like bronze filings sticking most of the way down his neck. He'd left his gun behind, I noticed. Abu Bhai squared off in front of him, as if he were expecting to wrestle. Mark offered his hand. Warily, Abu Bhai took it.

'And Akbar, isn't it?' he said, moving his hand to me.

'Ahmed. Akbar's my father.'

'Ah, yes. So you said.'

They'd heard reports of gunfire, he told us. Did we know that civilians were prohibited from utilising arms in this province?

'I see,' Abu Bhai said to me, 'so these bastards can go everywhere killing at us and we cannot even be defending ourselves?'

I swallowed, turned back to Mark. 'He said, yes, we do know that, but we were not using them against anyone.'

'That's not my concern,' Mark said, and went on to say that though he knew for every one he confiscated we'd easily get hold of another ten, he had to ask us to hand the arms over.

Abu Bhai wrinkled his nose in contempt for the white man. 'Tell him they will find them in the metal trunk under the settee. But tell him first that, yes, they can take them today, and tomorrow, and the day after that, but we will win in the end. We will wait, and we will win.'

I cleared my throat. 'They're in a box under the settee. Help yourself.'

He sent his men to fetch them. We turned to leave, but he called me back. 'One final thing. I've been checking the records, and there's no mention of an Ahmed Dustoor Khan entering Afghanistan from Great Britain. Can you think why that might be?'

And right then I felt everything speed up, horribly quickened by fear. 'I came through Pakistan. Yeah. I did stop off in Peshawar for a night. Hotel – what were it? – The Mahal Hotel? Yeah, that were it. The Mahal Hotel. Check it out if you want. I signed the register.' It's horrible, how easy it is to lie on the spot, all fluent. I were hoping like mad I'd done enough.

He ran his tongue over his greyish teeth. 'I did think of that – that you might've come via Pakistan – but I couldn't find you on the border-control list, either.'

'But how can it be!' I knew I were panicking. 'You've seen how many people cross that border every day.'

He folded his beefy arms over his chest. The green sleeve of his T-shirt rode up his bicep. I saw half a tattoo. C, L, A, R.

Clark, or Clara, maybe. 'Ahmed, please try and look at it from my point of view. This is a war zone. You're here from England. I can't find any record of you. But I do find you playing around with guns. Can you see why I'm a little concerned?'

'But you can take the guns! We don't want them. We were only messing about. I'm just here to see my family. God knows I might not get another chance.' I could feel my panic converting to anger.

'I understand that. I miss my family, too. It's just – obviously we can't rule out any possibility. We are faced with insurgents every day, you know?'

I heard some back-pedalling in his voice, enough to take advantage of. 'So? That means every brown person you see is against you? Take a look around, officer.' With a sweep of my arm, I took in the entire yard. 'Have a good hard careful look. You might see something you hadn't expected.'

He didn't look around. He just kept on looking at me. 'Okay. Well, I suppose that's that for now. But please be assured that we're not here to create any tension between us and you folks. It's vital for the future of the country that we work together, so, obviously, we want to maintain a good dialogue with the people here.'

'Oh, obviously.'

He let my sarcasm pass. 'And it's not just that that we're concerned about. We do also have a duty of care towards non-residents. If we feel their safety is in danger, then we can take them in. For their own good.'

'My safety's fine. There's nowhere safer than with my own people.'

He looked surprised at that, and that made me feel proud of myself. Not because I'd shocked him, but because it sempt to me like for the first time I'd stuck my neck out for everyone back home. I wondered if Aaqil and the others had noticed.

Mark swatted away a hovering fly. 'I've got a kid brother about your age and I sure know I wouldn't be comfortable if he was hanging around here.'

'Yeah, I wouldn't want anyone to see what you're doing here, either.'

The whole top half of his face sempt to flinch. 'We're here to help.' He'd looked away as he'd said it.

That evening, Abu Bhai crouched at the brass tap at the side of the house and soaped his arms all the way up to his hairy shoulders. His skin were coming up red he were scratching so hard. 'They are giving medicines, are they?' He snorted. 'It is like breaking a man's teeth and then offering to be his dentist.'

'Do you think he'll check out what I said?' I asked.

'Maybe,' Aaqil said. 'That's why we need to act quick.' He looked to Abu Bhai, who nodded, reached for a towel, and then told Aaqil to follow him inside. I heard them bolting the door after them. They didn't even think to ask me. I were just left out there.

I snatched up my mat and sloped off down to the field. The call to prayer came just as I got on my knees and lifted my face to the mountains. I began to recite. It were amazing how quickly the fear and anger just drained away, right out of my fingertips, and got replaced by this calm unhurried strength, that beautiful rising feeling we all want, of being truly known.

When I returned to the house, we ate in silence, the only sound the peel and suck of our sweaty feet on the polished floor. No one were eating much or very quickly. And then Faisal said he'd had enough. He handed me what were left of his roti and went and stood in the doorway, looking out.

'What's the matter?' I asked. 'Why's everyone so quiet?'

They looked at one another, then looked away.

'Aaqil? Charag?' They shook their heads. 'But we can get some more guns tomorrow, can't we?' Still no response. I threw my roti down. 'Will someone tell me what's going on?'

'It is them,' Charag said, with disgust. 'They are making Faisal do it.'

For a few beats I were confused, but then I understood, and felt my whole mouth dry out.

'He is being called simply,' Abu Bhai said. No one said anything. 'Oh, what is the matter with you? Rejoice, yes? Rejoice! It is a magnificent day!'

But no one moved. Eventually, Aaqil said, 'I still say it should be me.'

Abu Bhai sighed, like he were tired of going over the same argument. 'And how will they explain things back in your pindh, hain? The police will be looking tough for the camera. Interviewing all your brothers here. You must wait until Imtiaz is back in England.' Abu Bhai paused for a moment, then said, 'Yes, that will be the strongest way. Faisal, then Aaqil, then Imtiaz and Charag.'

Because they had also agreed that Charag would come with me. So I weren't fighting alone. Quietly, I asked how Charag would get over there, and Abu Bhai said he knew people who'd get him the papers. It'd cost, but it wouldn't be difficult to get him a visa for six months or so.

'And,' Charag added, too keenly now I think back on it, 'I thought while we are waiting for Aaqil, I could find a job there and maybe send some money to Abba?'

Abu Bhai stood up. 'Tomorrow I will make arrangements for you three to go back home, yes?'

I looked up and shook my head so hard I could feel my bottom lip wobble. 'We're staying with Faisal.'

He had been standing at the doorway with his back to us the whole time. But now he turned round and reached for the red-and-black blanket folded over the back of the settee. He said it weren't so cold tonight. He'd sleep on the roof. Ameen.

———

She were waiting outside with the kid when I got home earlier today. I didn't recognise her at first. She weren't wearing her headscarf, and she'd had her hair cut shorter, to just below her chin like when I'd first met her.

'My key doesn't work,' she said. 'Have you changed the locks?'

'Yeah, sorry. Forgot to say.'

'Why?'

'Can't be too careful.'

I let her in and, after one final look back down the road, shut the door. I'm sure I'd seen that Tarun, tailing me all the way from town. First in his car, and then through the park on foot. That's the second day in a row now. He thinks I can't see him, but I know he's there. I can feel it.

'You expecting someone?' she asked.

'What? No,' and I let the curtain fall back across the window.

Anyway, she were sorry, she said, for dumping this on me, but that interview? For that job in the uni library she'd told me about? Well, they'd brought the date forward and she couldn't very well ask her mam, could she? What with it being her one day at the Bingo and everything.

'It's fine,' I said. 'Course it is.'

'Great. Thanks.' She kissed goodbye to Noor, who still hadn't stopped crying. 'You haven't seen her purple toy, have you? That squidgy one? Usually shuts her up.'

'I think it's in our room. Back in a sec.'

I found it on top of the stereo, then headed back out onto the landing. Becka were coming up the stairs.

'Got it,' I said, holding up the purple whatever it were. I sounded like I expected some sort of reward.

'Great. That's great.'

The door to our room were right behind me. It'd been ages since we were anywhere near a bed together, and there were a horrible pause where we just looked at each other through the brownish gloom of the landing. But then she drummed her knuckles on the banister as if to say, 'Anyway!'

'Could you keep an eye Noor for a minute, please? Need to nip to the loo. Must be nerves.'

We shuffled shyly past each other at the top of the stairs, as if we were right back at the beginning of things, two awkward teenagers in the geography stairwell. I got a whiff of her pink-smelling perfume and I saw myself turning madly round and reaching out for her waist and pulling her down onto the stairs with me, right there. But none of that happened. I just watched her through the square white railings. The bathroom door closed behind her, and I felt a pang of sadness. She never used to do that when we were alone in the house. She'd leave the door open and we'd just carry on talking as she lowered her knickers and sat down. I don't think she ever realised how much I loved all that intimate kind of stuff.

Noor were clawing at my fist to try and prise it open when Becka came back down the stairs.

'Okay, missy, you be good for Daddy, okay?' She pulled on her blue raincoat, lifting her hair out from under the collar. 'I should only be a couple of hours. I mean, how long can it take for them to realise how wonderful I am?'

'You're not wearing your scarf,' I pointed out, just to keep her here a bit longer.

'Well, interviewers can be a bit funny about these things, can't they?'

'Is that why you've changed your hair?' I hadn't intended

on mentioning that. I hadn't wanted her to think I still noticed things about her.

'Summat like that.'

'Looks nice. Like how it were at uni.'

She looked to me, probably thinking how I looked nothing like when we were at uni. The cropped hair and beard, the kurta pyjama. It made me feel self-conscious.

'You've lost weight,' she said, out of nowhere.

I looked down, like I expected to see something else where my stomach were. I felt stupidly happy that she still noticed stuff about me too. 'You saying I used to be fat?'

'No, I'm just saying—'

'That I used to be fat. Sheesh, you know, if you're just gunna insult me then I think we need to be re-negotiating the terms of these visits.'

She laughed. I looked straight at her, waiting for her to stop laughing and then be swallowed up into my stare and come running to me. She just looked away. We tried to carry on as if nothing had passed.

'Actually,' I said, quietly, 'you're probably right. I have been skipping meals lately. Missed breakfast again this morning.'

'Oh, well, there's a few things in the fridge I noticed. Do you want me to rustle—'

But then she just shook her head, as if reminding herself that certain things weren't her problem any more. Ameen.

———

Faisal didn't say much during those last days. If anything, he just got quieter and quieter. He'd started sleeping on the roof, alone, and that's where he were one evening a few days before he became a shahid. I were coming back across the field from offering my du'a. I'd not seen him all day, I don't think. He'd gone out early with Abu Bhai. I waved, climbing up the bank. It took him a while to spot me, but then he beckoned me up.

He were sat on his menjha, hands locked around his raised knees. He'd seen the bomb, he said. It were small. Small enough to be hidden inside the lining of a thick waistcoat. He'd have to pull a cord. He said all this quickly, like it didn't really interest him, and then he went quiet again. We could hear Aaqil downstairs, doggedly arguing some point of scripture with Abu Bhai. I thought how different it would've been if it were Aaqil going first. He'd have gone on and on about the bomb and how it looked, felt. He'd have lapped it all up, all the attention, probably even have tried to get the village named after him. I bet that's what's taking him so long now. He's probably trying to convince everyone of the need for a statue of him in the middle of the courtyard. But Faisal weren't interested in none of that. People don't even think about that, do they? That there are different types of soldiers. That Faisal were different to Aaqil. But Faisal understood. He knew about love for his people and he knew that were the best thing in the world to feel because then their pain becomes as real to you as yours, and for the first time you realise you're not on your own.

'Did you ring your ammi and abba?' I asked.

He clucked his tongue, meaning he hadn't. 'What is there to say, yaar? Allah, Subhana wa Ta'ala, will look after them.'

'Don't you want to hear their voice one last time?'

'One last time? You don't think I will see them again?'

I'd been slipping up a lot lately. 'Of course you will. Inshallah,' I added.

He looked like he were wondering whether to say what he were about to. 'You have been very quiet for a while now.'

'I could say the same about you.'

'Are you becoming a shahid in a few days? No. I did not think you were. So what's the matter?'

'Nothing's the matter.'

There were a long pause that made me think the matter were dropped, but then he said, 'Abu Bhai asked me to speak

with you. He thinks you are wavering. That you're not praying as hard as you used to. And he is right. I was watching
you down there and you were not spending enough time to
be saying more than one raka'ah. So, I ask you again, are you
wanting to pull back from the fight?'

I had been doubting things. Ever since the night I'd been
told about Faisal. 'What makes you so sure? What makes you
so sure that He will let you in?'

'Because He loves me,' Faisal said, as if I were being thick.

'But if that's true, if He really loves us, then' – I turned to
Faisal, head on – 'then why does He let His children suffer
like this?'

'It is a test, isn't it? He is testing us to see who is good
enough to sit beside Him.'

I'd been afraid that were what he'd say. I looked over to the
mountains. I think Faisal guessed that his explanation weren't
enough, that no merciful God would insist that we suffer in
this life before letting us find happiness in the next.

'Is that what has been the matter?' he asked. 'Is that it?
Look, when you are back home, go see our ustaad, acha?
He will explain it all much better than me. All I know is that
it is not Him who is making us suffer.'

'But you don't know, do you? You believe. You don't
know.'

He sighed, losing patience. 'Of course I believe. I am a believer, yes? But I also know. And do you know why that is, Imtiaz? It is because even if someone told me now that when I get to the gates the swords will not uncross, that I will be turned away, even if I knew that for definite today, I would still be entering the fight.' I remember looking at him then, shocked at what he were saying. 'So He must be true, hain na? Why would I be happy to risk dying for nothing? Why would my mind be made that way? Because to die for nothing is the real hell. And there can only be a hell if there is also a heaven. And there can only be a heaven if there is . . .' He motioned for me to finish.

'If there is Allah.'

Faisal nodded. Someone were calling us down to dinner. 'It is the same question for you, yaar. Not is this true or is that true. But how true are you?'

—

Faisal must've had a word because later that night Abu Bhai shook me awake and told me to come with him.

'What? Where to?'

'Just come.'

My feet were freezing on the stone floor. I found my sandals in the dark, threw a blanket around myself and followed him to the jeep. We drove with the headlights off, in case Americans saw us. The only sounds were the faint running growl of the engine, or the raw squawk of a passing nightjar. My teeth were chattering slightly.

'Where are we going?'

But again he didn't say a word. There sempt to be nothing or no one around for miles. At the main junction we didn't turn west towards the town. We headed instead into desert. Somewhere I'd never been.

'Where are we going?' I asked again, more firmly this time. It made no difference. He just drove staring straight ahead. So they were going to kill me, I thought. They'd decided I couldn't be trusted any more. I remembered the rifles in the back, and I think I actually smiled a little. They were going to kill me, but I weren't scared. I didn't scream or beg. I just closed my eyes and rested my head back.

Abu Bhai said something, pointing up ahead. It were a building. And it were laid out against the night in a lighter shade of black. A compound of some sort, with a wire fence all round. We stopped a long way short. As we walked towards it, sand crawling over our feet, Abu Bhai sent a text, and a few moments later a man came prancing out on the other side of the fence. Keys jangled from his belt. He told us to walk further down, to where the door were. He didn't use his keys though. He drew out a white plastic card and passed it over the lock. A green light flashed and the door opened.

He were a guard. His brown face were pitted with scars. Smallpox, maybe. We followed him across the compound, passing wooden crates and barrels, even a trampoline. All of them said in blocky black print Property of United States Armed Forces.

Inside, we were led down a corridor with differently coloured light-bulbs, and then left into a narrow passage full of thick grey doors. The guard stopped outside one of these doors and unlocked the hatch. He held up five fingers – five minutes – and left.

Abu Bhai told me to take a look. I uncovered the hatch. It were on a spring, so I had to hold it up the whole time, and then I got on my tiptoes and peered down through the square grid. There were a man. He were curled up with his back to the wall and his knees pulled up to his chest. His white shirt were filthy, his green trousers stained yellow at the crotch. His eyes were screwed tight shut against the fierce white light that filled the room.

I looked to Abu Bhai. 'Who is he?'

'Abeed. They think he was working against them.'

'Was he?'

'Does it matter?'

I turned back to the man. He covered his eyes with one hand and turned over towards the wall. 'Won't they even let you sleep?' I took a step closer. My body were pressed up against the door. 'Bhaiji?'

'The glass,' Abu Bhai said. 'He cannot hear you.'

Neither of us said a word on the drive home, all the way until we climbed the track and arrived outside the house. Abu Bhai switched the ignition off.

'Everything alright?'

I nodded, and slid down from the jeep and into the house. I climbed under my blanket and closed my eyes. But I couldn't get back to sleep. I turned to the wall, my eyes now wide open. All I could see were him, closed up like a ball in that cell, trying to get through the cold night. Ameen.

———

There's a chance I dreamt it, but I think I remember waking up during Faisal's last night with us. I could see a softish figure through the veil of my lashes, on the other side of the thin curtain hanging down the doorway. It were Faisal, knelt on the ground with his back to me. For a second I thought I'd missed dawn prayers, but no, it were still dark outside, a rich heavy bar of blue running under the black sky. I flipped onto my elbows, too quickly because I remember the ropes of the menjha scraping across my knees. He had his new kufi on, I noticed. Me and Aaqil had gone down into Torkham the day before and brought a new one back. Pure white with intricate silver embroidery going round it. We didn't even haggle with the guy. It fit Faisal snug as anything and with him sat out there in the dark I remember thinking it looked like a fuzzy halo around his head. He looked to be burying something. Some bit of himself that he wanted to leave in the soil.

'What do you think it is?' Aaqil asked behind me. I didn't reply. It didn't matter what it were. And we never asked him about it the next day or dug it back up after he'd gone. We never even mentioned to anyone that we'd seen him. There's no need to know every last little thing about someone. We just carried on watching him pat down the clods of earth, and then bow down to kiss it. He offered a quick du'a, bringing his hands down his face, and then he stood up. Someone else stepped into view then. Abu Bhai. He'd been there all along, stood just a few feet away. He held Faisal's shoulder and said something which we couldn't hear. Then he pulled him close. Faisal let himself be held. His shoulders were shaking.

We stayed silent for a bit, the only sound the chattering of the rusting fan hanging off the wall.

Then Aaqil said, 'Bastards,' and I knew he meant them, the ones who were making Faisal have to do this. And then I heard Aaqil turning back round and sighing a sleepy, 'Allah hu Akbar.'

'Allah hu Akbar,' I replied, faintly. Faisal were still out there, and I don't know how long he stayed like that because a minute or so later I brought the blanket up over my head.

—

The next morning, fajr were as silent as the land, and no one sempt to be reciting with any enthusiasm. Breakfast were a quiet time as well. I pushed my plate to one side and said I weren't hungry. Faisal weren't allowed to eat. He were still praying, still fasting.

And then after midday prayers, Abu Bhai said it were time. Faisal and me put one hand on each other's chest and touched shoulders. As I pulled back, I nodded at him, and that nod were meant to say a hundred things. Me and Aaqil set off out the house then, down the road with the weeping red trees. We got ourselves a table at a chai-dhaba a long way down from the doctor's, on the opposite side of the road. I think we both felt we had to be there with him, to prove we were in this together, but truth be told, I felt relief when I saw that the

Americans weren't there. Maybe they wouldn't turn up today, and then Faisal could return to the house without anyone accusing him of quitting. It wouldn't be his fault.

'They should be here by now,' Aaqil said.

A tea-boy in an oversized grey-green kurta came to our table. His top were tied up in little knots around his waist to stop it trailing along the floor. He asked us what we wanted.

'Just go away,' Aaqil said.

'Arré, this isn't your abba's shop. Either buy something or you know where the road is.'

'Two teas,' I said. The kid sloped off, muttering. I reminded Aaqil that we were meant to be acting normal. He frowned, nodded, apologised, doing all things at once, the way you do when it feels like your heart's going too fast for your brain.

The kid thudded the teas down, sending half of it spilling over the sides. Aaqil glowered.

'Shukran,' I said hastily and paid the kid in full, with a tip.

He touched the notes to his forehead and left.

'Fucking little sisterfucking harami,' Aaqil said. 'If he knew what we're doing for him.'

'But he doesn't know. So let it go.'

We wiped our glasses on the table and drank our teas in silence. There weren't much traffic at the border that afternoon, and the street weren't as packed as it usually were. Maybe people were keeping out of the midday sun. It did seem to be burning down hotter than usual. My sleeves were stuck to my arms, I remember.

A truck loaded high with hay and goats came grumbling past, and I watched it all the way until it turned pale and vanished into the sun. Aaqil were looking off past my shoulder. His eyes did a strange dance then, growing and shrinking before resting down on the table. 'The Americans. They are coming.'

I didn't look round at first. If anything, I turned my face away from the road in case that Mark might have been in there. I heard them go past.

There were four of them, two in front, two in the back. They parked up outside the shack with the medicines laid out at the side of the road. The doctor came rushing out.

There were a dog, too, I remember. I had to squint to see, and it were more like an overgrown rat, but he were sniffing and weaving in and out of the jeep tyres. Stupidly, silently, I were willing him to move on, to just get out from under there, but he sempt to take a shine to the shade, and he snuggled down behind the rear tyre, paws over his snout.

I saw Faisal. He were slowly making his way to the Americans, acting like any other shopper because like we'd thought the two guys in the back of the jeep were keeping a lookout. He had his new kufi on. And he were carrying a small basket of okra – Aaqil's idea. To make it look like he is at market only. You couldn't tell he had a waistcoat on under his kurta, or that a long slit had been made into the side of his tunic so he could reach in for the cord. He stopped at a few stalls along the way, browsing, picking things up, putting them down, moving on. When he got level with us, I looked down at the table. I didn't trust myself. I wanted to call out to him.

'Did he see us?' I asked.

Aaqil said he didn't know.

One of the soldiers were helping the doctor unload the boxes and carry them into the back of his store. The dog were still there, sleeping. A couple of shops down, Faisal sempt to be asking after the price of a set of mirrors. But then he waved his hand at the trader – you are asking too much! – and carried on, even as the guy tried to call him back. It were all happening too fast. I looked down to try and sort out my breathing. When I looked back up, he'd walked straight past the jeep. And then, as if it were only an afterthought, as if he were only remembering at the last second that he had some business to do at the doctor's, he took a few steps backwards and put his basket down so he could take a closer look at the medicines displayed on the blanket.

The doctor were in the back of the store. No one were paying Faisal any attention. He were holding a bottle up to the sun, and then, as he crouched down to put it neatly back in its place, I saw his other hand slip inside his kurta. My arm lurched out towards him, as if it could stretch all the way down the street and pull him back. Again I wanted to call out. He stood up big and proud and the last clear image of him I have in my head is of him reaching for his topi, like he always did whenever he were running.

There were about half a second where there were only this silent dazzling yellow light in the space where Faisal had just been stood. That were when I saw the butterflies. Before the sound could blast through, the spiky tips of the light broke free into a million yellow butterflies flying skywards. Then there were this sudden contracting of the light, like an angry man preparing himself with a deep breath, and then this great unleashing flare of noise. Time sempt to judder and quake, and everyone around me jumped into their shoulders. And then they ran, throwing back chairs, jumping their carts, clawing one another out of the way. They came screaming down the road with their animal faces.

Me and Aaqil were tunnelling against them.

'Don't run away!' I shouted, all the time getting pushed further and further back. 'Let me through for fuckssake!' But

I weren't able to hear my own words, and even the screams all around me sempt to come in and out of focus, like noise in strobe lighting. It were then that these hard popping sounds rang out and suddenly the screams got louder, more panicked, and everyone were climbing over one another not caring who they trampled. The Americans were shooting. Someone – Aaqil – bundled me onto the side of the road, behind some sort of ditch, and shouted at me to just lie flat on the ground, flat! flat!

I laid there with my arms clasped over my head, just like the dog I'd seen earlier. Men were still rushing past, kicking up grit that made my eyes sting and water. When I did dare to look up I sempt to be seeing everything through the glazed end of a dirty bottle. I could just make out a man on all fours, groping about for his glasses. His hand got stamped on, and then the legs thickened round him and I couldn't see him no more. There were strange sounds coming from up the road, but all I could see were the blurred angry green shape of some sort of four-legged beast lumbering down the street. It were breathing fire. Bright watery flashes of orange were spraying out from its black snout.

'Get back you fucking bastards!'

I wiped the crap out from my eyes and looked again. One of the Americans had his arm around the other's waist, dragging him along. They looked to be heading for a small red Maruti parked a few shops up from me.

'Just keep still,' I think Aaqil said, breathing hard. 'They will shoot if you run.'

I kept my face turned towards them, my cheek pressed into the dirt. The guy being helped along were clutching at his eyes. Channels of blood ran down between his knuckles and pooled around his watchstrap. The soldier carrying him had his teeth bared and I remember that his gums looked bright pink out against the blackened face. He were firing at anything that moved. 'Get the fuck back, you hear me!'

Some guy – some frightened desperate idiotic guy – came running and screaming down the middle of the road, flapping his hands by his face like he were being attacked by bees. There were a shot. The man's shoulders jerked back and his eyes widened with surprise, as if he'd expected it to hurt more, and then his knees just crumpled softly underneath him. As he lay dying on the floor he stared straight across to me.

It weren't Mark being dragged down the road, and suddenly I were glad of that. But whoever it were I could hear him crying out when they reached the car, 'My eyes, Chris! My fucking eyes!' His friend said to hang on in there and they'd be back at base soon and then Johnson would clean up his eyes no problem. He used his gun to wedge open the

door and then eased the wounded guy into the front seat
before rushing round to the driver's side. Somehow he got
the car started and I heard it forced into gear and then race
off up the road as people scrambled out of its way. The
teaboy ran out and hurled a stone after them, but it landed
miles short.

Aaqil hauled me to my feet. The screaming had stopped
and people were slowly stepping back out onto the road.
There were this low-level whimpering coming up from the
men bleeding on the tarmac. The stench of burnt rubber filled
the air. There were bullet marks sprayed over the road – concrete flowers, they called them – but you couldn't tell which
were today's. I started hearing calls for blankets and water
and telephones. I left them to it and approached the burning
jeep. I made a wide circle round it, kept away by the hiss and
crackle of the flames. My face felt pink and hot.

The front tyres had burst and the engine had collapsed
down. The whole of the back end were under thick high solid
smoke. I got closer in as I went round, crouching, my eyes
watering from the heat. I couldn't stop myself from looking
for signs of Faisal. And then I saw that all along the back
panel of the jeep, seeping out of the exhaust and clogging up
the treads in the tyres were this bubbling lumpy grease. I felt
the sick rush up into my throat. Aaqil turned away and started

retching onto the road in these great spasms. Someone shouted at us to get away from there. I didn't move, but I didn't want to look any more, either. I wanted Faisal to come back.

Then I spotted something just inside the doctor's hut. I walked over, knowing it'd be Mark. His reddy-blond hair had been mostly burnt away. Clumps of dry frizz at the sides of his head. He'd lost his jaw. I blinked back tears. I weren't going to cry for him. Then I walked away. Back round the jeep. I saw the dog. I told you to move, I said. Why didn't you move? Ameen.

———

When I got back from the mosque last night, Charag were at the computer. He hadn't even changed out of his uniform.

'Everything alright, bhaiji?'

I didn't tell him I were being followed every day now. I'm still not sure if him and Tarun are in on it together. I seem to change my mind by the day. I watched him from the doorway. He looked to be checking his emails.

'Faisal taught you that, didn't he? How to use a computer.'

He said he did, when we were at Abu Bhai's. 'Sit down. I'll make some food in a minute.'

'I'm not hungry.'

He clucked his tongue. 'That is not good. You are already losing weight.'

'That's what your bhabhi says.'

He turned back to the screen, minimising the window.

I could feel my hand knocking against the doorframe. Shaking again. More so lately. I moved it to my pocket and squeezed it into a fist. It's all this remembering Faisal. It's hard.

'Why didn't you come with us? When Faisal gave himself?'

He didn't turn round, but I could see he were frowning. 'What difference would it have made?'

'Maybe it would've prepared you a bit?' His face darkened over. Sighing, I said, 'You're not going to do it. You were never going to do it. You were just using us to get here.'

'It's different for me,' he said quietly. 'If Aaqil and the others want to do it, then fine. It is their business. It is their fight and I wish them well. But it is not for me. Think how it would ruin everything for Qasoomah. Her new family would not want to be related to someone like me. They would send her back. How would Abba look anyone in the face? I cannot do that to them, bhaiji. And it is not the right thing for you, also. You have a life here.'

I felt proud of him if I'm honest, even if he didn't understand that it's not the life here that matters, but the one we're preparing for.

—

Abu Bhai said there were no chance of getting over the border that night, not with all the searching going on, so we'd better just put all our stuff back as it were in case the Americans came checking. In silence, we hung up our clothes back in the almari. It sempt to matter that we made the effort to pull out the creases in our pyjamas and check the coat hangers sat just so inside the shirt collars.

We convinced ourselves the Americans were on their way, so I went and stood by the oil tanker lying at the bend in the road. But as the night pulled in we accepted that there were no real reason for them to target us above anyone else. There must've been a hundred different groups they'd want to check out before they even thought of us. There'd been word that someone out there were already trying to claim it for themselves.

People left me alone that evening. I could hear motorbikes and rifle shots down in the main part of town. Off to the left, someone were sending off flares that made glittery lampshades in the sky. Small stones came bouncing past my feet. Abu Bhai, with Aaqil behind him. Abu Bhai held out a shawl, which I took and closed around me.

'It is on the computer news already.' He meant the Internet. 'Not on the TV yet, but maybe tomorrow. Inshallah, by then you will be going home. Away from all this.'

I just nodded: yes, maybe tomorrow it would make the TV. Yes, maybe we will be gone by then. Yes, Faisal had died. Yes, we had been called to join the fight. Yes, yes, yes. Abu Bhai gave a resigned sigh.

'Come and eat something, acha? You cannot stay here all night. Trust me. No one is coming.' He tugged at my sleeve. 'Come and try to eat something.'

I still had to look hard at them to make out what they were saying. My ears hadn't sorted themselves out yet.

'The ringing will pass,' Abu Bhai said, turning to go. 'Or you will get used to it.'

I followed him back up the track. Aaqil walked beside me. I asked whether he too had seen Faisal being lifted away. 'Right then. Just before all the noise. Did you see the butterflies? The way he were carried?'

Aaqil looked at me for the longest time, and maybe it were only because he could hear how much I needed someone else to say they'd seen it too, or maybe he really had seen it, just as I had. Whatever the reason, Aaqil nodded and said that yes, yes, no I wasn't alone, absolutely he had seen it too.

—

It were well past midnight when we climbed into the front of the van and belted up. A crowd had gathered to see us off. Everyone wanted to shake our hands, and kids were lifted up by their armpits so they could hand us gifts through the open window – handmade wicker rattles, mostly. I remember a camera flash going off.

Abu Bhai banged the roof of the van. 'Okay, men! It is time. You know the way out, yes?'

Aaqil started the engine and a cheer went up. We began to move away down the track, and as we did Aaqil started messing about with the dial on the radio and Charag said he were going to get some sleep. But I couldn't take my eyes off the wing mirror, and all those men sliding back into the distance, looking to us with their hopeful faces.

At the checkpoint the guard made us slow to a stop. It were the same guy who'd had us up against the van that first day. But this time he kissed our hands and then he blew his whistle and waved us on.

A few hours in, we stopped at some lonely roadside petrol station. It had just the one pump, and just the one attendant who lay curled asleep on the forecourt. His head were covered with a newspaper and with each snore it quivered a little further down his face. We filled up, left a few notes in his pocket and got back in the van.

It were a foggy dawn, and in the miles and miles of passing young green corn I could see women already at work. Aaqil switched off the headlights. I said we'd better park up or we'd miss fajr.

After prayers, Charag walked off down the road and drew out his phone from where it slumped in his shirt pocket.

'Arré, we'll be home soon enough,' I said. 'Save your money.'

But there were never any telling him. Every day he'd ring home – how were the land doing? have they sprayed it this week? how much credit do they have left in the bazaar? And I'd find myself thinking how similar we all were, how much we all wished for parents who, like the sun, were ever present, without forever making that presence felt.

'Qasoomah's getting married,' he said, climbing back in the van.

I think I smiled a genuine proper smile. 'Really? How come? When?'

'Which poor fool said yes?' Aaqil asked, turning the ignition.

'Someone from the next pindh. They only want a small dowry.' He sounded surprised, relieved even, and he sempt to be sitting straighter than before, as if he'd managed at last to shrug something off and leave it to rot out there on the road.

Noon approached, and the sun were spangling across the windscreen. We flipped down the visors. The dashboard had become too hot to touch, and Aaqil had to use a cool damp cloth to grip the steering wheel. But at last there were signs we weren't far from Lahore. Little roadside communities began shooting up, the shacks held up with tin and advertising. If you looked hard enough there'd always be some kid crouching barefoot beside a puddle, skimming the top off into a glass. The roads started to improve, and there were fewer miles between one tin-roofed garage and the next. And then, up ahead, Aaqil pointed out the dome of the Badshahi Masjid.

'Shall we stop?' he said.

Charag made a desperate face. 'Can we just go home? We're nearly there.'

So we drove on, bowing our heads as our masjid sailed by on a great lake of rippling heat. We turned left down a dry shrunken road dotted here and there with drooping purple trees.

'Do you know where we are yet?' Aaqil asked.

I did, I said, looking round me. It were like some kind of memory-rush, but with me not quite able to believe it were all still here just as I'd left it. Because there, sat at an angle in the field, were that white house with the painted orange gates. And there were the rusting shell of that abandoned red tractor.

And there went that man in the rainbow vest who spent all day every day grazing his cows up and down this road. It felt like they'd all kept their part of the bargain, and it were now up to me to keep mine. And I would, because the small white PepsoDent billboard had just come into view, and as we sped towards the smiling woman, and she in turn rushed forward to greet us, getting bigger and bigger with every moment, I don't think I've ever felt such a great feeling of solidness in this world, such a huge sense of finally coming home. Ameen.

———

I found out about Aaqil today. I were at the youth centre reading the noticeboard. I'd been about to leave – I couldn't keep putting off coming back to my empty house – but then Fahim came up to me. I think I beamed at him I were that stupidly grateful for some company. He held his pool cue behind his neck, arms flopping over the top like he were in stocks.

''S not like you to come to prayers,' I said.

'Yeah, well, I got the Friday feeling. You know how it is . . . You want a game?' But they'd already switched the light off over the table. 'Oh yeah,' he said. 'Forgot about that.'

He just stood there for a while biting his bottom lip. Blatantly, he wanted to chat about something. 'Is summat up?'

He frowned, said, 'I'm going back home again in a few weeks.'

'Yeah? What for?'

'I'm going with Ammi. Sonia – my sis? – she's preggers. So, you know.'

There were something else he weren't telling me. 'You getting married?'

He shrugged. 'Maybe. Got to sooner or later, so, you know, yeah, I might just chirps a few girls, lay it on the line, you know how it goes.'

'Yeah. It goes, alright.'

'So you got any tips? I want to stay for a bit this time. Really get to know the place.'

I looked at him properly. 'Why?'

'It's home, isn't it? You know, home home.'

I said that were the most sensible thing he'd said in years, which pleased him no end. And that made me have to look away again. It were horrible to see how important it were for him to know he pleased people. I took out my phone. 'Get this number down.' I gave him Abu Bhai's details and told him to contact him when he arrived. 'Just talk to him. See if you like what he says.'

He saved the number. 'Yeah, yeah. Deffo. I'll deffo do that. Thanks. Thanks a lot.'

I thought he'd leave then, but he stayed where he were. 'Anything else?'

'Talking about marriage and everything. I just wanted to say I were sorry to hear about you and your missus.'

'Me and my missus?'

'You know, that you've, you know, separated and everything. She's gone to stay at her mother's, hasn't she?'

I shook my head. 'It's just gossip, man. You know how shit gets spread. We've not separated. She's still with me. Her mother's just not well, that's all. She forgets shit. Alzheimer's, you know?'

'Sounds heavy.'

'Doctor said it were dangerous to leave her on her own, like. So Becka's with her for a few weeks. She'll be back with me soon enough.'

'Right,' Fahim said. 'Guess I heard wrong.'

He didn't believe me. 'You calling me a liar?'

He looked shocked. 'Course not. She's looking after her mother. I get you.'

'I can't believe you don't believe me. That's summat, that is.'

'But I do. Honest.'

'I'll take you round and you can ask her yourself if you want.' I took his arm. 'Come on, let's go now.'

He didn't move. 'Imz, you're acting crazy. I believe you.'

'I'll call her, then. You can ask her.'

I put the phone to my ear. Fahim took it from me, switched it off. 'Look, I believe you, alright? Believe me. And it's nothing to do with me, anyway.'

'Exactly. So make sure you don't go round spreading shit.'

'I weren't spreading anything.' He looked hurt.

'I'm just saying, that's all. I'm not having a go.'

He looked to his feet. 'Don't know why everyone has to have a go at me all the time. First Abba were in a mood because of those bombers, saying he'll be getting nowt but abuse when he goes out tonight, and then Jal had a go just because I borrowed his pod.'

'What bombers?'

And he told me it'd been on the news that morning how someone had walked straight into the British High Commission in Islamabad and blown themselves up. At least six dead. All British. He carried on talking, but nothing were getting through. I just kept staring at him. Already I were thinking how it were meant to be me next.

'Oh, here, look, can I get you a tissue or summat?'

'What? Oh, fuck.' I wiped the back of my hand across my eyes. 'It's nothing. It's just, you know, so sad and everything.'

He looked at me then, doubtfully, and it were such a blatant lie I couldn't hold back from pulling into a smile. And that set Fahim off as well, and soon we were both stood there, laughing nervously.

—

The minute I got back I were on the Internet and clicking through sites looking for the bomber's name. I didn't find it, but a video showing the attack did open up in a new window. Everyone's probably seen it by now. The one where the CCTV camera's trained on the steps of the building. One second the black-and-white scene's all still and calm, and the next thing you know the picture's juddering to fuck and lines are whizzing up and down as this silent cloud of smoke bursts out of the building like a cartoon experiment gone wrong. Near the end of the video, once things had calmed down a bit, there were movement at the bottom of the screen, something cutting across the corner. It took a couple of replays for me to work out what it were – a man with chalky white elbows in a short-sleeved shirt. He were on all fours, and the whole of his face and back were on fire. I logged off and went and sat on my bed and put my hands on my knees.

Later, I rang Abu Bhai to get confirmation, and then I just sat in the darkening front room, waiting for Charag. He were back late.

'Did you see?' I said, meeting him in the hall. I heard fear in my voice. 'He's done it. Aaqil's done it.'

He stood in silence for a while, then said, 'So it was him. I thought it might be, but I was not . . .' He moved past me and into the front room. I followed, flicked the light on.

'Eight dead. Maybe more. It's going up every hour.'

He slid his hat off his head and crumpled it into his fist. 'Are you sure? How can you be sure it was him?'

'I rang Abu Bhai.'

'You rang Abu Bhai? What did he say?'

'He said it were our turn now.' I could tell what Charag were thinking. 'I didn't tell him about you. Don't worry.'

He nodded, then suddenly angry, he brought his knuckles down against the wall. 'But what was he thinking? He's got three unmarried sisters back home. Three! Did he not think how will his abba manage on his own? Did he not think of any of this?'

'Maybe he were thinking of all the sisters who're being killed. Who'll never have a chance of getting married.'

He grabbed the TV remote, searching furiously for something to watch. 'I have known Aaqil since we were small. He was never caring about anyone but himself. Always chasing his own glory.'

—

When we got back from Afghanistan we still had a couple of weeks before the flight to England. I started doing more work around the farm. I wanted to. I didn't ask if I could help like I'd done before, I just got up one morning, tied a loose turban around my head and set about emptying the sacks of grass into the troughs. I were nearly finished by the time everyone else woke up.

'Arré, what are you doing?' Tauji said. 'You don't have to do that!'

I didn't say nothing. I just carried the iron bucket over to the pump so I could wash the animals while they ate.

Qasoomah laughed. 'He must've been learning some sense while he was away.'

Every day I'd help Tauji out in the fields, spraying the wheat or turning over the earth or carrying the huge sacks of long leaves down the track and to the farm. I'd then run the leaves through the cutting machine, turning them into feed for the buffaloes. I enjoyed that the most, my bare foot pressing on the pedal and the druk-druk of the rusting thing drowning all other sound out. I'd be there for hours, pushing bundle after bundle through the wheel and watching the silver spokes slice up the leaves. Sometimes the current blown up would be so strong that all the millions of tiny chopped bits of leaf would

hang suspended and quivering in the air, like some strange shoal of green and yellow fish.

I were at the machine when Charag came through the archway, beeping his scooter. He were waving a padded blue envelope. 'My visa has come!' Tauji, Ammi, Qasoomah, they all came out into the yard to coo over the papers, as if they were some rare find. I stayed where I were, at the machine with my hands and wrists and arms covered in grass. Charag looked over. 'Bhaiji! I am coming with you!' I nodded, then went back to my work.

Just like Faisal had, I started sleeping on the roof, alone. I preferred it that way, lying on my menjha with the stars curving all round me, like I were on a different plane to everyone else. I think it were the same night Charag got his visa when I heard some dull banging noise that had me up and looking over the veranda. Ammi, Tauji, Charag were all asleep in the courtyard below, on menjhe half tucked in shadow. But Qasoomah's blanket were pulled back. I could see her though, picking her way back to the house along a trail in the neighbouring field. The moon tipped the corn silver. She must've been for a shit, I thought, but then I saw how she were bent off to the side as she walked, like a determined reed in a strong wind, and it were only when she stepped out of the field and came through the archway and into the yard that I saw the iron bucket in one hand. She put it down by the mud oven, then squatted on the flats of her feet and began working up a fire. She must be hungry. I went back to my bed, but soon enough I heard footsteps on the concrete stairs. I raised my head off the pillow.

'I knew you were still awake.' She sounded pleased she'd been proved right. 'Have some hot milk. It will help you sleep.' She stood at the end of my menjha, blowing over the top of the steel glass to cool it for me.

'You didn't have to do that. You didn't have to go to all that trouble.'

'What trouble? It is milk only.'

Except it weren't just milk, no matter what she said. It were a whole midnight trip across the field to fetch the milk from the barn, and then carrying it back, and then walking up the track to find some dried cowpats, and then using them to try and work up the fire . . .

'You shouldn't do things like that for me. I don't deserve it.'

She pointed to the glass. 'You do not like milk?'

I sat up properly. 'Here. Just pass it here.' I downed it in two goes, wiped my mouth, and passed back the empty glass. 'All done.'

'More? There is more.'

'No, no. I'm done. Thanks.'

'Teekh hai. Then I will go. You will be wanting to sleep.' I started huddling back under the covers. 'But seeing as you are awake,' she said, and nearly knocked me clean off the bed as she sat down and made herself comfy. 'I want to speak with you. It is about Charag.'

And she started on about how worried she were for him and this whole going to England business. She didn't know how in God's name he would be coping, or who would be looking after him. Did I think he would be alright over there? Because she'd heard, you see – the other day? in the bazaar? – she'd heard that goreh were not always kind to people coming to their country for work.

'If they do not like us, then that is fine. He does not need to go. We do not need to go where we are not welcome.' She stopped, her face set in some proud look of defiance.

'But he's not going to be on his own. He's going to be living with us. And I'll be there. And Becka – your bhabhi? remember her? – you heard how excited she were when we told her.'

'She were calling him a "visitor" only,' Qasoomah said, with real distaste.

'She didn't mean it like that. That's just how the English speak. Believe me, it's his home as much as mine.'

A smile came to her face. That sempt to be all she'd wanted to hear.

'But what do you care anyway? You'll be married off. Living with your new family. Too busy pleasing your janum to think about us.'

'Oh, what nonsense,' she said, in English. 'I am already having these nightmares about the whole jing-bang tamasha. Did you know Abba is booking the Lucky Palace?'

'Have you seen his photo yet? What's he look like?'

'Like an oaf. I am not surprised they only want a small dowry. They should be paying me to marry him. And why you are not staying for the wedding? Are there no more planes going to England that you have to catch the next one?'

I fell back onto the menjha. The stars looked so close all of a sudden. It felt like all I had to do were stroke my hand across the night and I'd have a pocketful to take with me. 'No, I should head back.' I tried to not sound too sad about it. Ameen.

———

Yesterday he were in a silver saloon. Today it were a red Nova. Changing cars. Thinks he's being clever. That I won't notice. But I did. I'm not thick. All the way back from masjid he were tailing me. When I turned a corner, he turned as well. When I ran, he speeded up. And when I stopped, waiting for him to pass, he didn't. He just stopped as well. I had enough. I went right up to him and knocked on the window. It sank down. Some turbaned dude with a bucket of fried chicken wedged between his thighs. He asked me what the fuck I wanted.

'In the back, is he? Tell him to get the fuck out.'

'You what?'

I tried the back door but it were locked.

'Oi! Get the fuck off my wheels!'

'Too scared, or what?' I peered into the tinted windows, squinting. 'Too shit-scared?' I think I were shouting.

'What the fuck you on, bruv?' and then the lights changed and he roared off.

Back home, I locked the door and drew the curtains. I tipped back the kitchen drawers until I found the masking tape and went through the house taping up all round the windows. He's not gunna get in. Afterwards I rang Abu Bhai and told him what were happening.

'They know everything. Don't ask me how, but they do. They know about Faisal, about Aaqil. About me. It's all over. It's all over.'

The line were crackly. I moved to the window. He were telling me to calm down, to just calm down and not panic.

'But they know!'

'No one knows. Now you just calm down, you understand me? Are you ready?'

'We don't have the vests yet.'

'Why don't you have them? What is keeping you?'

'I just haven't had time to collect them.'

Things went quiet for a bit, then Abu Bhai said, 'Imtiaz—'

I cut him off. I didn't want to hear it. 'It's not that. I'll get them this week.'

I saw Becka through a gap in the curtains, pushing the pram up the hill. She were leaning over the top of it to speak to Noor. I opened the curtains wide again.

Abu Bhai were still talking to me. 'Imtiaz?'

'Yes?'

'I said, when?'

I moved to the middle of the room, thinking hard. 'Sunday,' I said firmly. And then I said I had to go.

I let Becka in and then just stood around the room like a spare part while she sorted Noor out – getting her out the pram, making her feed, changing her nappy. 'She didn't sleep well, so she might be a bit grumpy today.'

'Same as usual, then.'

She frowned, and I worried I'd said the wrong thing. On the TV some government troll were getting interviewed about the attacks. 'Crazy, ain't it?'

She glanced at the telly, then went back to sorting Noor's nappy out. 'Why? What's gone on now?'

'The bombing. The British Embassy got gutted, didn't it?'

She looked confused. 'Here?'

'Islamabad. In Pakistan. You've not even noticed it?'

She put Noor in the baby-walker. 'I've been kinda busy, you know, what with looking after our kid and trying to get a job.'

That reminded me. 'How'd the interview go?'

'I got it. Start in a couple of weeks.'

'But that's fantastic,' I said, sounding more pleased than I felt. It turned out she were perfectly capable of getting on with her life without me. She didn't need to depend on me. There were a moment of awkwardness, but then I leaned in and kissed her warm cheek. 'Congratulations.'

I followed her down the hallway. She paused at the door, one hand lifted to the lock. 'Actually, Imz, I've been meaning to say something. Now I'm starting a new job, we probably need to talk about where we go from here. You know?'

'Where we go?'

'Well, I can't expect me mam to look after Noor whenever I'm at work.'

'No. Right. Yeah. Absolutely. So, yeah, let's work out some sort of timetable, then, I guess.'

But she already knew what she wanted to do. 'I spoke to a lawyer at the Citizen's Advice and it turns out it's probably best if we start formalising things a bit. Get a separation order. It'll make things easier in the long run.'

'A separation—?' I felt a stab of hatred. 'Why? You seeing someone?'

'Oh, don't be ridiculous,' she said, and her look of disgust were enough to shame me back down.

'Sorry. Sorry. So what you want to happen next? You seem to have it all worked out.'

'The lawyer said it'd be best if we can come to an agreement between ourselves, and then they'll just write it up, pretty much. So how about I ask me mam what day she can look after Noor and then we go somewhere? For a coffee or something and . . . you know, see what we can come up with?'

I nodded, and maybe I looked as sad as I felt because she said, 'I know this isn't easy for you.'

'Whatever you think, B, we do belong together. You and

me.' Last-ditch, pathetic, hopeless. I were embarrassed for myself. But I didn't want her to leave. It were like if she were around then death stayed away.

'It's too much over.'

'It can't be. I'm still missing you.'

But she just opened the door and left me again.

—

The last time I spoke to Aaqil face to face were the night before I caught the plane back to England. We were walking through the muhalla. He had his arms folded loose over his chest. A thoughtful look, maybe even a smile on his face. We stepped aside to let a couple of scooters pass, and then carried on slowly down the cobbled lane.

'How long is the flight?' he asked.

'Seven. Eight hours. We should be there by noon.'

He nodded. 'It will be cold. Take something warm to wear for when you land.'

At the end of the bazaar, the thin dark lanes opened out into the sun. I turned to Aaqil, smiled as best I could, and held out my hand. He took it between both of his. I wanted to say something but couldn't think of what. Goodbye sounded so flimsy. And maybe he knew this, because he shook his head and said, 'I shall see you very soon.'

He patted me on the back, half comforting, half to send me on my way.

Instead of going straight home, I stopped off at the mosque. Ustaadji were sat cross-legged against the wall.

'Young Imtiaz!' He folded up his newspaper. 'Sit, please, sit. I hear you are leaving us?'

'Tomorrow, Ustaadji. The wife, you understand,' and we shared a laugh. 'But also, it is time, you see. I have been called.'

He didn't flinch. 'Aaqil has told me.'

'About Faisal as well?'

'I am sure he is being rewarded as we speak.'

I nodded, looking to the floor.

'Imtiaz, my question for you has always been that you are joining the struggle for the right reasons. He will know if you are not.' I stayed silent. 'But I do not think you are here to have your mind changed, yes? What can I do for you?'

It had sempt like a good idea at the time, but now I felt embarrassed to ask. 'I wondered if you had any books I could take with me to read?'

'A Qu'ran? Yes, yes, I have many. What kind would you like?'

'No, I mean – do you remember those stories you used to tell? About all the great old battles we fought? I'd like to hear those again.' I could feel my cheeks glowing red. 'For Noor, my daughter,' I tried, but it were too late and he looked at me with such sadness in his eyes that on my way home I crushed the stories he'd dug out for me deep into a rubbish pit.

—

The next morning, while everyone were still asleep, I took out my kufi from the suitcase and went barefoot across the courtyard and round the back of the house. I knelt down beside Abba, where I imagined his feet to be. It were still dark, just turning. I could feel the soil and stones against my knees. I stayed like that until the sun began to rise grubbily on the horizon, and the air started to twitch with life. Then I brought my hands up to my face and closed my eyes. The last thing I did were take a handful of Abba's soil and let it fall over my head.

By the afternoon, the courtyard were packed. They'd all come to see us off – friends, relatives, people from the village, even families just passing through stopped at the road, leaning on their bicycles or staying their tongas to see what were going on. Charag were calling out make way! make way! as he carried the cases on his head and to the van. He had on his new jeans, the ones he'd been saving up for, and a green silk shirt.

'Where's Ammi?' I asked.

'In the kitchen,' Qasoomah said, dabbing at her eyes with the end of her dupatta. She'd been crying on and off for most of the morning.

Ammi were by the concrete sink, wrapping rotis in crinkly yellow paper. 'For the journey. There is lime pickle too, but do not have too much, acha? You know how it makes you need the toilet.'

I wanted her to come with me, but Tauji had asked her to stay until after the wedding. He said someone had to take charge of things and prepare Qasoomah, and she were the nearest thing to an ammi the poor girl had left.

'Pass me that bag, beita. No, the other one. The brown leather one.'

I took the flask and the tiffin box and the rotis wrapped in yellow paper from her and packed them away in the bag. I slung the bag over my shoulder. We could hear the crowd outside.

'Ready?' she asked.

I nodded, and came forward and touched her feet. She gave a tiny gasp of surprise, but then rested her hand on my head and offered a blessing.

'I see Kashmir was good for you,' she said as I stood back up.

We went back outside together. Tauji were coming to the airport to see us off, and he waited in the front seat while we said our goodbyes.

'Come back every year,' Qasoomah said. 'Promise? And bring bhabhiji and Noor next time also.'

Some people – people I didn't even know that well – came forward and gave me money as a parting gift. I tried to protest, hand it back, but they said no boy of this village would be leaving empty-handed.

I hugged Ammi last of all, tightly, and I think maybe she sensed something. But I smiled at her when I finally let go, and I hope she were reassured.

—

On the plane, I sat there waiting for take-off with the Qu'ran open on my lap, but I don't think I read it once. I just stared out the window, at the woman on the tarmac supervising the luggage. She wore a bright green waistcoat over her salwaar-kameez.

We began taxiing, and soon the plane were mustering up speed and the engines' splutter grew into a roar. And then, as I felt myself being pinned back into my seat, I looked out the window, at our plane peeling off the runway, and it felt like someone who'd been holding my hand were now letting me fall.

All through the flight Charag kept on rising out of his seat to look at the screen-maps, and then leaning across me to match that up with what he could see out the window.

'It's no different to when you looked five seconds ago,' I said, irritated.

'It is exciting, hain na?'

If he weren't doing that, he were worrying over his clothes. Should he leave his top shirt button done up ('What is the rule in England?'), or combing his jeans for the tiniest speck of dust ('These are just like the ones they are wearing in England, yes?').

I were sleeping when he shook my knee and woke me up. 'We're here!' His eyes were wide. He sounded thrilled. But when I looked out I just saw squares of disappointed brown ghostly fields floating up through the mist.

While we waited for our luggage to come I stared around me – the shiny tiles, the flashing signs, the sparkling windows, just the wasteful meaningless brightness of everything. None of it felt real. Even the people didn't have proper faces with eyes and noses and smiles.

'There are our bags,' Charag said, struggling with a trolley that made a rubbery squeak on the grey tiled floor.

We got a taxi from the airport, and I remember how the driver tried to get a conversation going. Where had we been?

Did the weather stay nice? But he soon got the message I weren't up for a chat. Charag stared fascinated out the window. I just looked down into my lap and tried to breathe.

Even the house looked different, thinner and bleaker somehow. If it weren't for Ammi's figurine things in the window, I don't think I'd've recognised it. I stepped out of the fake car and went up the fake path and buzzed the fake doorbell, but it felt like only my arms and legs were working, the rest of me, all the important things inside, were refusing to take part. Behind me, I could hear Charag and the driver bumping the luggage over the kerb. And then the front door swung open and Becka stood before me. She'd done her make-up. Put on something decent. She didn't look like the other girls. She looked like Becka, and I were so grateful for that it made me smile with relief. It were the smile that convinced her it were me. Until then she'd been struggling to see past my beard and clothes, but when I'd smiled she jumped forward and threw her arms around my neck.

'Imz! You're home! I'm so glad you're home!'

But something were wrong. Her voice, I thought. Why has she changed her voice? Ameen.

————

My mobile rang in the middle of last night. I didn't answer it at first. I just watched the green shadow it cast across the wall. I thought it might be them – Tarun and his friends. Then it stopped ringing. A few minutes later it started up again. Don't be a coward, I told myself. It were Abu Bhai. He wanted to know why I still hadn't been to fetch the vests. Were I changing my mind?

'I'm going to get them in the morning. I called him about them yesterday. Honest.'

So just before lunchtime today I zipped up my parka and locked the front door behind me. As usual, I slid in a tiny piece of card beside the lock so I could tell if anyone entered while I were out. Then I looked down the street, but I couldn't see that Tarun anywhere. Maybe he'd got the message. I called the Bradford number on my way to the cash machine. He answered with a rough, snappish, 'Yes?' but as soon as he heard it were me his voice collapsed into a girlish simper. 'Yes, absolutely the suit is ready, mai baap. Of course you can come to collect it. Whenever you would like is absolutely A-class fine with me. My house is your house . . .'

The vests were laid out waiting for me when I arrived.

'No rush, ustaad. Please take your time. The missus is at a wedding.' His half-moons were hanging on a gold chain, swaying stiffly out from his chest like an ornamental swing. His eyebrows were lighter, almost white, his hair too. 'The chemicals, huzoor. They are getting everywhere.'

I turned back to the vests. 'I thought I said I only needed one?'

'But both were ready. I thought I would give you the choice. Has the other brother changed his mind?' His voice went sing-song as he tried to keep it casual.

All the wires and crocodile clips were now hidden behind a suede black lining. The only thing I could see were a tough knotted black cord that hung like a zipper near the inside pocket. He told me I'd still have to do a few things on the day – peel back the lining like so and connect the green clip to the brown wire, and make sure I tightened the screws on that black box there. The brother's eyes widened when I slid the vest on. I'd expected to feel my chest fill out a couple of extra inches, but I hadn't expected the shudder. It felt reassuringly heavy on my shoulders, and the box pressed against my ribs but not in an uncomfortable way. Turning away, I caught my reflection in the TV, and that stayed me. Here was me, in this room, preparing to die.

My thumb hooked into the loop at the end of the cord. I looked to him.

'Go ahead, huzoor. Nothing will happen yet.'

But I didn't. I removed my finger. 'Is this one mine, then?'

When I left, I still had the vest on under my jacket. No one sempt to notice. I were watching all the hundreds of people I passed on my way back to the station, but no one had a clue, not even when I boarded the train and slid into an empty couple of seats. The train pulled out, and I let my hand trace its way round the outline of the vest. I started mouthing the final prayer, testing how well I'd memorised it. The words came easy, and when I got all the way to the end without going wrong once I let my hand move inside the vest and up to the tough little cord. As I twirled the ribbed material around my finger, the weirdest thing happened. I got this light-headed feeling of rising above my body and being able to watch myself. I saw my pupils disappear into the tops of my eyes. I could see myself still reciting the prayer. I didn't like that. I didn't want to see myself. I wanted it to end. I pulled down hard on the cord, and something inside me lurched up, desperate and thirsty, like a hand stretching for another whose hand was not quite in its reach. Ameen.

I don't think I left the house once the first week I got back to England. I spent most of the time just laid out on our bed, my face across the pillow, eyes open. I could see out the window and to the sour grey sky. Everything sempt to have dulled since I'd got back. I'd been shining in Pakistan, but I now knew the brightness hadn't been coming from me. It were a reflection of something in that land.

At first Becka put it down to jet-lag, and she'd make an effort to keep Noor quiet because Daddy was sleeping it off. But after a few days her patience went and she'd stand at the end of the bed with Noor hanging off her hip.

'Your uncle rang. He were wondering when you were coming back to work. I told him you'd give him a call.'

I didn't say nothing. I heard her sigh.

'I need to go to the shops. Can you look after her for a bit?'

'Ask Charag.'

'I'm asking you.'

I groaned, turned over.

'Oh, for chrissake, Imz. You're acting like a lovesick teenager.'

I only properly left my bed to come downstairs when I heard Becka's mam in the front room. She'd come to pay a little visit, see how we were getting on now the wanderer had returned.

'We're getting on fine,' I said, coming through into the room.

'Oh, Imtiaz,' she said, and she took a few seconds to look me over – the clothes, the beard – but she didn't say anything. Probably Becka had already warned her not to. 'Did you enjoy your holiday?'

'Is it still called a holiday if you're only going home?'

She gave Becka a look, as if to say, 'I see what you mean.'

Charag came in then. 'I have put the tea on, bhabhiji.'

'Oh, thank you, Charag. Good to see at least one of the men in this family has some sense.'

He turned to me. 'Salaam, bhaiji.' The oily quiff had been lopped off. His hair were now short, messily spiky, the sideburns tapering.

'When'd you do that?' and maybe there were something hard in my voice because Becka came to his defence.

'That were me. You can't expect him to find a job looking like he did.'

'And aren't those my jeans?'

'Planning on wearing them, were you?' Becka asked, all sarcasm.

Theresa spoke up, to ward off an argument. 'I think you look lovely,' she said to Charag. 'I'm Theresa.' She were pointing to herself with one hand, extending the other.

'Rebekah's mother.' He weren't used to shaking hands with women, but he shook it cheerfully all the same. 'My, aren't you a handsome one?'

'Oh, you should've seen them at the hairdressers, Mam. Couldn't keep their hands off him. He even got a date out of it.'

'A date?' I said, looking from Charag to Becka. 'Who the hell with?'

'Yasmin,' she said. 'That one with the lisp and tits.'

Charag grinned, then quickly sobered up. 'I have to go. I might have found a job.' He took his – my – jacket from the coat rack and left.

I turned to go back upstairs myself, but Becka spoke. 'Do you think you can put the bins out?'

'I'm busy,' and began climbing the stairs.

'Yeah, yeah. You go back to your hovel.'

But I think you soon began to realise something deeper were wrong, didn't you, B? Because late one evening you came and sat on the bed beside me. You pushed your hand through my hair. 'What's the matter?'

I shook my head.

'Well, something's up. I've never seen you like this before.'

'It's nothing. I'll be fine.'

She laid herself on top of me, her breasts gently spreading into my back. She kissed the space behind my ear. 'Charag said something about a trip you went on while you were over there?'

'So you've been talking about me now?'

'Did something happen? On that trip?'

'What's with the third degree?'

'I'm just interested. You seem to have got a lot out of the visit, that's all. That's all I'm saying, Imz. Nothing more.'

And then there were one horrible time a week or so later when I were knelt beside the bath with the tap on full blast. The door opened. She were in one of my old grey T-shirts. She leaned against the doorknob.

'Imz, it's the middle of the night. What are you doing?'

'We need a new boiler. This one's taking ages to heat up.'

'Okay. We can do that,' she said, like she were trying to talk someone down from a tall building. 'But can I ask what for?'

'I need to wash, don't I? The sun's gunna be up soon.'

'Right. Well, in that case,' she went on, putting on a happy voice, 'shall we pray together? I don't think I've done the early prayer once since Noor was born.'

'We can't. Men and women can't pray together. You just go back to sleep.'

'That hasn't stopped us before.'

'This isn't before. Didn't you hear me? Just go back to bed.'

But she didn't. She pushed off the doorknob and sat on the lip of the toilet. She leant forward with her knees pressed together and feet discarded to the sides. 'Imz, I'm not having a go or anything, and tell me if you don't feel you can talk about it, but I am your wife, you know. I'm not some stranger off the street.'

I could feel her looking hard at me, willing me to look at her.

'Did something happen to you over there? Did – I don't know – did you do something or see something or go somewhere? Because something's not been right ever since you got back.'

There were a long minute with me just staring straight into the white tub, until it sempt like the white were breaking off into different colours. 'Seriously. Go to bed.'

Her head flopped onto her knees, and I noticed the centre parting down her lovely-looking skull, her hair falling over those loose slender shin bones. She said quietly, 'What are those dreams you're having?'

I chuckled, shook my head, as if to say now she really were talking like she were crazy.

'Don't do that.' She looked up. Some anger had come into her voice. 'Don't treat me like I'm stupid. I'm not blind. You're having bad dreams, aren't you? Did they start over there? We'll get it looked at. There are people who know about these things. Are they the same dreams?'

Just thinking about the violent dreams makes my head start to vibrate. 'Look, how many times? I'm just trying to wash. Go to bed.' I hated how rough my voice sounded.

She straightened back up. I knew what she were going to say next and panic rose inside me because I hoped she wouldn't say it and I even twisted the tap so the water drummed even harder and maybe then she'd get the message and just please leave me here alone. She said it anyway.

'You really hurt me last night.'

I were waiting for more, but nothing more came. I nodded, still not looking at her. She leaned forward, cupping my bristly chin in her hand, and gave me a sad damp kiss across the corner of my mouth. Then she left, dragging the door over the carpet ridges and putting it to. Ameen.

––––––

My phone's been ringing again tonight. Same as every night. It's Abu Bhai. Wants to know what happened last

Sunday. Why I failed. He can wait. Everything can wait. How did it come to this, B? How did we end up like every other miserable lying couple in this griefhole of a town? But I'm going to try and keep it together. I've been thinking about it all week. I haven't been writing, but boy have I been thinking. I thought we were different. But it were your feet again. Last Saturday, when you came round to pick Noor up. You were all excited because you were starting your new job on Monday and you'd just bought the perfect top to wear on your first day. A bargain off the market. You fetched it out of your bag.

'Only fifteen quid. And see the beading? That's hand-stitched.'

'It's lovely.'

She frowned and crushed the top back. 'I don't know why I bother sometimes.'

'Sorry, sorry. It's really nice. Honest.'

'This job actually means a lot to me.'

'And I really hope it all works out for you, Becka. I hope everything works out for you.'

She looked a bit spooked by me saying that, as seriously as I did. 'Right. Thanks. Thank you. So, what's with all the tape? Around the windows?'

'What? Oh, I were thinking of decorating. Painting. I were just marking stuff out.'

She looked amazed. 'You? Painting?' She shook her head. 'Anyway, when you want to get together?'

'Get together?'

'Remember me saying we need to talk about next steps? Lawyers and stuff? How about tomorrow? Me mam can take Noor.'

Tomorrow were the Sunday. I thought to Abu Bhai and what he were expecting me to do, and I weighed that against an evening with Becka. 'Tomorrow's fine. I'll pick you up. It'll be like our first date.'

She were quick to set me right. 'Let's just keep it to a coffee, yeah? Nothing major.'

The front door went, and Charag came whistling down the hall. He turned into the lounge, but then stopped. 'Oh, sorry. Hi, bhabhiji. I'll just go and get changed for work.'

'Where've you been anyway?'

'Out.'

'Hear that?' I said to B. 'He has a different girl every weekend.'

She smiled. 'I'm sure.'

'It's not like that,' he said.

Becka squashed her handbag into the wire basket underneath the pram. 'I'll miss the bus.'

'Your bhabhi's starting a new job on Monday. You might want to wish her luck.'

'Good luck,' Charag said.

'Thank you,' she replied.

It's only now that I remember how the two of them had been looking past each other the entire time, as if to look might bring the whole thing falling down. But then Becka turned the pram round, and then she did look, and something terrifying passed between her and Charag. Something in the second too long he spent looking at her, something in the way she were gripping the pram, as if she needed it just to stay upright. I looked from Becka to Charag. And then I looked down and saw Becka's feet pointing towards him. Her body may have been turned towards the door, but it were clear where she really wanted to be.

—

He'd know, I'd thought. Tarun'd know if something were going off. Next morning, I put my coat on over my kurta and started on down to the shopping centre. But halfway down the hill I realised it weren't even six thirty yet. I couldn't face going back to the house. I zipped up the snorkel-hood of my parka and spent the next two hours sat at the kerbside by some long straw grass.

Tarun were drinking from a plastic cup when he saw me running down the escalators towards him. 'Imtiaz, my colleague! To what do I owe this pleasure?'

I think I actually laughed, because I had this stupid notion and I know it's ridiculous and everything but would he just confirm to me how wrong I were?

'Imtiaz, is something the matter?'

'It were just something you said. A while back.'

'Something I said?'

'Or maybe you didn't. I don't know. About Becka?'

'Oh,' he said, very slowly, and he tipped his hat off his forehead so the beak pointed up. He put his tea down. 'We better find a table.'

And that were when I noticed it weren't packed like normal. The whole place were clean empty of everything – people, tables, shops, the lot. It were just me and Tarun and the shifting white floor. I felt tiny inside that huge emptied space. He led me to the only two chairs in the middle of the giant hall. 'Where is everyone?'

'Don't worry about that. Take a seat.'

He told me it were true. He'd seen them, together, in the park, at Becka's mother's. He weren't sure how long it had been going on, but a few months at least. It may be over by now, though. He carried on talking, but I'd stopped listening. All I could hear were the noisy rambling confusion in my own brain. Image after image kept on swimming up and dissolving. He said he'd been working late. She asked when he'd be leaving. He gave up on the fight. She visited the hospital.

'Imtiaz?' Tarun clicked his fingers. 'Anybody home?'

I looked across. 'How'd you know all this? Who are you?'

'I'm your friend, Imtiaz. Your only one by the looks of it, so you'd do well holding onto me.'

'You a detective or something?'

He made a so-so move with his head. 'You could call me that.'

'What else do you know?'

He leaned in, so close I could see the gaps between his teeth. 'I know everything. I even know what you're going to do here next Sunday.'

I shifted in my seat, looked up, looked down. 'I'm not doing anything next Sunday.'

He relaxed back into his chair, the backrest sagging under his weight. 'Well. We'll see, won't we?' He smiled then, and took a bite out of his apple.

'Where'd that come from?'

'You want one? Hang on, I'll go see if they've got any left.'

I watched him go, swallowed up into the crowd. The crowds. There were crowds now. And tables. All around me people were eating and slurping and talking and shopping. I got out of the chair and vaulted up the escalators and ran out the automatic doors.

I don't know where the rest of the day went, but it were dark when I got home and let the stairs take me to my bedroom. I went to the window and pressed my forehead to the cold wet pane. That light. The flashing red light were still there, spreading across my forehead. It reminded me of being a kid, of reading stories of Ala-ud-din. And now someone over there were twisting their clocks against the burning stars, trying to get my attention. Someone over there were needing to be rescued.

—

A night passed, maybe two, but it were light outside when I came round. It took a few seconds to get my bearings – front room, settee – but I weren't sure how I'd got there. My neck hurt from being bent over the armrest for so long. I wondered if that were really her stood at the end of the settee with a glass of water.

'Here,' she said. 'And take these too. Paracetamol.' I didn't move. 'Just take it. It's what the doctor said.'

My body creaked as I unfolded, sat up. I put the pills on my tongue. I could see her out the corner of my eye, both hands holding her hair back off her face.

'So are you going to tell me what you were up to or is it all a big secret?'

'Where's Charag?'

'He had to go to work. He's knackered. He stayed up all night beside you.'

I nodded. 'Nice of him.'

She sat on the armrest. 'Are you going to tell me, then?'

'Tell you what?'

'What you thought you were doing out there. In the dead of night.' I stayed silent. 'Were you looking for someone? Was it something to do with the mosque?'

I lifted my head a little. 'The mosque?'

'I don't know. I'm just guessing. That's all I can do. You've hardly said a word these past days.'

I looked back down. 'It were nothing to do with the mosque.'

'What, then?' Silence. She sighed, exasperated. 'The ambulance driver said something about a light? You were saying you had to get to the light?'

'Ambulance driver? You mean Tarun. Tarun brought me here.'

'Who the hell's Tarun? Did he put you up to it? Were you going to meet this Tarun?'

'You've met him,' I said. 'You met him here.'

She shook her head. She reached for her coat. 'Have it your way. I've got to get to work. Just do me a favour,' she went on, buttoning up. 'Next time you decide to go off on one of your little adventures, let me know first, will you? I were waiting all evening for you to show up. We were meant to be going out, remember?'

I remembered. 'Sorry.'

'I can't keep on leaving Noor with me mam. It's not fair. Not at her age.'

'I know. Way too young to have to listen to your mother.'

'I guess a sense of humour's always a good sign,' she muttered. She were fumbling in her pocket for something – her watch – which she snapped back around her wrist. 'How about we try again this weekend, then? Sunday?'

I nearly said yes, but caught myself. 'I can't Sunday. I'm busy.'

'Doing what?' she asked, dubious.

'Stuff.'

'Well, would his highness happen to have a window free on Saturday, then?'

It'd be a chance to say goodbye to her. I agreed to meeting her on Saturday. I expected her to leave then, but she stayed where she were. I could sense her watching me. She took a step forward.

'Is everything okay?'

'You'll be late for work.'

'Your mam rang.'

I'd been waiting for that. I had a feeling Ammi'd call.

'Yesterday. She's worried. She's been trying to call you.'

'What did she say?'

'I think you know.' But when I didn't say nothing, she went on, 'She said you'd called her. That it must've been around two in the morning over here and that you sounded really upset. She said she couldn't make out what you were saying but that you kept on asking her to come home. You wanted her to come and hold you.'

'She must've not heard right. You know what she's like.'

'She said you were weeping your heart out.'

'It were a bad line.'

She let out a little laugh. 'She actually asked if you'd taken up drinking.'

'If only.'

She groaned, saying there were no point in trying to talk to me when I were in this mood. 'I'm gunna call me mam and then I'll be off. She must be run off her feet with the kid.' She moved into the hall. Her voice rose. 'I don't suppose you'll feel like cooking – do you want me put some dinner on before I go? I can leave Charag's in the oven for him. What time's he finish these days?'

'Just call your mam.'

I heard the click of the receiver being taken up. 'You'll never guess what she's got into her head.' She came back into the room. She held the beige cordless loosely in her hand, her wrist bent out. 'She seems to think she's got a stalker. You know the green opposite the house? Over the road? She says she keeps on seeing someone sat on the bench at night, all hooded up like a snorkel. She swears it's true. I told her, Mam, it's a bench, it's what it's for is sitting on. But, anyway' – she began to dial – 'it were probably just a tramp.'

Ameen.

———

This morning I went back down to Meadowhall. A final scout around the place before I return for the last time on

Sunday. I didn't stay long. I spent most of the time on the first floor, looking down into the atrium below. Before I left I went over the route again. Through the automatic glass doors and down along the right-hand side of the walkway, avoiding the guard stood inside the door of that jewellers. Take the second set of escalators down into the food hall. Move round – not through – the diners and stop under the TV screen. I checked my watch. One and half minutes. I were getting faster. But I'll have to take care to pace myself. Can't let the adrenalin just take over.

I came back home and sat on the bed in the empty room. I dreaded that I had nothing to take my mind off things, but then I remembered how I still hadn't finished preparing my vest. I jiggled the waistcoat free off its hanger and opened it out across the bed. From the kitchen I fetched a screwdriver and tightened the last two screws in the side of the box. Then I hid the thing back inside the lining. I put the vest back on its hanger and closed the wardrobe door. It was ready.

'Knock, knock.'

I turned round.

'Sorry,' Tarun said. 'Didn't think you'd mind me coming straight up. The kitchen door was open.' I ushered him out the room. 'Ooh, something in there I ought to know about?'

'No. Nothing.' I shut the door.

'Doesn't look like it.'

'What did you want? I thought I'd seen the last of you.'

'Easy,' he said, taking his elbow back. 'New shirt, I'll have you know.' He shot his cuffs. 'Where is everyone? Becka? The other one – what's he called?'

'How should I know?'

'Temper, temper. They're probably at work. Let's hope so anyway.' He smiled. 'I saw you earlier. I thought you might've stopped to say hello.'

'Thought you only worked weekends?'

'Why? Avoiding me, are you? Hope not. That'd be no way to treat a friend.'

'You're no friend of mine.'

He offered me some gum. I told him to fuck it. 'Suit yourself. You know, what do you think your abba would make of you?'

'You don't know anything about my abba.'

'Wife wants a divorce, kid doesn't live with him, no job to speak of. Not exactly much to show for yourself. If you don't mind me saying so.'

'Fuck you.'

I heard a key rattling in the door. I went to the window. It were Charag. I turned round, but Tarun were already disappearing down the stairs. 'I'll see myself out the back. And I'll guess I'll see you on Sunday.'

I found Charag bent into the fridge, easing out a bowl of yesterday's sabzi.

'I don't have long. Double shift today. You hungry?'

I said I weren't. I sat down at the table, watching him. He peeled off the clingfilm. He spooned the potatoes and cauliflower into a plate. He put the plate in the microwave and turned the machine on. Then he took two slices of bread from the breadbin and set them on the worktop. Finally, he poured himself a glass of water and put this beside the bread.

'Remind me to buy some more kitchen foil tomorrow,' he said.

I said I would.

The microwave pinged. He took the plate out, clutching at it with his fingertips. He ate standing up at the counter, angled away from me, hand under his chin to catch any breadcrumbs. Every now and then his tongue darted out to fetch a stray bit of potato. I could see his thin curved lips closing round her hard pink nipples. His dark brown hand on her splayed white thighs.

'I'm telling you, bhaiji, nothing can beat our home-cooked food. So much chemicals there is in the pre-cooked stuff, hain na?'

'Chemicals. Pre-cooked. Kitchen foil. All these new words you're learning. Turning into a proper little English sahib.'

He smiled, thinking it were a compliment.

'Before I forget, I'm not going to be in tomorrow night. I'm going out with your bhabhi.'

He looked to me. He'd stopped chewing. 'Oh? Where?'

'Just the Leadmill. There's a few things she wants to tell me.'

'What kind of things?'

'Dunno. I guess I'll find out soon enough.'

'Tomorrow?'

'Tomorrow.'

The clock on the microwave buzzed, right by his ear. He nearly shit himself. 'I'm going to be late.' He dumped the dishes into the sink and left.

I staggered round the front room hunting for my phone. Throwing up cushions, pulling out settees. I found it in my pocket where I thought I'd looked already. I needed to speak to Aaqil. He were the only one who could set me right about everything. But I couldn't get through. I tried again and again, but every time the line were dead. And then I remembered. There were just me now. Alone in this darkened room, with all the shadows on the wall closing on me. I got out the room. Out the door.

I walked the whole way and maybe that'd been a blessing because by the time I rang the doorbell the drizzle sempt to have doused off the worst of whatever I were feeling.

Becka answered. There were an instant of panic in her face, which she quickly turned into surprise. 'Imz! Wow. Is everything okay?'

'That video camera? Could I borrow it?'

'Course you can. Sorry, I were meant to bring it last week, weren't I? You should've just rang, though. I'd've brought it tomorrow.'

We stood there for a few seconds until I pointed out that it were raining.

She came to life. 'Oh, shit. Yes. Sorry, please come in, come in. Here. Give me your jacket.'

I glanced around the room, maybe for signs of him, but it were the same as ever. Doilies and too many porcelain figures with top hats and bonnets. Noor were sat up in her baby-walker, playing with some toy. I kissed the top of her head. Her grandmother came in from the kitchen.

'Who is it, Rebek—?' She stopped dead.

'What's the matter, Mam? You know Imz, don't you? Or do I really have to make the introductions?'

Theresa shook off her surprise and came and kissed me wetly on the cheek. She left a nice powdery smell.

'How are you, Theresa?'

'I'm fine, love – it's the rest of them. But it's lovely to see you. Really, it is. Take a seat, won't you?'

I perched on the edge of the settee, legs apart, elbows on knees.

'Imz just came round to borrow our camera. Anything in particular you want it for?'

'I just thought it were time to record a few memories of me and her. Before she's all grown up and I forget what she were like. Or she forgets what I'm like.'

'Aw, that's nice. Ain't that nice, Rebekah?'

'While I'm here,' I went on, because I'd been going back over everything lately, 'she's been touching her ear a lot. Thought I'd get her to the doc's. Don't want that infection coming back. What hospital were it?'

I saw terror in Becka's face, and that told me everything I needed to know. 'Oh, I doubt it,' she said hastily. 'That were all cleared up.'

'What infection?' her mother asked.

'Her ear infection. You remember.'

'I most certainly do not. When was this? And why wasn't I told?'

'Mam. You do.' She sounded helpless. 'Remember when I first came back and had to take her to the hospital?'

Finally, her mother understood. 'Oh, that infection. Well, why didn't you say? Oh, yes, Imtiaz. I remember now. But Rebekah's right, that was all cleared up. I'm sure it wouldn't return. But – you know what? – that doesn't mean we should take any chances, does it? So thank you for letting us know. I'll make an appointment tomorrow morning. Just in case.' She were babbling. She thought she could just dupe me like that. That I were that simple and stupid. 'But you two chat. I'll take the little one upstairs. We can finish that jigsaw we started, can't we, darling?'

We were left alone. But no one spoke. This were pointless. I got up, all decisive. 'I should go. I'll see you tomorrow night, then, yeah?'

'Night? We're just going for coffee.'

'I thought we'd make a night of it. Go to the Leadmill.'

'The Leadmill? But I've told me mam.'

'It's where we first got together.' She looked at me with

her mouth open. 'We might as well finish things where they started.'

'That's a bit dramatic,' she said, smiling. I looked away. 'Alright, then. If it means that much to you. I guess I could do with a night out. And I can wear my new top.' I nodded. 'Obviously, I'm only telling you now so you can get your compliments ready.'

'Pressure's on, then. I better make sure it's a good night.'

'A good night would be the very least I'd expect.'

'Like you said, one doesn't go out a lot.'

'This is true,' she said quietly, sadly. 'Well, I do hope we'll have reservations.'

I nodded, with difficulty. 'At a very exclusive establishment.'

'A good table, I trust?' Her eyes had filled.

'With the most perfect view, Rebekah.'

She walked with me to the door. I turned round on the step. 'B, I were never – I were never mean or anything to you, were I? I don't think I've been a bad husband.'

Her shoulders fell. She sighed like she were tired of life. 'Imz, you say that like it's something to be proud of.'

When I got to the road, I looked back, maybe hoping she'd be watching me from the step, like a woman seeing her man off into battle. She weren't though. She were back in the yellow window of the front room, bending down to gather up Noor's toys. Ameen.

———

I cut myself today. Just a paper cut, but it's left a polite trickle of blood around my thumb and down to my wrist. I won't let a little thing like that stop me. Not when I'm so close now. One more night of writing to go. And then I'm going to put these pages away and just sit at the window and wait for the day to turn and face me.

Don't worry, Abba, everyone's here now. Tarun, Aaqil, Faisal. I'm not on my own. I found them in the end. I thought they were still at the Leadmill, but they'd come back home, you see? Faisal ran up to greet me, one hand on his topi. He asked me what I were so happy about. But she were so nicely dressed, you see. When I came to take her out. Really, she looked so different. Pretty. And I got to make the joke I'd planned already in my head, asking if it were new, and she laughed and said, What? This old thing? She even noticed that I'd gone to an effort, that I'd shaved my beard off and were wearing jeans and a shirt for a change. Old times. She said I looked even more handsome if I could imagine such a thing, and that made me think that, yeah, we can make this work. And I know she were looking forward to it, because her mam said that were the third pair of shoes she'd tried on, and that she'd been like a mad giraffe deciding what to wear all day. It felt good queuing outside the club, too, even if the line were full of shivering blondes and blokes looking for fights. And I told Becka to look how the red Leadmill sign had been fixed at last and how it were now taking long cosy gaps between each flash. I remember thinking that were a good sign as the bouncer waved us through.

I got us drinks. Found us somewhere to sit. When she said she must be getting old because she used to be the first up 'bopping away', I looked around, asking if I'd just walked into nineteen fifty-five, and she laughed and touched my shoulder. And even when she wanted to talk, I didn't mind. I looked serious and said I'd go along with anything, even if it were because I knew none of it would actually come to pass. But then she had to mention Charag. Asking how long he were planning on staying. I didn't like hearing his name, not out of her mouth. It sent my mind flaring. But it were okay. I didn't act like a wanker or anything. I just said I needed to go to the toilet. I wanted to get myself together, and then we'd get back to how we were. But there were someone blocking me at the toilets. Tarun. And I were frightened at first and turned away, but then he were in front of me and said it were okay. He weren't going to stop me. And he told me to look who else had come to see me. So I turned round to where he were pointing. It were Aaqil and behind him were Faisal. They were laughing and they had this green mazy light all round them. I called to them, but they started moving away from me, Abba. Into the crowds and the harder I tried to follow the more and more people just kept on pushing me back. I shouted and waved and begged them to let me through but they wouldn't let me get to them. And then I couldn't see them anymore, but they'd just come back to the house to wait for me. When I saw the yellow butterflies come flying past, I ran to Becka and said we should dance. Can you believe it? I never dance. I hate dancing. And even Becka were shocked at first but then I grabbed her hand and pulled her through the crowd. She kept on saying she wanted to talk, but I just wanted to dance with her. And you should've seen us, Abba. She were just swaying from side to side at first, like she didn't want to be there, but then I twirled her out along my arm, and that made her laugh. We kept on doing that. Twirling and twisting and spinning and all that kind of stuff. Making fools of ourselves, but it felt good, Abba. We were both of us laughing hard and we didn't care who were watching us, because it didn't matter how much I turned and twisted I never once took my eyes off her. And then she fell against me after a few songs. And I held her up in my arms. She were knackered. She were leaning on me. She needed me. I weren't going to let her down. I even told her I'd forgiven her, but she didn't seem to hear. I wanted to tell her everything then. About back home and what I were going to do tomorrow and how I needed her to be strong for me after I'd gone. I were ready to tell her everything, Abba, and when we waited at the bus stop I thought I were gunna let it all out to her at last. But summat kept me back. It were how she kept on saying that I didn't need to see her home. But I wanted to. It were like when we'd just started out and I'd wait with her at the bus stop. This time I even got on the bus with her. But when we got off she said I had to go home now. She didn't want me coming to the house this late. I said I wanted to say night to Noor, but she said she'd be asleep. I could come round in the morning. So I just watched her walking off up the road. I could hear her heels on the pavement, sharp and thin. That's when I called out and said I couldn't come round in the morning or ever again. She stopped, turned round. I said that we weren't going to meet again for a long time now. That this but just sit next to me. And then just let me lie on my old bed. But don't go, okay? Just stay sitting there. Right next to me on my old bed. And don't go. Just please don't leave my side till you're sure I've gone to sleep.

picador.com

blog
videos
interviews
extracts

was it. What are you talking about? And I told her that I was talking about us and me and back home and Faisal and Aaqil and how it were my turn tomorrow. By the time I stopped she were standing in front of me again. She knew I weren't messing. She knows me too well. I didn't have to do that, she said. That we could get help. But I told her I didn't need anyone's help. A car dipped its lights behind us and she took my elbow and moved us to the pavement. She wouldn't let me do this. She'd tell someone, the police. How could I do this to Noor? She were going to call her mam and tell her she weren't coming home tonight. She didn't want to leave me alone. I told her she didn't have to do that. I didn't need her. I were going to do this on my own. And then I were running away from her, down the road, and all I could hear were her calling my name in a desperate sort of voice.

I saw Faisal when I rounded the last corner and he walked the rest of the way home with me. And then Aaqil and Tarun showed up when I got inside. I'm glad they're here. Really I am. But I wish you were here instead, Abba. I feel so on my own right now. You, Ammi, Becka. There's no one. And I know one day I'll work out why things ended up like this. But tonight it doesn't make any sense to me. And these aren't tears. I promise you I'm not crying like some kid. I wouldn't do that to you. It's nothing. And I don't need anyone here with me. I don't. Just like you haven't needed me for the last year. Haven't thought about me or called me or anything. And that's fine. If that's the way you want it.

But, Abba, I do want to ask something of you. If it's not too late to be asking for favours, you know? But if you can pull this one out the bag I'd be really grateful. It's all going to end tomorrow. Something I got to do. But when I've done it I'll come and see you. I'll get the bus, walk up the path, knock on the door and come and find you sat in the front room with your paper. It'll be tomorrow morning sometime. I know I'll have to wait till you're back from work. But then I'll go and sit in my old room in the middle of all my kids' stuff. And after that, if you still want me around – and I'll get it if you don't, I wouldn't blame you or nothing – but if you do still want me around then just do me a favour please, yeah, Abba? It's only a small one. And even if you don't want me to stay and want me to leave then just do me this one favour anyway and I promise I'll go in the morning. First thing. You won't even have to see me go if you want 'cos I'll make sure I go before you wake up. But if you can do this for me, Abba, then just come upstairs into my old room and sit next to me. You don't have to touch me or hold me if you don't want to